D0001912

An Attraction
to Danger

His gentleness vanished, submerged in the molten fierceness of the black-souled ruffian she'd come to know. Silken tones caused a shiver to run through her.

"Now my precious little imp, tell me, my well-bred lady, my sweet, who else knows your secret."

"I—" Her voice cracked and she had to start again, wishing she didn't sound so fainthearted. "I decline to tell you."

He moved nearer then; she was forced to step back and landed in the chair. Nightshade swiftly bent down and placed his hands on the arms of the chair so that she couldn't escape. He was so close she could feel the heat of his body and catch the spiced-wood scent of him. Prim shrank back, all the while trying to meet his dark-eyed, vandal's stare.

"Miss Dane," he whispered. "I've persuaded many to do what I wish. Don't make me have to persuade you."

❧❧❧

The
Rescue

Suzanne Robinson

BANTAM BOOKS

New York   London   Toronto   Sydney   Auckland

THE RESCUE

A Bantam Book / February 1998

ISBN: 0-553-56347-5

Published simultaneously in the United States and Canada

Bantam Books are published by Bantam Books, a division of Bantam
Doubleday Dell Publishing Group, Inc. Its trademark, consisting of the
words "Bantam Books" and the portrayal of a rooster, is Registered in U.S.
Patent and Trademark Office and in other countries. Marca Registrada.
Bantam Books, 1540 Broadway, New York, New York 10036.

PRINTED IN THE UNITED STATES OF AMERICA

OPM   10 9 8 7 6 5 4 3 2 1

This book is dedicated to
my niece, Stephanie Woods.

When I create my female protagonists,
I favor qualities like bravery,
intelligence, humor, and creativity.
Stephanie combines all these
with grace and beauty.

The
Rescue

1

London, 1860

Nightshade. The word spread throughout the low districts of the city. It floated like a whisper in the black fog, slid down alleys on oily bricks and cobbles, and burned in the fumes of tallow candles—*Nightshade.* Nightshade had returned, as if from the dead.

A pauper sitting on a stoop in Shoreditch thought he caught a glimpse of Nightshade's shadow. He muttered his suspicion to a basketmaker, who shivered and passed the word to a herring-hawker at Billingsgate. There in the fish market, word hurtled from mouth to mouth with the bawls of the vendors: "Now's your time, now's your time! Cod here, cod here! Who will buy my fine grizzling sprats? Who will buy? Fish alive, fish alive, fish alive alive-o!"

In Houndsditch Street, not far from the docks, the fog turned yellow, and the gaslights grew dim near the

Black Fleece Tavern. Inside, the light wasn't much better, but the fog was kept at bay. It wouldn't have dared enter, for the place was guarded by Big Maudie, its owner, and among the clientele were the worst ruffians London's slums had to offer. Big Maudie, who was six feet in height, shoved her sleeves up over her red elbows, toyed with the cudgel she wore stuck in her belt, and surveyed her patrons.

Something was wrong. She couldn't quite understand what it was, though, for no one was fighting. Lobster Bill and his mongrel dog were asleep by the fire. A few of Inigo Ware's gang were drinking in a corner while a group of sailors sang off-key with Mayhew banging at the piano. Maudie shrugged and was about to return to her place behind the bar when she glimpsed a tattered silk skirt. At a table near the door lounged Alice Treacle and Ha'penny Hazel. What were they doing here so early? There was still plenty of trade on the streets.

It was chilly for October, and Maudie's nose, cheeks, and chin were redder than usual. She rubbed her nose and glanced around the front room again, noting that Gin Ginny was already on her third glass. And there was Fanny Milch. As Maudie scowled at Fanny, a woman bearing a tray stacked with meat pies, custards, and beer joined her. Larder Lily. That made five, and every one of them taking care not to be seen watching the door.

At that moment, the door opened. Yellow mist floated into the tavern and evaporated. Candles sputtered, and conversation ceased. A short figure trotted out of the fog with a knock-kneed gait, ginger hair dripping from the moisture. Badger Scoggins. Badger was followed by Cyril Prigg, one of the countless dealers in stolen goods who infested the city. Maudie sucked in her breath as she realized the significance of the two being together. Badger and Prigg. She skewed her gaze around to the expectant women. Even Ha'penny Hazel's dull eyes had a bit of spark in them, and they all looked like eager magpies after a bit of ripe fruit. There was but one who excited that mixture of nubile anticipation and anxiety in her jaded street friends.

"Nightshade!"

A gentle voice behind her said, "Yes?"

Maudie yelped and whirled around to scour the shadows. "Nightshade." Her throat was dry and her lips stuck together. "Nightshade."

"I already know my name, Maudie," came the whisper that sent tiny, sweet spikes of pain into her muscles.

Maudie licked her lips, then licked them again because her mouth was so parched. Finally she was able to speak. "You back again, then?"

"I do so detest people stating the obvious. You know that."

He hadn't moved from the shadows. Maudie recovered enough to be annoyed with herself for allowing Nightshade to get the better of her so soon. But how could she be blamed for it? He was but a tall shadow topped with gleaming ebony hair. Most of his face was shrouded in darkness; dim candlelight revealed his eyes, dark and hard, like topaz in desert sunlight. They said he got his dark coloring from a grandfather who'd been a Spanish sailor. Perhaps his disturbing intensity, that air of being on the verge of violence, derived from his grandsire as well. Whatever the case, Nightshade himself had earned his name, for he was as deadly and as subtle as that herb.

Some said he'd been given the appellation because, like nightshade, he was the servant of the devil. Who but a servant of the dark one could appear and vanish at will? He certainly made people think of Satan—dark of color, vicious of tongue, with all the benevolence and mercy of a guillotine. And he was back after having vanished for so long that Maudie and everyone else had thought him dead. Only the devil could do that.

Rubbing her hands on her apron, Maudie eyed the tall shadow. "Inigo Ware's men is here. You know him, always ready to do you a mischief since—"

"A curse on his head and black death on his heart. Inigo Ware's of no interest to me."

At last Nightshade moved out of the shadows, and it was as if a sorcerer had fashioned an incubus from the blackest void. Maudie's senses sharpened as he drew alongside her. She felt the tug of his physical presence, the pain of meeting a gaze that captured, mastered, and commanded in the length of a sigh. Then he was past her, and she was released from that glinting prison of the soul. Maudie cursed herself as always, irritated that a woman of her years could let a younger man turn her into a slack-jawed twit.

She watched Nightshade drift like mist into the crowded room. His name hissed its way around the tavern, but was soon given tongue by Gin Ginny, the first woman to catch sight of him.

"Nightshade, my love!"

"Choke me dead, it's Ginny," Nightshade said with a grin.

Ginny shrieked and hurtled at him, throwing herself into his arms and planting a gin-soaked kiss on his lips. In an instant he was surrounded by women. One or two of Inigo Ware's men scuttled into the shadows and vanished. Badger Scoggins trotted over to the shrieking group of women surrounding Nightshade. He was followed by Prigg and most of the sailors. Nightshade called for a round of ale for all, and a shout of approval rose throughout the tavern. Revelry erupted, fed by Nightshade's liberal use of his purse, and not many hours passed before Maudie had an establishment full of stumbling, befuddled customers. Then the moment came for which she'd been watching. Nightshade untangled himself from Ha'penny Hazel and Alice Treacle and strolled over to her.

"Same room as always, Maudie?"

"Right."

Without looking back, Nightshade vanished into the back room that led to the kitchen. A few minutes later, Badger trotted after him, then Prigg. When she'd made certain that their leaving hadn't been noted, Maudie left the bar in Mayhew's charge, went through to the kitchen and up the back stair. In the last room down a dark hall, Nightshade was sprawled on a rickety bed, his legs crossed at the ankles on the footboard, his gaze fixed on the tips of his boots. His head was propped on his arms, which rested on a pile of her best pillows. Her only good pillows. She scowled at Badger and Prigg, who scuttled to the other side of the room.

Maudie shut the door, put her back to it, and crossed her thick arms over her chest. "Why are you back, Nightshade?"

"Dear Maudie," Nightshade said without looking at her. "As subtle as pig's dung. I've missed you, too."

"You only come back to make trouble for the rest of us. So I don't see no reason to make merry. Last time you showed your pretty face, Chokey got his throat slit for you."

"Chokey went with me for his own interest."

"He went with you for the same reason poor old Badger here does, and Prigg, and the rest of your followers. You twist them and beguile them until they don't know day from night, and then you use them. You're the worst of the leaders, Nightshade. You use us like you use your boots."

Nightshade sat up so swiftly that Maudie would have backed away if she hadn't been against the door already. He swung his long legs off the bed, rose, and drew near her. Fixed on his mobile, dark lips was a smile of little-boy sweetness. He stopped in front of Maudie and cocked his head to the side.

"Usefulness is a virtue." He bent and whispered, "And since you profit the most from this virtue, you'll keep your complaints to yourself or I'll give you better reasons to reproach me."

Maudie's palms began to sweat, and she nodded. But Nightshade had already turned, with that swiftness of movement that recalled the acrobatics of a hawk in flight. He walked to the center of the room, raised his arms, and uttered a chimelike laugh.

"Good news, my perverse imps. There's blunt to be made. Easy, quick and lots of it."

Badger knocked his knees together in his eagerness to join Nightshade. "How much, governor? More than a quid?"

Nightshade ruffled Badger's ginger hair. "Much, much more."

Prigg joined them at this news.

"How much?" he asked with breathless anticipation.

"Ah," breathed Nightshade, "that's my greedy fellow. You'd sell your infant sister to a brothel for a quid, wouldn't you, Prigg?"

Prigg scowled at him. "You're a born devil, Nightshade. How much?"

"If you're quick and silent, ten pounds each."

"Ten!" Badger began to dance from one foot to the other.

Maudie interrupted. "What's the line of work? It can't be a crack, or we'd get a share of the loot. And it's got to be dangerous, for the price speaks of peril."

"You're good at selling watered ale, Maudie, but never think you're flash at the better sort of crime." Nightshade resumed his pose on the bed and surveyed the group with malicious benevolence. "An easy style of work, my imps. All we got to do is find a lady what's got lost in the rookeries."

His listeners exchanged glances. Then Badger spoke.

"Some toff's lady's got herself lost in St. Giles or Whitechapel, and we're to find her?"

"You're looking sharp," Nightshade replied as he fluffed his pillows.

Maudie shrugged. "If she's been gone for more than a day, she's either dead or in some brothel."

In one smooth movement Nightshade sat up and twisted around to face her with a nasty grin. "Not this one."

"Why not this one?" Maudie demanded.

"Because, my fine mistress of spirits and drunkards, she's a spinster, an old maid, plain, fussy, timid, and dowdy. Depend upon it. She's hiding in some dark, quiet hole of a place, quivering and whimpering."

Prigg snapped his fingers. "Wait. I heard tell that Mortimer Fleet and his dogs is looking for some woman. This her?"

"I doubt it," Nightshade said. "What would Fleet want with an old spinster lady? He's probably looking for one of his harlots what's took her wages without giving him his toll."

Prigg exchanged uneasy glances with Big Maudie, who turned a suspicious gaze on their leader. "You certain about this?"

Nightshade tossed his hair back from his face and laughed a soft laugh with all the sympathy of a viper. "It will be easy profit, my hounds. How difficult can it be to hunt down an old maid?"

❦

Eight nights later, the old maid scurried from a butcher's shop in Whitechapel. She was carrying a basket laden with food, tightly packed with its lid tied down. Glancing up and down the road as if fearful of being seen, the lady slipped into the blackness of

Knife Lane. She hurried past rows of neglected, once-elegant houses, and turned into an alley between the lane and a mews. There she set down the basket, stooped, and searched through yards of skirt for her back hem.

Had she not been wearing a threadbare, hooded cloak and been concerned with secrecy, Primrose Victoria Dane would have attracted attention from the street vendors, harlots, dock laborers, and char-women of east London. Few charwomen appeared distracted or had a distant gaze that seemed fixed on a dream just out of everyone else's sight; fewer still wore fashionable silk dresses.

Beyond her dress, Primrose would have caught the notice of anyone who appreciated hair with as many shades of blond as a bird has feathers and merry eyes whose gray-green depths were ringed with teal. Her refined appearance gave an impression of meekness not often met in Whitechapel. This impression was supported by the delicacy of her carriage, the fluidity of her walk, and the air of apologetic hesitation Prim often wore in company. Certainly none of her ac-quaintance or the inhabitants of east London would expect Miss Primrose Victoria Dane's soft hands, with slim fingers that ended in pink, rounded tips, to be employed in the tasks they'd undertaken lately in or-der to survive.

Those pink fingertips finally found the hem of her gown and pulled it up between her legs. Prim stuffed it into her front waistband. Now she could move and climb without tripping over her skirt. Picking up her basket, she hooked it on one arm and got into a wagon with a broken spoke that had been left in the alley beside the mews. Balancing on the seat, she gripped a window ledge and began to climb.

Prim wasn't nearly so frightened as she had been two weeks ago when she'd first run away. Not that she'd meant to run away, but that's what one did when one witnessed a murder and the killer chased one into the rookeries of St. Giles. She had been on her way to teach the poor Kettle children their weekly lesson, and she'd been late because Lady Freshwell had once again objected to her "going about in the company of rude persons," meaning little Alice Kettle, who had come all the way across London by herself for the honor of accompanying Prim. Lady Dorothy Freshwell, whom Prim had secretly christened "the hedgehog" for her unfortunate resemblance to that snout-nosed and prickly creature, was her aunt.

Prim had finally escaped the hedgehog, and she and Alice had taken the Freshwell carriage. But the delay had brought them into St. Giles at dusk. Since Aunt Freshwell needed the carriage back at once, Prim got out a few blocks from her destination and sent it back. Alice knew a shortcut to the house where the informal school was held.

They were hurrying through the darkening streets when they turned down a narrow passageway beside a tavern. Prim didn't know what made her stop; perhaps it was the men's voices—meat-grinder hard and vicious. She saw three people ahead, clutched Alice, and shrank against a wall. Slowly, so as not to attract the attention of the group, she slipped behind a stack of crates that came up to her chin.

Why had she stayed? In those moments of hesitation, when she could have retraced her steps, she'd glimpsed the face of the woman. Cheeks red with garish rouge, lips a gash of crimson, the woman's features contorted as she saw the first man raise the knife over her head. Frozen in horror and disbelief, Prim had opened her mouth to cry a warning, when the second man grabbed the woman. Nothing came out of her mouth, and the knife plunged.

Prim paused in her climbing. She squeezed her eyes shut and fought the return of images. What came to her instead was the vision of the second man, a man she never expected to see in St. Giles. She heard his words again: "Do it, Fleet." Three words that had wrought such evil. Why hadn't she left the alley at once? If she had, she would never have heard the second man give the order to kill, would never have seen how he watched the murder he'd ordered with the placid expression of a visitor to an art gallery.

She knew his name, the one who had caused murder with three calm words. He had attended her aunt's ball only last month. He should have been in some silk-draped drawing room or on a bench in Parliament. Prim bit her lower lip and made herself forget the man's face for the moment. Her object was to get back to the Kettles' bare apartment alive and unnoticed.

She gripped the top of the wall and climbed up to balance on the gutter of the mews. Alice Kettle's younger brothers, the twins Hal and Hugh, had taught her the art of roof traveling. Prim inched her way across the mews. Reaching the next building, she stepped up to a window, climbed to a higher roof, and crossed its flat expanse. Prim almost smiled as she wondered what Lady Dorothy Freshwell would say of this activity, if indeed she could even recognize her charge. No doubt she would turn prickly and lament the demise of the real Primrose, that retiring, bookish dreamer who gave no trouble and seldom put herself forward. Her dire situation had occasioned the change. She had managed to adapt in order to survive, but Prim was certain Lady Freshwell would rather see her dead than climbing roofs and living with the Kettles.

She continued her progress for some minutes without having to descend, but eventually was forced to use a crooked passage that would take her past a street full of taverns, a music hall, and a brothel—the existence of which she had recently learned from the twins. She hurried to cross an intersection with an alley off the main road, for it contained a gaslight. As she stepped into the open, a man smoking a pipe and wearing an ugly green-and-red-checked waistcoast passed the light.

Prim suppressed a gasp and shrank back into the shadows of the passageway. The man paused in the yellow glow to tamp down some tobacco in the bowl of his pipe and light it. His face was grimy, as if he worked in a coal mine, and his hair, which might have been blond, was greasy and clung to his head and ears. When he drew on his pipe, Prim could see that his front teeth were brown near the gums. She knew this man.

Jowett was one of the ruffians sent to hunt her

down. The two murderers had seen her in that alley. They'd chased her, lost her, and now had sent their hirelings to find her. Which was why Prim couldn't go home. She'd never reach the West End of London alive. It was difficult enough to fetch food for the Kettles, who had taken her in and hidden her, but she was determined to succeed. Betty Kettle had just given birth to her ninth child. The poor woman was exhausted and undernourished. She needed the mutton and fresh milk Prim had purchased; she wasn't likely to get help from her husband, who drank most of his wages.

Prim waited until Jowett continued on his way before she crossed the intersection. Then she took to the roofs again. Jowett had a partner named Stark. Prim had been chased by them several times. They always moved together, so she would have to keep alert for the pair. She hurried across another flat roof and was about to leap down to a lower one when Jowett appeared. She crouched and watched him skulk down the road to stand almost directly below her. He stood there and turned his narrow, dirty head in a half circle, like some questing vulture. Then he leaned against the wall and dug out a tobacco pouch.

Prim waited a while, but Jowett had taken root. The longer she remained outside, the greater the chance she would be found. Prim set her basket down and glanced over the roof. It was littered with old newspapers, broken glass, and straw. Here and there lay bricks and chunks of mortar. Prim picked up a brick. Its surface was rough against her hand. She hefted it, but glanced up when she caught movement out of the corner of her eye. Seeing nothing, she chided herself for being so excitable and looked over the roof at the top of Jowett's head.

Still hefting the brick, she noted that the man wore a cap, but it was made of thin material. Prim stood with her feet planted apart and raised the brick in both hands. She had always been good at playing catch and throwing a ball with her younger brother. Pray God she still had the skill. Prim kept her eyes on her target, gripped the brick tightly, and hurled it down. The missile hit Jowett square on his greasy skull. He dropped to his knees and then to the ground, without uttering a word, his pipe and pouch still in his hands.

Prim rose and dusted her hands. Taking up her basket, she put her foot on the edge of the roof, preparing to spring across to the next building. She bent her knees and leaped, but something snaked around her waist and pulled her back. Someone had grabbed her! She sailed through the air and was set on her feet, but in her panic she lost her footing. The basket flew out of her grip and her skirt came loose from her waistband. She landed beside the basket on her bottom, her skirts above her knees, the hood of her cloak askew. Ignoring the pain in her bottom, Prim wrestled out of the tangle of her cloak and skirts and grabbed a nearby brick. Scrambling to her feet she backed away from the dark figure looming over her.

"Come nearer and I'll bash you!"

If she had ever imagined the laughter of a demon, it would have been the sound that came tumbling at her. All mockery, chapel chimes, and evil, just like

what would issue from a fallen and corrupt angel.
Fear wrapped a sheet of ice around her body. The
man who had grabbed her sauntered closer, close
enough for her to see him in the light of the moon.
Silver illuminated his face. Slim, mobile lips curled
into a smile that almost gave her relief. But she looked
into his eyes—and was almost dragged into the depths
of a black and perilous sea. It was then that Prim
knew she was going to die.

The man put his hand beneath his coat and withdrew something. Prim nearly dropped her brick in
her alarm that he had a knife, but he wasn't even
looking at her. He was looking at a picture. His gaze
lifted to her face, and his brow furrowed. Then his expression changed again; the mockery and ruthlessness
returned. She heard a soft murmur that should have
allayed her terror but fed it instead.

"Choke me dead. It's the old maid at last."

2

This was one ruffian she hadn't seen before. She would have remembered him: that air of amused menace, those eyes that rivaled the night in their darkness and malevolence, that loose, careless stance that belied the agility and speed of his movements. She would have remembered him, too, because he was clean. Black-haired, black-clad, black of spirit, he nevertheless wore his rough clothing as if it had been tailored for him. His hair was long, nearly touching his shoulders, and he had a habit of tilting his head down and looking up through a curtain of silken blackness. The gesture should have made him seem coy; the absence of a hint of conscience or pity in his eyes made it frightening instead.

The brief moment in which she glimpsed her attacker passed, and she realized that he was smiling at her. Old maid? This hound of hell had called her an old maid! Ever since she'd witnessed the murder, Prim had been discovering things about herself. One was that she had little use for propriety and good manners in the rookeries of London; the other was that she liked not having to curb her conduct. While the ruffian continued to smile at her, she slowly bent and grasped her basket.

"You're not near as ugly as your picture shows," the ruffian said.

"I hope I may be pardoned if I don't think you for the compliment."

Prim waited for him to reply while she straightened, but his gaze dropped. She looked down to find that part of her skirt was still tucked into its waistband, exposing her legs. One stocking had ripped to reveal an expanse of white flesh from thigh to calf. She lifted her gaze and found that he had done the same. There was that habit again—his head was down, but he was looking up at her. And something violent and disturbing erupted in his eyes.

Whatever it was provoked a strange response in her. For an instant she wasn't frightened but drawn, excited, and then he smiled again. The infamous creature knew what she felt! He'd given her that look deliberately. Her susceptibility frightened Prim, and her fear made her angry. She hauled the basket up and swung it, hitting the ruffian in the stomach.

"Ooffh!" He doubled over.

Following Hal and Hugh's advice to hit an enemy when he was down, Prim then bashed her attacker on the head with the basket. He dropped to his knees. As she raced across the roof, she heard a curse that would have earned the man a place in hell had he not already been assured one. She increased her speed as she neared the edge and sprang over the gap between her and the next roof.

She heard running steps. He was after her already, and he was too fast for her to outrun on the rooftops. Prim veered to the right and leaped to another roof that was lower by a story. Then she thrust herself over the side and half climbed, half slid to the ground. Not looking back, she ducked into the shadows, away from a gaslight, and slid between a stack of crates and the wall of the building from which she'd just climbed. Setting down her basket, she pulled her cloak hood over her head, flattened herself against the bricks and breathed deeply and quietly. She waited.

Her breathing hadn't calmed when she heard a soft footstep above her head. Moments later a slim shadow seemed to melt down the side of the building not a yard from where she stood. Prim forced herself to breathe steadily. The ruffian stood still in the dim gaslight; his black silk curtain of hair swung as he turned his head, tilted it, listened. He turned toward her, and Prim nearly screamed. When he looked away, she silently thanked Providence.

Then, in the time it took her to blink once, he disappeared. That he could accomplish such a feat was more frightening than being chased. He would come upon her, and she would have no warning. Prim began to tremble and had to talk sternly to herself.

This is no time to lose courage. Take heart. What did Hal and Hugh say? When they're chasing you, circle around so that you come behind them. Circle, Primrose Victoria, make a circle.

She waited a few more minutes before setting out. Eventually she traversed a section of the dock district, but it was a long trip. On the journey she saw no more of the black-haired ruffian, and she made her way back to the cramped dark apartment shared by all the Kettle family without further trouble.

She saw no more hunters for the next two days. Her time was taken up with nursing Betty Kettle, who was not recovering well from the birth of her ninth child, little George. The provisions Prim brought helped, but the family lived at the edge of an abyss created by the drunkard father.

Frightened, uncertain about how to remedy her dangerous situation, Prim spent much of her time alternating between trying to solve her difficulty and staving off terror that she would be discovered and bring ruin to the Kettles. The third day dawned, as dim and cheerless as a November day could be in a tenement with no water or facilities. The family shared an outhouse with the entire building. The communal water pump was down the road and often foul, as its water came from the Thames, which was used as the city's dumping ground.

At the moment Prim was climbing the stairs to the third floor with two buckets of water. The younger children were playing in the street, and Sidney Kettle, Betty's husband, had gone to the docks to hire himself out. Hal and Hugh were pursuing their nefarious occupations and wouldn't be back until after dark. Prim

set the buckets on the landing and opened the apartment door. Alice Kettle met her holding baby George.
The child looked too thin and weak to support the
weight of the infant and his blanket, but Prim had
learned that her appearance concealed strength of
character as well as body. Alice managed all the children. Indeed, she managed the entire family, quite an
accomplishment for a girl of ten.

"Mam is asleep," Alice whispered. "She looks much
better since you give her that meat, miss." Alice hefted
George onto her shoulder and patted his back.

"I'm glad."

Prim set a bucket down and brought the other to
the iron brazier that served as the family's only stove.
She poured water into a pan and set it on the brazier.
It would take a long time to boil, but she had heard
that heating the water would make it healthier.

"Now," she said to Alice, "where is that mending?"

Alice pointed to a heap of clothing on one of the
pallets that served as bedding for the children. While
Prim sewed, she drew from Alice more of the family's
history, their hopes and their adventures. She listened
at first, but after a while Prim's thoughts returned to
the black-haired ruffian, as they had too often since
she'd first seen him. He'd been so different from all
the others who had hunted her. His person and clothing had been clean; Prim had discovered long ago that
poverty made cleanliness difficult. Therefore he was a
successful ruffian.

And he was alarming in his perfection of form.
Prim was ashamed of herself for dreaming of the man.
She had created pleasant fantasies before, but these

dreams had little magic in them. In them she felt no sweeping, selfless love; she felt desire. Well-brought-up young ladies shouldn't dream of touching a man as she imagined she touched this black-eyed villain.

Her dreams began with him standing over her, half in darkness, his head lowered in that mysterious and menacing attitude. His hair concealed all but his eyes. These were raised to look at her with that strange expression that frightened and attracted her at the same time. What was it about his eyes that gave him such power? When he assumed that stance with his head lowered, he didn't smile. One might think he was about to threaten murder from the severity of his expression, but in her dreams, that look seemed the precursor to pleasure, dark, wild and forbidden. She hoped never to see him again.

"Are you still going to the fish market tonight, miss?"

"We must have something to eat."

"But I can go, miss. I done it lots."

"You do too much," Prim said as she set a mended smock aside. "Tonight you must get some rest."

Alice nuzzled her face against the sleeping baby's head. "Pa wants more rent."

When she had sought refuge with the Kettles, Sidney had demanded payment for room and board, then promptly went to the tavern down the street to drink until he'd used up the entire amount. If Sidney wasn't supplied with drinking funds, he became violent. Alice and the children spent much of their time scrounging for money to keep him inebriated and pacific.

Prim lifted her skirt and withdrew a shilling from a pocket in her petticoat. Handing it to Alice, she said, "Give him this."

Alice gave her solemn thanks and slipped the coin in her apron pocket. "You should go home, miss. It ain't' right you being here. This place isn't good enough for you."

"This place isn't good enough for you, Alice, or for anyone. And you know I can't go home. The man we saw knows me, and he'll be watching Lady Freshwell's house."

Prim had no family except her brother, John Harold, who was at Oxford. After her father died, John Harold had inherited the family estate, and it was in trust for him while he was at university. As the son and heir, he had gotten almost everything. Like Sidney Kettle, Prim's father had been fond of liquor and left his family with little upon which to live beyond the entailed estate.

Prim had a meager sum of her own, not enough to purchase her own home, but enough to provide her with food and clothing. With John Harold away at university there did not seem to be enough money to support Prim at home. A manager took care of the estate, but John Harold was to close the house. Eventually, out of duty, her aunt Freshwell had offered Prim a place as her companion. In desperation, Prim had accepted.

By now Lady Dorothy Freshwell no doubt thought Prim dead. Prim assumed her aunt had sent servants to search for her when she didn't meet the carriage at the appointed time, but they had, of course, failed.

What she and her son Newton, Lord Freshwell, had done to recover their relative after that Prim couldn't guess.

Whatever it was, it would have been discreet. Lady Freshwell had a horror of scandal, especially now that Newton was being considered for a place in the queen's household. To become a member of such an exalted community was the lodestar of Newton's existence. It was the primary reason he and his mother entertained so much—currying favor took a great deal of effort. And it was expensive. Prim wished him success, for Newton was an irritating, pompous little whiner whose presence she wouldn't miss if he were to spend months at court.

Prim brought her mending closer to see it more clearly. Then she realized the light was fading. Setting the garment aside, she said, "It's time I was off if we're to have fish pie for our supper."

She went to the corner of the room near the window. There, a patched curtain had been suspended from an old rope to form a partition. Behind it slept Betty Kettle in the only bed the family possessed. Betty wasn't much older than Prim, but the births of so many children, combined with backbreaking labor as a charwoman, had taken her health.

Having ascertained that Betty's childbirth fever hadn't returned, Prim donned her cloak. Before she picked up her basket, she assured herself that her treasure was still safe in its secret pocket in the lining of the cloak. She felt for the shape of the book. It wasn't much bigger than her hand, but it was worth more than the sum of all her other possessions, at least, to

Prim. Satisfied that the book was safe, she set out for Billingsgate fish market.

She could have purchased fish pies from a vendor in Whitechapel, but the street hawkers were known to use inferior, sometimes spoiled ingredients. It was safer to go to the huge dock market where a friend of Betty's gave the family an excellent price. As darkness fell, she joined the teeming crowds that moved ceaselessly along London's streets. The city had spewed the human contents of workhouses, banks, parks, squares, taverns, and shops. The din of countless horses, wagons, carts, omnibuses, and trains rose up to meet her along with the noise of street vendors and urchins.

When she reached Billingsgate, the crowds thinned a bit, but the smell of mountains of fish pervaded everything. She could hear the cries of the sellers: "Five brill and one turbot. Have the lot for a pound! Look here, look here! Here's your fine Yarmouth bloaters! Who's the buyer? Who's the buyer?"

A vast shed rose up before her, and as she entered it, she beheld long tables piled with shining carcasses: pale-bellied turbot on strings, lobsters, baskets full of herring with glittering scales. She was jostled by men bearing heavy hampers and women with cod strung from their aprons.

Prim looked for Betty's friend, who sold cod and wore a green apron. She threaded her way among the stalls, baskets, and hampers, nearly running into a man with ginger hair who suddenly appeared in her path. He dodged aside quickly, and Prim glimpsed a green apron beyond a table crawling with lobsters. She was rounding the table when a thin, cold hand clamped on her wrist and spun her around. The ginger-haired man stood there grinning at her.

"Hallo, missy, now you just come with old Badger."

Prim froze and stared at Badger, whose pale complexion resembled the belly of a turbot. He tugged at her wrist. Prim dropped her basket.

"Release me, sir." Surreptitiously she stretched out her free hand while glaring at Badger.

"Not a chance, missy. You're worth too much. Now come along."

To her horror, Badger looked over his shoulder and raised his voice over the cries of the market. "Got her, Nightshade, neat as a new candle."

A man emerged from a crowd at a nearby stall, his clean black suit a contrast to the rough wool-and-leather-clad fish hawkers. Prim's eyes grew rounder than the fish staring up at her as she recognized the black-haired ruffian.

"Oh, heaven!" She picked up a lobster and smacked Badger on the head with it.

Badger cried out as the creature locked a claw onto his nose. He let Prim go, grabbed the lobster, and stumbled backward into Nightshade, who in turn fell against a man bearing a hamper. The three tangled together and fell beneath the hamper, which spilled turbot onto the floor. Prim was already scampering between aisles of fish. She didn't dare look behind her as she cleared the market. Her heart pounded, and she dodged customers and groups of people huddled together to divide their purchases.

Breaking free of a knot of women carrying pails of fish, she began to run. This wasn't Whitechapel, where she knew some of the streets. They would catch her and throw her in the river! Prim had always feared drowning. The feel of water in her nose, her throat and lungs, suffocating. They would tie her up so that she couldn't swim, so that she would be unable to save herself.

Horror gave her speed. Prim raced through the streets, taking back alleys, crossing through mews and abandoned warehouses, always heading north toward Whitechapel. Finally she ran out of breath and was forced to stop. She ducked into a doorway situated well away from any streetlight.

While she fled, the night had grown black. Clouds obscured the moon with a yellow-green haze, and their cousin, the dirty mist, returned to the streets of London. Prim's chest heaved. She wiped her damp face with a kerchief, and it came away begrimed with the soot that seemed always suspended in the air. She was parched; her hair was limp and damp, and she shivered, although more from fear than the cold. Someone was coming!

Prim shrank back until she pressed against the door. A carriage came down the street, and she didn't breathe until it had gone by. Then a man stumbled around the corner. He took a swig from a bottle in his hand and wove his way across the street. Prim watched him, ready to bolt should he suddenly come at her. The man steadied himself by placing his free hand against the walls of the buildings he passed.

She was still watching him when the door at her back opened and she fell. Arms grabbed her, lifted her off her feet, and she was trapped in a relentless grip as frightening as being bound by ropes and drowned. A hand covered her mouth before she could scream. She kicked hard, hitting a leg and provoking a curse, and she kept kicking. She heard a light, amused voice over her head.

"You're a precious sly and deceitful creature, and if you kick me again I'll give you a tap worse than you gave poor old Badger."

Prim stopped kicking. She could feel his hand rubbing her ribs.

"That's better. Choke me dead if you're not the damnedest old maid that ever was."

3

He hadn't expected this at all. Nightshade tightened his hold on Miss Dane while he waited for Badger and Prigg to bring the hansom cab they'd borrowed. He'd been asked to find a gently reared spinster lost in the East End of London, and he'd been put to more trouble than if he'd crossed his old enemy Mortimer Fleet. She squirmed in his grasp, and he hissed a curse under his breath. Plain she might be, but feeling her against him scraped across his desire like a file against glass.

"Rot Badger and Prigg," he whispered to himself. "They're late."

There was no response from his captive. Not that she could speak with his hand over her mouth—her warm, soft, pink mouth. What was he thinking? Old maids didn't have warm, soft mouths. For certain they didn't have pink ones with gently rounded lower lips and a habit of allowing the tip of a rosy tongue to peek out from it when thinking.

Rot her! She was the cause of him coming back to a place he wanted to forget. And she'd got away from him. Nobody got away from Nightshade. Big Maudie and her crew would laugh if they knew this little creature had led him a dance over the roofs of Whitechapel.

They'd enjoy his defeasance. That was a new word of his. Defeasance; it meant defeat. He'd got himself one of them dictionary books. Interesting things, dictionary books. They had great lists of complicated words that meant something simple like defeat.

The old maid started squirming. Her hips rubbed against him, and Nightshade felt a spike of sensation shoot through his body.

"Defeasance!"

She tried to turn her head, as if to question him. Nightshade lowered his voice. "You get one more warning, Miss Primrose blighted Dane. You quit rubbing your arse against me privates, or you'll end up on this floor. It's wonderful what a man will do when his blood is up."

From that moment she became as rigid as a tomb effigy in Westminster Abbey. Luckily the hansom cab clattered up to the door, and Prigg jumped out. Nightshade swept his captive into the carriage before she could protest. He threatened her with grievous consequences if she even tried to speak, and lapsed into an ill-humored reverie that lasted until they reached the Black Fleece Tavern.

He had Badger and Prigg bundle the lady into a room and lock the door. Then, remembering her talents, he ordered the room's window barred from the outside. Maudie grumbled at the trouble, but sent the boy who did the washing-up to nail a board over the shutters. Badger went to the kitchen where Prigg attempted to repair the damage done to his friend by the lobster.

Out front, while Larder Lily sat on his lap and ate the meat pie he'd ordered, Nightshade spent an hour mastering himself. It had been many years since he'd suffered the torments of a boy's ungovernable urges. How this plain and troublesome spinster could have turned him fruity in the brief time he'd been near her mystified him. She irritated him; no, she made him furious, causing all this trouble for him. He hated coming to Houndsditch, and he hated her for being the cause of his return. He would get rid of her.

Maudie appeared, hands on hips, and glared at him. "I don't want no trouble here. You brung that woman to my place, and I don't want no trouble."

"Don't get your petticoats twisted," Nightshade snapped as he shoved Lily off his lap. "She's going to disappear sprightly."

Turning his back on Maudie, Nightshade swept upstairs and let himself into the room where his captive waited. As he shut the door a chair sailed at him, knocking his shoulder as he ducked to avoid it. The chair slammed into the door. A candle stand nearly hit him in the face as he rose. He leaped aside and raced across the room as the young woman hurled a pitcher at him. It hit the floor and shattered as he sprang the last few feet and tackled her. She cried out, and they fell to the bed, which collapsed under their weight.

Nightshade heard running steps, but he was too busy trying to avoid scratching nails and kicks from small, booted feet. She landed a slashing blow on his neck.

"God rot you!"

"Nightshade?"

He grabbed both her hands and looked over his shoulder at Badger and Maudie while his captive tried to kick him senseless. "Get out, damn you. Badger, lock the door and wait for me."

When the door was shut, he closed his eyes. The old maid was rocking back and forth, thrusting her body against his in an attempt to shove him off her. Setting his jaw, he hissed at her.

"Stop it! Just bleeding stop it! You must be perfectly blithering mad, or desperate to get tupped."

The struggling ceased, but he counted to twenty before he opened his eyes. She was staring up at him, her eyes wide. That tight little bun she wore had come loose, and her hair had fallen about her shoulders and across her cheeks and temples. Some of the strands were pale gold, others a darker, old-wheat color, some light amber, and some the color of bleached almonds. He'd never seen so many colors in a person's hair. When he found himself trying to count them, his anger returned. It didn't help that she was breathing so hard that her chest kept pushing his. It was like being teased by an experienced and talented harlot. Nightshade kept his grip on the old maid's wrists, but he shoved himself up on his elbows so that there was enough distance between them for him to keep his sanity.

This measure gave him a chance to really look at her for the first time. Primrose Victoria Dane hardly resembled the sketch he'd been given. The sketch must have been taken from a portrait done about ten years ago, for her cheeks no long puffed out from childish plumpness. No, the sketch had been bad. Beneath him lay a young woman who would never be called beautiful, but who with age had acquired a neatness of feature that pleased him. He liked her eyes, the rings of teal surrounding a burst of gray-green. He liked the way, if one looked closely, her nose seemed just a tiny bit off center. He especially liked her generous breasts. Too bad he didn't like her.

He growled at the cause of all his grievances. "Are you going to behave yourself, or shall I throw up your skirts and paddle your bottom till it's red?"

"Infamous creature!"

"That's not a promise," he said lightly as she began to fight him again. He let her struggle until she wore herself out and lay beneath him panting and defeated. "Now, do you admit defeasance?"

She frowned at him. "I beg your pardon?"

"D'you admit defeat, defeasance?"

"I shan't throw anything at you if you will release me."

Nightshade got up, discovered that he wasn't presentable, and turned away from her while he got himself under control. When he faced her again, she had put the collapsed bed between them and was gathering hairpins from the floor and blankets. She stopped when he moved. Her hand clenched around the pins as if she might use them as a missile should he threaten her again.

"Never heard of no lady who preferred the noisome stews and dens of the East End to a toff's house."

"What are you talking about?"

"Oh, never mind, Miss Primrose blighted Dane. I don't care why you're here. You're going home to Lady Freshwell's, so don't throw nothing else at me."

Miss Dane's tongue appeared at the corner of her mouth, and she appeared to be confused. Then her expression grew contemptuous. "I understand. That man Fleet has finally realized he must question me before he kills me. I did not credit him with the intelligence, but perhaps his master issued the decree."

"Fleet?"

Nightshade's thoughts went blank. The name meant more to him than she could know. Mortimer Fleet was as black a soul as the rookeries had ever produced, and Nightshade owed him much—curses, plagues, all manner of evil. He thrust aside his hatred as he realized something he'd have noted sooner if he hadn't been distracted by a pink mouth and multicolored hair. And flying lobsters.

"Choke me dead, Miss Primrose, you ain't lost. You're hiding. From Mortimer Fleet."

"I congratulate you, sir, on your theatrical capacity. However, I am quite capable of perceiving your rather simple trickery."

"Oy! What's this about trickery?"

"Do you think me so simple a creature as to trust you and tell you what you want to know?"

Miss Dane squared her shoulders and lifted her chin. She clasped her hands before her, and Nightshade blinked at the change. Somehow she had acquired a simple dignity that placed no reliance on fine clothing or palatial surroundings. This was dignity of breeding, of heritage, and above all, dignity of the soul.

"I decline to tell you anything, sir. I hope I am not so selfish as to risk the lives of others for my own sake."

"You was hiding from Fleet, and you think I work for him."

All he got was a slight nod.

"Why?"

"I find this pretense tedious, Mr. Nightshade."

"Not Mr. Nightshade, just Nightshade."

"In polite society, ladies do not address gentlemen so familiarly."

"Well, you're nowhere near polite society, but you soon will be. I'll prove I'm not Fleet's man by taking you home."

"You know very well I cannot return to my aunt's house."

"And why not?"

"I really do grow weary of this game, sir. Perhaps you toy with me to wear me out. Perhaps you threaten to take me home because you want to remind me that if I return, I'll be dead by sunrise."

She said this so simply, so without emphasis that, at last, he believed her. Miss Primrose Dane had been running for her life ever since she vanished. If he took her home and she was killed . . .

"Well, damn and blight me," he said to himself.

"I have no doubt of it."

He grinned at her. "Watch your tongue, Miss Prim, or you'll get that hiding I promised. No, don't say anything. I'm thinking."

"A task that requires your utmost effort, I'm sure."

He heard her, but pretended not to notice. "Hmm." He shook his head. "There's no helping it. If going home will get you killed, I got to take you somewhere else."

"Now we're closer to the truth. You're taking me to Mortimer Fleet."

"Bleeding hell, woman. How is he in this?"

"How can he not be?"

"You don't know what Fleet is, Miss Prim. What you seen so far is naught to what he can do if he's pushed."

"You know your master well."

"Stupid woman, what have you got yourself into? I didn't bring you here in secret, you know. By now, the streets are full of the news." Nightshade went to the door. "Badger, tell Prigg to get a few of the boys and set a watch. Fleet's got his fingers in this pie. And tell Maudie we'll be leaving sooner than I thought. She should be pleased."

From the other side of the door came a loud reply that faded as Badger trotted for the stairs. "Fleet? Fleet? Fleet? Ooo. Terrible trouble, bad, bad luck. Cursed luck."

Nightshade came back to stand by the bed, thinking hard about the next few hours. When he looked at Miss Dane again, she had pinned her hair back into its neat little bun at the nape of her neck. He almost smiled at the way it made her look like a girl of sixteen trying to masquerade as a dowager.

"Mr. Nightshade, I will pay you to let me go."

For some reason, he was offended. To cover this weakness, he scoffed. "You got the blunt to pay me?"

"Not at the moment, but I have a small independence. If my solicitor will allow it, I can touch the principal."

"I hear you got a brother who's set. What about him?"

"My brother's fortune is bound up in the estate, and he is at Oxford. You cannot know how much is required by such an education."

"Wait," he said with suspicion. "You mean you got a brother with an estate and the blunt to go to university, and yet you're living on the charity of this Lady Freshwell."

Miss Dane's expression grew cool. "I have no wish to confide in *you* the intimate particulars of my family's affairs. Will you accept payment?"

"No."

"It would be a great deal."

"How much?"

She answered eagerly. "Fifty pounds."

"Ha! Not enough, Miss Prim."

Miss Dane gasped. "You never intended to accept!"

"Just wanted to know how much you could afford.

Now I know one of them intimate particulars you was so anxious to hide."

She uttered a long, wordless cry of disgust. He grinned at her, and all dignity deserted Miss Primrose Dane. She stooped and reached beneath the bed. Nightshade saw what she had in her hands and bolted for the door. He dodged aside just as the chamber pot crashed against the portal, and blessed his luck that the vessel was empty. Porcelain shattered in all directions. A shard bit into his cheek. He shouted a blasphemy and called to Badger. The door opened. He hurtled through it and slammed it shut seconds before Miss Primrose Dane threw a pitcher of water at his head.

When the noise of the pitcher's demise had ceased, he yelled through the door. "You're getting awfully close to that hiding, Miss Prim. Think how much it will hurt to make a bumpy carriage journey sitting on a sore bum!"

He listened for her response, but all he detected was shocked, maidenly silence.

4

Larder Lily shoved Alice Treacle off Nightshade's lap. Alice hit the floor and screeched as she lunged up and smacked Lily across the face. Nightshade rose, dumping Lily and grabbing Alice's arm before she could strike again. All around them Maudie's customers turned to whistle, shout encouragement, and clap. Lily ducked under Nightshade's arm and would have kicked Alice had Nightshade not grabbed her by the hair.

"Here now!" He shook the two. "Any more of this, and I'll not be having with either of you."

"Bleeding whore," Alice muttered, and spat at her rival.

A shrill exchange of insults followed, escalating into the far reaches of vulgarity. Neither woman saw Nightshade's eyes roll or the way his finely drawn lips curled in distaste. If they had, perhaps they would have curbed their rough conduct, but they were too deep in their jealousy. Finally, Nightshade dragged them to the kitchen and out the back door, and shoved their heads in a rain barrel. They came up spluttering and shivering, but Nightshade whirled and stepped inside, slamming the door behind him.

Both women rushed back into the kitchen to warm themselves by the fire. Alice couldn't get warm, and she went in search of her cloak, vowing to return to her room and dry her hair. Larder Lily bullied a scullery girl into giving her a kitchen cloth. She dried herself with it, and crept to the doorway of the main room in time to see Nightshade finish a whispered conversation with one of his men. They went upstairs together, and Lily was certain they were going to the room where Nightshade had secreted that strange young woman.

Since his return, Lily's hopes of capturing Night-shade's interest had renewed. There wasn't a woman in east London who didn't want him. Lily was simply one of the more persistent, even in the face of his vicious tongue and the indifference he never bothered to hide from any woman. She had never known Nightshade to bring a girl to the Black Fleece. She didn't like the idea of another rival.

Walking casually through the tavern, Lily glanced around to make sure Maudie wasn't looking. Then she followed Nightshade upstairs. If he'd succumbed to the wiles of some fancy tart, she'd know what to do about it. She knew too well how easy it was to make someone vanish. No one was going to come between her and the most beautiful and successful thief in London.

Lily slithered up to the door to the woman's room and listened. When she heard nothing, she dared to open the door a tiny crack, but upon seeing no one, she pushed inside. The door hit something on the floor. Lily kicked aside pieces of porcelain, and noted the toppled furniture and collapsed bed. She was looking for some clue to the stranger's identity when she heard voices in the hall.

Rushing to the door, she was in time to see Prigg shove Nightshade's coat and a woman's cloak into Badger's arms. She followed the two at a distance down the back stairs and spied a hansom cab. Badger handed the garments to Nightshade, who was in the cab, and jumped up beside Prigg in the driver's seat. Lily tried to see beyond Nightshade to the other occupant, but Nightshade had thrown the cloak over the woman, and her face was concealed.

Suddenly Nightshade leaned out of the hansom and stared straight at her. Lily shrank inside and didn't dare look until she heard the cab roll into motion. Her last sight was of Nightshade's dark head withdrawing to the interior of the vehicle. She heard his voice.

"All speed, my imps. To Woolwich."

Lily shut the door and made her way upstairs, her steps slow as she thought. What business had Nightshade in Woolwich, a district far to the east of Houndsditch? Lily didn't know, but she smelled a chance for profit, if she brought this bit of news to someone's attention. Someone who could pay well. Nightshade and a mysterious woman.

Lily's sly brain worked steadily. Perhaps she could profit and get rid of Nightshade's woman at the same time. The trick would be not risking Nightshade— and keeping him from discovering her part in revealing his activities, of course.

⁂

Prim's eyelids felt like book weights. She had scooted as far away from Mr. Nightshade as the cab would allow and maintained vigilance. Certain that she was being taken to her death, she had decided to leap from the cab, even though they were going at a speed that would assure her injury. Just as she prepared to jump, the black-haired ruffian grabbed her wrist. Prim gasped, but he gave her an irritated snort.

"Daft creature. You'd break your neck."

It had been her last opportunity, for he'd kept hold of her wrist from then on. Now she was having great difficulty keeping her eyes open, for the journey was a long one, and being terrified all the time was exhausting. She fought to keep awake, and almost succeeded when she realized that they had traveled to Woolwich only to turn back. Mr. Nightshade was circling, just as she'd learned to do. Prim's eyes closed as she reflected upon the irony of their knowing the same tricks.

The sounds of the carriage and horses faded, then transformed into a waltz played by the musicians hired by Aunt Freshwell for this evening's ball. It was last summer, and the ballroom was packed with guests.

Prim looked on as the dancers whirled in a circle beneath glittering crystal chandeliers. The crowd of bodies made the room even warmer, and ladies were fanning themselves not just to draw attention to their white, rounded shoulders and bosoms, but to keep from perspiring. Ladies did not sweat.

The heat made it hard to breathe, and it made Prim's discomfort at sitting out so many dances all the greater. She had danced with Newton, but he didn't count. Newton's idea of cleverness consisted of looking down at her blue ball gown and remarking, "I say, isn't your dress blue?" If she had to listen to his inane conversation during another dance, she would stomp on his foot to escape.

The dancers spun in a great circle, turning as they went. Her head felt heavy from the heat. If she narrowed her eyes, the silks and brocades of the women's dresses blurred together, and she could imagine they were dancing jewels. Her game came to an abrupt end when she heard her name called. She opened her eyes to find David Acheson, an undersecretary for foreign affairs, approaching. Acheson was an acquaintance of Newton's, but not a friend. No one of Acheson's intellect and refinement could find Newton attractive as a companion. He came toward her, smiling, his lean elegance and poise a contrast to her own diffidence and moist stickiness.

"Miss Dane, Harcourt is coming to join us, if you have a moment."

"Of course."

"So kind of you, for you see, he's anxious to speak with you about an old book he's found in his father's library. He asked me, but I'm hopeless about historical things, and I knew you'd be just the person to talk to."

Acheson talked on, and Prim listened while trying to hide her humiliation. Acheson was a married man with a kind heart who had taken pity on her several times before at Society functions. He'd spotted her decorating a wall at an afternoon dance and made her his charity ever since.

"Before Harcourt comes, Miss Dane, I beg you to do me the honor of dancing with me," Acheson said with a graceful bow.

And so she danced. And spoke with Harcourt, who obviously had made up his story of an old book just to be able to oblige his friend and dance with her. Harcourt was almost as well tailored and mannered as Acheson, and more handsome with his chestnut hair, blue eyes, and the glamor of being a cavalry officer. Prim began to forget being the object of charity and enjoy herself. She even enjoyed dancing with a third victim snared for her by Acheson, the Honorable Robert Montrose, who was indeed the prize of the three, even if he was also married.

Montrose combined charm, elegance, and breeding with an almost French appreciation of arts. Unlike many of Society's male members, his conversation wasn't limited to sport and gambling, and he actually knew the difference between a psalter and a book of hours.

"Miss Dane, I find it fascinating that you care for old books. I have a fine collection, you know. I have a book of carols, fourteenth century, I think."

And so, in that hot ballroom, she became the object of attention from these three kind gentlemen. Their good deed, their protégée. At almost every ball, she could be assured that they would attend her and corner their eligible young friends to dance with her. Grateful and yet embarassed, Prim could think of no way to refuse their kindness.

After all, she didn't want to stand against the wall and endure looks of pity and condescension. Indeed, dancing with her gentlemen friends was such pleasure, and dancing with Robert Montrose the greatest pleasure. He was the most graceful of the three, and the most handsome. They whirled and sailed around the ballroom, faster and faster. The heat grew stiffling, but they didn't stop. On and on they danced, until Prim was so out of breath that her corset felt like a steel press.

Prim was awakened by a jolt of the cab. It had stopped, and her captor was moving. Her head fuzzy, suffering from the feelings of suffocation in her dream, she struggled to pull herself from the fog of confusion in which she found herself.

Nightshade descended and held out his hand. She blinked at him, afraid and too weary to do anything else. He sighed and lifted her to the ground. Dropping her unceremoniously on her feet, the ruffian shoved her ahead of him.

Prim glanced around at a world of fog that was rapidly turning a dim gray with the approach of morning. They were in a rear courtyard of some great deserted town house. When she saw the pitched roof high above her head and the dormer windows she hesitated. This was the residence of someone of great wealth, but not of the person she expected. That person's town house had no magnificent central dome resting on a base of Corinthian pilasters.

"Get on with you," Nightshade said.

She turned on him. "Mr. Nightshade, you've broken into this house."

"For a spinster you got a lot of fanciful notions."

He shoved her down a flight of stairs, into a vestibule, through a series of uninhabited service rooms. As she passed the butler's pantry, a man stepped into the hall, startling her and causing her to back into Nightshade. She trod on his boot. He swore, pulled her aside, and addressed the newcomer.

"Featherstone, is everything ready?"

"Yes, sir. If you will come this way?"

Prim was half escorted, half shoved after their host. Featherstone was a surprise to Prim. He cut a tall, kingly figure with the proud set to his head and his thick shock of silver hair. Prim had spent her life in houses like this. There was only one inhabitant who had such dignified bearing and manner of polite condescension. Featherstone was a butler. The ruffian had corrupted a butler!

Shaking her head, Prim almost forgot her own danger. Then she began to wonder why the ruffian had dragged her to this deserted place. At first she thought it was to murder her; then she realized he wouldn't want a butler for the purpose. By the time they reached a vast hall and mounted a staircase of white Italian marble, she was growing even more confused. Her mystification reached new heights when

Featherstone stopped outside a pair of doors and opened them.

"I thought the Blue Boudoir would suit your needs, sir."

"Thank you, Featherstone."

Prim turned to stare at Mr. Nightshade. In their short acquaintance, she had never heard him speak so civilly, or so grammatically. When he shoved her through the doors, she realized that his civility was limited to Featherstone.

"Bath and clothes," he snapped. "You'll have to make do yourself. No lady's maids around here. Don't take long. We're leaving quick."

As she stared at him, he closed the door and locked it. Prim gaped at the place where he'd been. All at once she burst into motion. Rushing across what had to be a sitting room, she thrust aside blue silk curtains and searched for the lock to the tall windows that formed one wall of the room. Then she stopped, for beyond the glass, the windows had been fitted with decorative wrought-iron grillwork. She hurried into the bedroom and found the windows the same.

Pounding her fist on the sill, Prim sank down on a bench beneath the window. It was some time before she could master her frustration and renewed fears, but when she noticed her surroundings, she was again surprised. The room was free of dust and looked as if some great lady was in residence. It boasted an antique bed of state, complete with a carved gilt canopy and blue silk damask upholstery.

She rose and walked to the bed. On it lay a traveling dress of a shining bronze fabric with braided trim and

matching jacket. There were a bonnet, gloves, and un-
derthings. Prim noticed gaslight coming from another
room and found a bath prepared in what had once
been a robing room. Steam from the water rose and
beaded the surface of a mirror sitting on an eighteenth-
century vanity. Prim glanced from the bath to the
traveling dress on the bed. The ruffian had not only
broken into the house but stolen clothes from the owners as well.

Her gaze drifted back to the bath. It, too, was
stolen. She would be stealing if she used it. But her
entire body felt caked with soot, and her arms and
legs were sore from running and struggling with Mr.
Nightshade. Nightshade! What if he were to come in
while she bathed? Prim went to the door between the
bedroom and the bathing room and closed it. There
was a key in the lock. She turned it and faced the
steaming bath. If she was going to be killed, at least
she would spend her last hours clean.

The bath felt as good as it looked. Sitting in the tub
with the steam rising all around her, Prim's weary
mind drifted away from thoughts of danger and death.
This house was the kind of place to which she was accustomed. She had been born to a life in such houses.
The past hadn't prepared her for Whitechapel or the
black-haired ruffian, for her parents had been Lord
William Harold and Lady Frances Dane.

Prim would be the first to admit that her birth had
been a disappointment. She could hardly miss the fact,
since her mother talked of it often. There was a
memory of being seven years old and allowed the
privilege of coming downstairs when her mother's

friends called. Prim, who spent most of her time with her nanny, was escorted into the drawing room to make her curtsey.

Lady Frances turned to her dear friend Lady Sarah with a lament Prim had overheard before. "I shall consider myself a failure until I have a son."

The declaration had little effect on Prim. She was used to hearing it from time to time. The first occasion had been when she was five. Until that day, she had thought herself the center of her little world. That one sentence had sent her crashing into the depths of bewildered misery. Her birth had been a misfortune, unwelcome, a disappointment.

When she was eleven, John Harold had come along, and the entire household rejoiced. All at once, her mother was jubilant. She held her head high and beamed her pride for all to see. At first Prim could see no reason to celebrate. All John Harold did was eat, sleep, and squall like a cat in a sack. Later she became acquainted with this little intruder and fell in love with his chubby face and golden curls. He would go for walks with her, his little hand clasped trustingly in hers. He came to her when he fell and bumped his head. He depended upon her to teach him how to tie his shoes.

And she tried hard not to take her feelings out on him when her mother would gaze upon John Harold with rapture and say, "My dear little John has rescued me from the catastrophe of a daughter." Or, "If I hadn't had a son, my life would be a blank."

In the years that followed, three more children were born to the Dane family. One was a boy, and his death was much lamented. Two were girls, whose appearances and deaths were barely noted. But the family title and name were safe, for John Harold was strong and would continue the Dane lineage.

William Harold, Prim's father, never lamented her birth as had her mother. Sir William was too busy attending to his horses, his gun dogs, his rents, and his liquor and gambling. However, Sir William's most abiding interest was in the position of his family and name. In his library, the most valued books were those mentioning the Dane name. The most precious documents were those proving how old the title was, and that there wasn't a draper or cobbler in the entire lineage.

And his daughter? Prim was certain that her father loved her. He had said so, in that offhand, fashionable way of his. He had said it in passing, as he was on his way to his club for an evening of cards and liquor. "You'll be a comfort to your mother in her old age," Sir William had said. Prim had rejoiced in her father's approval. Her spirits had been high for weeks.

Prim worshipped her parents as one did remote gods on top of mountains. She gave her love to her nanny, Mrs. Peace, and to John Harold. Left to herself much of the time—her company hardly ever necessary to anyone—Prim grew up creating her own friends and occupations in daydreams and pursuing adventures through her studies and reading.

By the time she was eighteen, Prim was comfortable with her place in the family. She came first with Nanny Peace, and first in the family—after her father, John Harold, and her mother, that is. She was the one whose engagements were canceled should anyone else need a carriage. She was the one whose preferences were asked last, if at all. Her place was to listen in admiration to her mother's social triumphs, to John Harold's tales of hunting rabbits and learning to jump a horse.

Prim sometimes offered little stories of her own, such as those of how she mastered French pronunciation, learned a piano sonata, or discovered a manuscript in the vast collection in the library. But her stories never seemed as interesting as the others. If they had been, her father wouldn't have interrupted so often. Her mother wouldn't have gotten that vacant look when Prim began, and John Harold wouldn't have made fun of her. By the time her mother died, giving birth to a stillborn daughter, Prim had ceased almost entirely to recount her own adventures to the family.

The growing chill in the bathwater distracted Prim and called her attention to her wrinkled fingers and toes. She washed her hair, left the bath, and dressed. It was impossible to put on her old clothes. She couldn't bear the idea of the soiled fabric next to her clean skin. She donned the traveling dress and vowed to repay its owner, should she live.

To distract herself while her hair dried, Prim found her old cloak and removed the book that had lain within it all this time. She slipped the small tome from the lining with exaggerated care, for the book was centuries old. It was an illuminated manuscript she had borrowed from her father's library, quite valuable. Some might say she had no right to take it, as the house and its contents were John Harold's. But her brother hardly set foot in the library. He didn't even know the book existed, while Prim loved it and knew its contents by heart. It was called *The Book of Hours of Yolande de Navarre*.

Ten years ago she'd come upon it while exploring the library, and she'd been studying illuminated manuscripts ever since. She dreamed of one day being able to write a treatise on the subject. But who would read it? Such a work would be of little use if no one saw it, and unless she could persuade some scholarly journal to publish it, no one would see it. Her chances weren't good. While the world accepted ladies as novelists, Prim knew what reception lady scholars received.

At the moment she needed a place to put the book. She finally slipped it into a drawstring bag that had been set out with the gown. It was made of fabric matching the traveling dress. As she pulled the drawstrings, she heard the lock in the sitting-room door turn. Prim was tempted to rush into the bathing chamber and lock herself inside, but there was no other way out, and Mr. Nightshade would only break down the door.

The sound of his voice made her jump. "You might as well come out."

Gripping her bag, Prim walked slowly into the sitting room. Nightshade wasn't even looking when she came in. He was turning the key in a traveling trunk beside the writing desk. Prim had been too preoccupied to notice it. When her captor rose and pocketed the key, Prim was startled at the change in his appearance.

His hair had been swept back from his face and was still damp from washing. He wore a suit of fine wool, woven with threads of black and dark forest green. The fawn brocade of his waistcoat contrasted with the dark suit, as did the fine linen of his shirt. The details of the cut of his coat, the semifitted waist, the slight flare near the hem, the lapel slant well above the waistline, all spoke of some little, unpretentious, and horribly expensive shop in the Strand.

Prim glanced at the gold watch chain that looped across his waistcoat and sniffed. "I suppose you chose this house because its owner's clothing fits you."

He gaped at her for a moment before grinning. "You're a right clever little thing, you are. Me and the old buster are right of a size together." He pointed at the trunk. "Got some duds for you too. Didn't steal them though. Featherstone got them for me."

Not believing him and having exhausted her store of remarks, Prim merely stared at him, wary and alert. When she didn't speak, Nightshade continued.

"Right. Now, we're leaving. Stayed too long in the city as it is. But before we go, I'm going to save meself a bit of annoyance by explaining how things are going to be. You can ride with me in the coach as long as you're quiet and don't give me no trouble."

"I shan't be any trouble, I assure you."

Nightshade gave her a skeptical stare. "Right. But the first time you give me trouble, you go in that." He pointed at the trunk.

Had he known her intimately, he couldn't have chosen a more terrible threat. Prim paled at the idea of being shut in that wooden box, locked in without any way to get out.

"Here!"

Prim felt a hand on her arm and realized Nightshade was supporting her. "I'm quite all right."

"You don't look too chirpy."

In spite of her protests, he guided her to a chair. Prim lay back in it with her eyes closed, but only for a moment because he knelt in front of her. Her eyes flew open to find him subjecting her to a severe examination. Then he raised his voice.

"Featherstone, you can come in."

The butler appeared bearing a tray. Prim smelled roast beef, which made her realize that her stomach was burning from emptiness. Nightshade pulled her out of her chair and guided her to one in front of the writing desk. Featherstone set the tray down and vanished at his master's command. Weariness was overwhelming her, and Prim just stared at the food, the china, the silver teapot, the white napkin. Then Nightshade gave her a gentle shove.

"Eat quick."

How could she be so hungry when she might be killed at any moment? Well, not at any moment, but soon. Prim gave up trying to understand her own inclinations and stuffed a forkful of roast in her mouth. While she ate, her captor poured tea and thrust the delicate china cup at her.

"Drink this."

Prim took the cup and poured half the little pitcher of milk into it. Then she heaped sugar in after it.

"Oy! You're ruining it. That tea is dear, I'll have you know."

Prim ignored him and drank the whole cup. Nightshade shook his head and walked to the window. He gazed out at the grounds until she finished. Then he came back to her.

"You want any more?"

"No, thank you," she said.

"Feeling better?"

She nodded.

"Well then, what's it to be—the coach or the trunk?"

Prim glanced at the trunk. "I should have known you would devise some such revolting scheme."

"That's right, you should have. Now give me an answer, Miss Prim."

"I shall ride in the coach."

She rose, ready to bolt as he approached her. "Just you remember that trunk's coming with us."

He was close now, too close for Prim to remain anything like calm. She smelled soap and freshly washed linen. Then she started as he took her hand and placed it in the crook of his arm. The gesture was disorienting, for it was one to be expected of a gentleman toward a lady in his care. He was escorting her out of the room as if they were a husband and wife on their way to the opera or a drive about the town.

All the way downstairs she could feel the warmth of his body, the hard mass of muscles beneath the expensive wool of his coat. In the entry hall, she received another surprise. Featherstone and a footman were waiting. The butler handed his master a woman's

mantle. Before she could protest, Nightshade whirled
it around her shoulders, and Prim found herself enveloped in velvet and fur. Her captor donned an overcoat and tall hat, then escorted her from the house.

When she stepped outside, Prim beheld a shining
black town coach drawn by four matching bays. A
footman and coachmen were loading the trunk, but
what caught Prim's attention was the heraldic arms
painted on the coach door. Before she could ascertain
whose arms they were, the footman opened the door
and she was hurried into the vehicle.

Setting such a house and its inhabitants at the service of a ruffian, even one like Mr. Nightshade, spoke
of wealth and power. As she scooted to the far side of
the seat, Prim realized the implication. The killer had
devoted his entire resources to finding her. He wanted
her in good health long enough to question her, and
the black-haired ruffian was just the kind of elegant
yet ruthless villain to accomplish the task.

She had her back pressed against the carriage wall
when her captor got in. He rapped a walking stick on
the roof, and the horses set off. As the carriage wound
its way around the curved drive and out the gate, the
ruffian reached for her. Prim threw up her arms and
cried out.

"Quit squawking."

She felt him grip her wrists. Despite employing her
full strength, her arms were forced down. Turning her
head aside, Prim strained away from this frightening
man. He held her wrists in one hand and leaned close.
When she felt his breath on her cheek, she gasped and
turned to face him. His gaze locked with hers, and she

thought she glimpsed the stirring of hell's fires. His hand moved slowly from her arm, up to her shoulder.

The feel of his hand caused Prim to shiver. He noticed and smiled. His hand neared her throat, and Prim nearly whimpered. Then he reached up and tugged on her bonnet, pulling the veil down so that it covered her face. While she goggled at him with her mouth hanging open, he released her and sat back against the leather squabs.

"Now, Miss Prim," he said softly. "You're going to tell me what's drove a fine-bred lady like you into hiding in the stews."

Fear was making her stomach queasy, but Prim sat up straight and said, "Mr. Nightshade, I should be an ill-conditioned wretch indeed if a bath, new clothes, and a little food caused me to forget my duty."

Her answer didn't appear to annoy him. Holding her gaze, he pulled off a pair of buckskin gloves, revealing hands with long fingers with whose strength she was too familiar. Slowly, with deliberate menace, one of those hands strayed to the top button of his overcoat and unfastened it. The second was undone, then the third. All the while Prim remained trapped in his dark stare.

"I can wait, Miss Prim. We got a long journey ahead, and I got plenty of time to think of a way to persuade you to talk." He slipped the overcoat off and put his hand on the button of his suit coat as he gave her an evil smile. "Choke me dead if before we're through, I don't have you pattering and babbling."

5

Nightshade unfastened the last button of his suit coat and leaned back in the carriage seat. "Well, Miss Prim. You going to save yourself a deal of trouble and tell me why you were hiding in the stews?"

"I should have thought you more clever than to repeat the same lies, Mr. Nightshade."

"I told you, I ain't in with Mortimer Fleet. Choke me dead. I never saw a lady more averse to getting herself rescued." He waited for her to answer, but she appeared to have fixed her attention on his hands. Her own clutched her bag as if it tethered her to safety. "You still don't believe me, after I put myself to the trouble of cleaning you up and giving you clothes and everything."

"I am not in the habit of believing the tales of

persons of furtive manner, ill-conditioned acquaintances, and revolting language."

Nightshade flushed and sat forward, propping his forearms on his knees This slight change in his position caused Miss Dane to gasp and throw herself against the carriage door. She fumbled for the handle. Nightshade was almost too late to stop her from turning it. He snatched her hand and dragged her back from the door. She fought him and landed a kick on his shin.

"Ouch! Blighted little tart, that hurt."

He thrust her into the opposite seat and rubbed his shin. She remained where she landed, staring, her eyes like small planets, her color fading. Nightshade grumbled to himself while he nursed his sore leg. When he glanced at his captive, he grew alarmed. He'd seen children that pale, usually after a beating or something worse. And she was trembling.

"Oy. Don't you go fainting on me."

Miss Dane's tongue appeared at the corner of her mouth and she straightened her shoulders. "I assure you, I have no intention of becoming vaporish. Nor do I consent to tell you anything about my situation."

"You still look bad." He eyed her complexion, searching for a hint of the pink that usually enhanced her cheeks and the glitter of determination that enlivened her gray-green eyes. He felt guilty for having been the cause of her present misery. "Now see here, Miss Dane. I'm not going to hurt you." He had to strain to hear her reply.

"But your master will."

All his irritation at the inconvenience she'd caused

him faded. He'd underestimated her fear, which meant he'd also underestimated the danger. "Bloody hell, Miss Dane. What's wrong? Oh, don't bother with that condescending retort of yours. I see I got to explain myself before you'll come out with the truth."

"I doubt any explanation of yours would suit, Mr. Nightshade."

"That's the first thing we got to change. My name isn't Nightshade. It's Luke Hawthorne."

"I'm sure you have many names."

"Well, that's the one I'm sticking at."

She didn't answer him, but he noted that she wasn't trembling so much. He'd distracted her.

"As to me being in somebody's pay, that's all wrong. Your aunt, Lady Freshwell, asked a friend of mine to help find you. He called on me, and here we are."

Miss Dane regarded him skeptically. "My aunt knows a friend of yours, Mr. Night—Hawthorne?"

This was the problem. He hadn't expected to have to convince the lady he rescued that he was an ally. Still less had he expected to be forced to prove himself respectable.

"Yes, well . . ." He cleared his throat and employed the grammar he'd abandoned so easily upon returning to the Black Fleece. "I suppose I'd better explain. You see, I'm not really Nightshade. That is, not any longer. I left Nightshade behind when I quit the East End. Years ago, I made my fortune and became a gentleman."

"Indeed."

"Oy! Don't you be sneering at me, Miss Prim. I

was better at thieving than most toffs is at guzzling wine. I got out of the stews and got me a gentleman's occupation. I even got me an education—some of it, leastways. And you can call me Sir Luke, 'cause that's who I am. Sir Lucas Hawthorne."

Miss Dane stared at him for a moment before looking out the window at the city traffic. "How long will it take us to reach your master?"

"Now you see here, Miss Primrose blighted Dane. I got no master. My friend Ross Scarlett come to me when you vanished and asked me to find you. As a favor to him, who I owe for his part in helping me get out of the rookeries. A proper gentleman is Ross Scarlett, and he knows your aunt."

"I have never heard of this person."

"Blow that. You ain't heard of most people, but they still exist. Choke me dead if you're not a proper sneering little dried-up nut of a creature."

"I find this conversation useless, Mr. Hawthorne."

"It's sir. Call me Sir Luke."

"I doubt if I could without feeling absurd."

"Absurd, by God. What's absurd about my name? Didn't you see them arms on my carriage door?"

"The door of this stolen carriage?"

"And my house. You saw my house."

"I saw *a* house."

"Blow the house, Miss Primrose blighted Dane."

Luke subsided, muttering and cursing to himself. He never expected such a devil of a time as he'd had doing this favor for Ross Scarlett. His friend had come to him with a tale of a vanished spinster and asked him to search east London for her. Luke hadn't wanted to go back. To him, Nightshade was dead and unlamented. If he could, he'd forget most of his past.

His earliest memory was of a woman too busy with her male visitors to take care of him. He remembered her skirts the best, because they were what he saw at his eye level. Limp, worn skirts of thin wool, their dark brown faded to something closer to dingy gray. He would cling to them and lean against her legs, until she shoved him away.

Between these memories and those of his foster parents was a nightmare. One day his mother had pushed him out the door, and when he came back, she was dead. The landlady had her body taken away. Luke tried to go with it, but the men who put it in a wagon shoved him back and drove off so fast he couldn't keep up. After that, his home was the streets, until the Hawthornes took him in. His new ma was a charwoman, and Pa had worked the docks until he was injured. Then he became a rag-and-bone man who riffled through garbage for old cloth and bones. The Hawthornes could barely support themselves. When they adopted Luke, their meager resources were insufficient.

Luke grew up hungry and desperate to save his parents from the fate of many of the East End's elderly poor—becoming pure-finders. These unfortunates gathered dog dung. A bucketful would buy a day's food and shelter. Fear of the workhouse drove many to such disgusting occupations. Luke promised himself that neither he nor his own would ever resort to such extremities.

The threat of the pure-finder and the workhouse

drove him to seek apprenticeship under Inigo Ware, the most notorious thief in London. It had been a bargain with the devil. Inigo exacted payment for his training in a percentage of Luke's spoils, and in cruelty. Inigo had given him the name Nightshade, and Inigo liked to pit Luke against another of his apprentices, Mortimer Fleet.

"Fleet, my dear," Inigo would say. "Do you think you'll ever be as pleasing to the eye as Nightshade? Or will you always be a dried-up stick insect?"

Or he would meddle. "Luke, my pretty. You're fond of our young Jenny, but so is Fleet here. Which of you is going to have her, eh? I'm sorry, Fleet, but my money is on Nightshade. But if she can't make up her mind, you can always fight for her. I'll sponsor the match. Knives are the proper weapon for a duel between two rivals."

By the time Luke was sixteen, Inigo had turned him into his most talented protégé. He could slip into rich town houses, plan and execute daring daylight jewel robberies, and pick pockets at society weddings and balls. Around him Luke gathered talented sorts like Badger, who could climb the highest building laden with housebreaking tools, and Prigg, a master forger. Of all of them, Jenny Jenkins had been the best. Pretty, saucy Jenny could pretend to turn her ankle in the street in front of a fat, well-dressed gentleman and come away with his watch, his money, and his calling cards.

He'd loved Jenny, but she'd fallen for Mortimer Fleet's lies and blandishments. Fleet became Inigo Ware's right-hand man. Jenny left Luke to follow

Fleet, and ended up floating in the Thames. Fleet always claimed some toff she'd robbed had done her. Such an end wouldn't be surprising; they all risked their lives every day. However, Luke had always suspected Fleet of killing Jenny, because not two days before she was killed, she had promised to leave Fleet and return to him. If he ever discovered the truth for certain, he would do for Mortimer Fleet.

Thinking of Fleet reminded Luke of Miss Dane. She was sitting stiffly opposite him, watching him with a cat's fixed gaze, tracking the movements of his hands, ready to spring out of his reach should he attack. He was never going to convince her of the truth with words. Not when those words came out in an east London accent lacking in beginning H's and sprinkled with thieves' cant.

She had stopped trembling. No, her hands shook when they moved to adjust her bonnet or her mantle. The dark bronze of her dress accented her pallor. He'd been rough with her. His irritation at having to become Nightshade again had caused him to resent her even before he'd found her. When she gave him the devil of trouble catching and keeping her, his pride had been hurt. Now that he bothered to notice, she was strung tight and near the limit of her strength.

Something powerful evil was worrying her. Something that had to do with Mortimer Fleet. Once he'd realized this, he'd sent people to make inquiries about events occurring on the day Miss Dane vanished. He'd instructed Badger and Prigg to nose around the taverns and gin shops to find out about Fleet's doings. There was no direct link between his old gang and his new life, but Luke had a method of receiving reports. He should know something in a few days.

Meanwhile, he would take Miss Dane home with him. He was looking forward to seeing her face when they arrived this evening. Her shock and discomfort would repay him for enduring her sneers.

"You just wait," he said, but Miss Dane wasn't listening.

She had fallen asleep sitting upright. Annoyed that he couldn't tell her how much he looked forward to her embarrassment, Luke withdrew a small volume from his inner pocket. It was his traveling dictionary book. Several years with tutors had given him some education, but he was still left with his old manner of speech, which reappeared if he wasn't careful.

He was determined to improve. It was but a part of his life's plan, the ultimate goal of which was to put down roots. He wanted a family and a substantial home, for these meant safety, freedom from the terrors of a life spent in poverty and dread, never knowing when the chap walking past you might try to shove a knife into your belly.

"Spinster," he murmured as he looked up the word. " 'An unmarried woman of gentle family, past the common age of marrying, who seems unlikely to marry.' That's her all right. Unlikely to marry, with her 'Mr. Nightshades' and 'I decline to tell yous.' " His finger moved down the page. " 'Old maid, maiden, lone woman, virgin.' Humph, virgin. Not a wonder. Nothing interesting there."

He was searching for a more gratifying word to memorize when the carriage went over a bump and made him lose his place. They had left London and were on their way west through the countryside. Luke put away his book and looked out at the fields and villages, always a spirit-enriching sight to him after all his years in the grimy, belching cesspots of London.

The carriage clattered around a bend and hit another hole. The entire vehicle jolted. Luke braced himself, but Miss Dane was tossed out of her seat and landed on him. He heard her cry out, but was too late to do more than catch her as she fell, pressing her body against his.

They ended up face to face, staring at each other, their mouths slightly rounded in identical expressions of alarm. Then Luke became aware of her chest against his, of her hand braced on his thigh. Out of nowhere came a thought: Was her cheek as soft as her breast? He'd never expected to know the feel of a lady's breast without ever having touched her cheek.

Miss Dane was still staring at him. She seemed transfixed, as if she was afraid to look away. Her cry of alarm signaled her recovery, and she pushed herself back so that their chests no longer touched. In mid-movement, she stopped and looked down at her hand where it gripped his thigh. Luke followed her gaze and noticed how her fingers sank into muscle. Under her hand, his flesh burned.

Clamping his teeth together, he said, "Miss Dane."

She continued to stare at her hand and didn't answer. His hands were wrapped around her waist now, and he squeezed as he said her name again.

"Yes?" came a faint reply.

"Miss Dane, could you refrain from squeezing my leg? I'm trying to be a gentleman."

She blinked at him, then gasped and turned crimson. Scrambling out of his lap, she shot backward into her seat and slid as far away as she could. Turning away from him, she stared out the window.

Luke shifted so that his body leaned in the opposite direction, staring at the scenery without seeing it. His thoughts were jumbled, flitting from memories of Miss Dane's hand on his thigh to speculation about her troubles. Eventually he realized that the sun was low. They were driving down High Road, in the village of Langley Green. They were almost home.

He glanced over his shoulder at Miss Dane. She was still braced against the corner, but she was having a difficult time keeping her eyes open. As he watched her, she frowned and bent so that she could see the shops and houses of High Road.

"This isn't . . ."

"Isn't what?" he asked.

"The place I expected."

"That's what happens when you think you know everything. I told you we were going to my house."

Miss Dane looked at the small cottages that marked the end of High Road. "Which of these is it?"

"Oh, it ain't none of them. I live in the country."

He let her wonder as the carriage turned off High Road into a lane that wound its way down the side of a valley thick with trees in their autumn colors. They crossed the valley basin and climbed the gentle opposite slope. Then the carriage turned into a dense forest. After a few minutes, the trees began to thin until they parted to reveal a rushing stream. The horses slowed to a walk and clattered over a stone bridge with three supporting arches. In the middle of the bridge, Luke knocked on the roof with his walking stick. The coachmen halted the carriage.

Turning to Miss Dane, Luke said, "I want to show you something."

"You're going to drown me."

She was staring at him as if he were a Thames water rat, and he was growing tired of her suspicion.

"If I am, at least you won't have to dread it no more."

He could see her make up her mind. Her tongue sneaked out to pose at the corner of her mouth, then vanished. She pulled herself up straight, her spine rigid, and gave him a slight nod. Descending to the stone bridge, he offered his hand to her. She stared at it without moving from the doorway.

"Damnation! You think I'm going to throw you off the bridge." Before she could answer, he gripped her hand, slipped an arm around her and swept her from the coach. He heard her suck in her breath. Knowing what she expected, he took satisfaction in releasing her as soon as she was on her feet. "There. You see? You're still alive."

Clutching her bag, Miss Dane eyed him warily for a few moments. When he failed to rush at her and toss her into the stream, she let out a long breath and glanced around her. She dared a peep over the edge of the bridge into the waters that danced over rounded stones and pebbles.

He joined her there, causing her to ease out of

reach, but Luke merely gestured toward the water. "Now don't you feel a proper wooden-head, thinking I'd toss you into such a shallow stream. Can't be more than five feet deep."

"You might have tied my hands and—" She bit her lip.

Luke shook his head. "Afraid to give me ideas? Choke me dead if you're not determined to suffer on this journey. Well, it's almost over. All I wanted was to show you that."

He pointed in the only direction Miss Dane hadn't looked, straight ahead, and watched her. Beyond the bridge, rising out of the forest as if it had grown from it, lay a sheer mass of gray stone, the base of a castle tower. A defensive wall extended from it, its crenellated battlements marching out of sight.

Festoons of ivy hung from the tower and the wall, while trees and climbing vines hugged the castle base and cast long shadows across the stone. Beyond the defensive wall rose the shell of some ruined structure, broken by long rows of windows with pointed arches. A broad road extended from the bridge to a gatehouse formed by two monumental towers. A drawbridge lay across the gap of a water-filled moat, and over the drawbridge came a cart driven by a lad wearing a smock and munching on a hunk of bread.

"That, Miss Dane, is mine."

"What?"

"I told you I was taking you home, and that's my home, every last battlement, tower, and wall."

Miss Dane gestured toward the castle. "This—this is yours?"

"Why, you look struck all of a heap." He was grinning now, for her mouth hung open and she was gaping at the castle in a dazed manner that was most gratifying. "Come along. The household will be expecting us because it's almost dusk."

He helped his confused passenger into the coach. As they set off, the cart passed them, and the lad in the smock doffed his hat. Luke returned the salute with an inclination of his head and noticed that Miss Dane was staring at him again.

"Have I sprouted a second nose or something?"

She shook her head, and as they drove into the gatehouse, beneath tons of stonework, he couldn't resist gloating. "Don't worry, Miss Prim. I promise not to throw you in the moat or lock you in the oubliette."

6

Prim tried to preserve what little composure she still retained by forcing herself to attend to her surroundings. Otherwise she would go mad trying to understand how Nightshade the thief and ruffian could own a castle. She stared intently at the ramparts as the carriage passed beneath the portcullis and plunged into the darkness of the gatehouse. Overhead she glimpsed the murder holes, through which defenders poured pitch or fired arrows at invaders.

When the carriage clattered into what had been the outer bailey, she beheld a vast expanse of green lawn, and behind it, a hill upon which sat a Norman shell keep. All around them rose the massive enclosure walls, their expanse broken by drum and square towers. Beyond the shell keep, nestled against the northern half of the surrounding walls, stood a conglomeration of buildings. In spite of her confusion, Prim was fascinated. The gradual change from Norman to Gothic architecture in the structures spoke of centuries of building by an endless succession of owners.

As the carriage drove around the shell keep mound and along the gravel road to the central palace at the north end of the castle, the buildings seemed to grow out of each other in a continuous U shape. The jumble of residential and defensive structures boasted a soaring, buttressed chapel and residential palace, squat service buildings, and gargantuan blocks and towers that must have once been armories, barracks and treasuries.

At last the carriage stopped in front of the palace. She looked at the man who claimed to be Sir Lucas Hawthorne, and to her surprise beheld someone almost as reluctant to get out of the carriage as she was. He sat slumped against the squabs, his walking stick gripped in both hands, frowning. He didn't move even when a footman from the house opened the door.

Prim ventured to address him. "Sir Lucas?"

He glanced at her and managed a wry smile.

"I forgot about Mrs. Snow."

"Who is Mrs. Snow?"

"A blight upon the scenery of my life, Miss Dane. Mrs. Snow is my housekeeper. Been at the castle since she was a underhousemaid, which by my figuring must have been about two hundred years ago, the old besom. Ah, well. Have to endure it, I suppose."

He got out and offered his hand to Prim, who had recovered her astonishment at the news that this ruffian seemed to fear his own housekeeper. She put her hand in his, and in the moment before she stepped down from the carriage, he squeezed it and whispered to her.

"Pleased to see my castle has brought the color back to your cheeks, Miss Prim."

Prim felt her face begin to burn, so she withdrew her hand and moved away from him as soon as she could. As she turned from him, the double doors at the head of a shallow staircase swung open, and a woman descended, followed by a gaggle of maids and several footmen. The footmen scurried to the coach and began unloading luggage, while the woman and her attendants bore down on Sir Lucas and Prim.

It was like awaiting the landing of one of those new ironclad ships. Soaring, black-clad, severe, the woman anchored herself before Sir Luke. Prim blamed exhaustion for her immediate dislike of Mrs. Snow. The housekeeper couldn't help her looks—the beaky nose, the way her small incisors peeked from beneath her upper lip when her mouth grew pinched, her gaunt face that reminded one of Jacobean woodcuts depicting condemned sinners. Prim chastised herself silently while Sir Luke spoke to his housekeeper.

"And we'll need something to eat."

Mrs. Snow had fine eyes of light blue that seemed to bore into the soul looking for wrongdoing. They glared at her employer down that long, buzzard's-beak nose. "I had no warning of your arrival, Sir Lucas."

"I regret it exceedingly, Mrs. Snow."

"There is nothing prepared in the kitchens. The guest rooms haven't been aired. There are no fresh flowers about. I am not used to such precipitance.

When his lordship was in residence, everything was done without haste and with decorum."

Sir Lucas stared at his boots and mumbled something into the collar of his coat. Waiting beside him, Prim found herself amazed. Where was the dashing, ruthless Nightshade? Where was the man whose smallest word caused the denizens of the Black Fleece to cringe and Prim to cower in fright? In his place was a man who, although improved in grammar, seemed afraid of a servant.

With a jolt Prim awoke from the dazed state she'd been in since crossing the stream. The attitude of the servants and housekeeper made this man's true position certain. This was indeed Sir Lucas, a man of property and legitimacy—of a sort. All this time, he really had been trying to help her. Providence only knew what would have happened to her had he been trying to do otherwise. She contemplated Nightshade in the role of savior. Doing so only added to her confusion. Prim found herself gawking at him and turned her attention back to the housekeeper, who was still complaining.

"Under his lordship, a proper manner was expected of all who lived at Beaufort."

Clearing his throat, Sir Luke said, "I regret—"

"Sir Lucas." Prim stepped forward before he could commit the folly of apologizing to this officious creature in front of his other servants. "You haven't introduced me."

Startled, he glanced down at her as if she were a stranger. "Oh, yes. Miss Dane, may I present my housekeeper, Mrs. Snow. Mrs. Snow, Miss Dane will be my guest."

"As I said, there are no rooms prepared."

Before Sir Lucas could respond, Prim lost her patience. Turning to him, she said, "May I deal with this?"

After a hesitation, he nodded rapidly.

Prim turned and walked past Mrs. Snow with Sir Lucas close behind. The woman was left to rush after them. Inside the entry hall, Prim removed her bonnet and handed it to a maid without looking to see of the girl was ready to take it. She was slipping her mantle off as Mrs. Snow arrived. Prim held it out to her, and the woman took it without thinking.

"Mrs. Snow, Sir Lucas will require that his rooms and a guest room be made ready at once. You will also please see that the most comfortable sitting room is prepared so that we can rest while we're waiting. We'll have tea, I think. With whatever you have that is fresh—bread, scones, cakes. You may serve dinner at nine o'clock this evening, as you'll need time to lay in a few fresh provisions." Prim sighed and glanced around the foyer at the carved wood and suits of armor standing sentry. "Yes, I think that's the best plan. You may show us to the sitting room, Mrs. Snow."

The housekeeper seemed frozen in place, but in the face of Prim's absolute confidence that her orders would be obeyed she snapped out of her daze. Thrusting the mantle at a housemaid, she said, "Yes, miss."

Without a grumble or a mention of "his lordship," she escorted them across the great hall to a room on the second floor of the west wing. She left them in a chamber of warmth and light. Done in white and gold, it had a west-facing wall consisting of mullioned windows with pointed arches, a high, beamed ceiling, and a fireplace with a mantel of Italian marble.

While in the presence of the housekeeper, Sir Lucas was quiet and grim, but as the door closed on Mrs. Snow, Prim beheld a transformation. Sir Lucas Hawthorne's worried frown vanished. Dark brows arched; his chin lowered and his gaze lifted along with the corners of his mouth. Prim edged away from him as he swept across the room to collapse with un-studied grace into a baroque tapestry-covered chair.

"Bless your bright eyes, Miss Prim, you struck old Snow all of a heap."

Seeing that Nightshade had no designs to annoy her, Prim sank into a chair beside a boulle mosaic cabinet and studied its gilded bronze fittings. How could this man be Sir Lucas, and how could Sir Lucas be Nightshade? Young thieves from the stews of London didn't acquire titles, never mind knighthoods. But this one must have. Gathering her wits, Prim addressed her captor-host.

"Mr. Night—Sir Lucas, I think we should begin anew. Would you please tell me where I am and who you are?"

"You going to believe me this time?"

"Mr. Nightshade, I have seen you at your worst, and now I want an explanation. Where am I, and who are you?"

"I told you. You're in my castle. Castle Beaufort is what it's called. And I'm Luke Hawthorne."

Faint furrows appeared between Prim's eyebrows. "Perhaps you would be so good as to explain how a person of your . . . station, came to acquire a knighthood."

"After Ross Scarlett helped me get out of London, I done some work for Her Majesty's government."

"What kind of work?"

Twisting sideways in his chair, Sir Lucas gazed up at the gilded white plaster garlands and scrollwork on the ceiling. "In government, especially the foreign ministry, there's all sorts o' situations that calls for my kind of skills. Ross had lots of occasions to acquire items in secret, ones foreign folk wouldn't want us to know about. Documents and such things."

"These documents must have been important to have resulted in such an elevation."

Sir Lucas didn't say anything. He twisted back around in his seat, planted his boots wide apart, and propped his elbows on his thighs. Clasping his hands, he lowered his chin and looked up at her. At that moment, he was so much more Nightshade than Sir Lucas that Prim thrust her fists into the billows of her skirts to hide their sudden trembling. She jumped when he spoke softly.

"Don't."

"I beg your pardon?"

"I really am Sir Lucas Hawthorne, not some bloke sent to murder you."

Prim threw up her hands. "You must expect to meet with skepticism, Sir Lucas. At our first meeting you pounced upon me like a wolf on a goat!"

"I had to. You'd been right hard to find, and I

wasn't going to let you get away." He forestalled her next comment by standing and walking to the fireplace. "Lady Freshwell asked Ross Scarlett to find you, and I done him the favor. That's all. And as long as we're asking questions, suppose you tell me why your blighted aunt waited three days before she called on Ross. He said she was more concerned with avoiding scandal than finding you. She'd already put it about that you'd gone to visit friends in the country."

Prim brightened. "Then my brother still doesn't know what's happened."

"Oy! That's right. You got a brother. Why didn't you go to him?"

"He's still at university. Oxford."

"What does that matter? Why are you living with your aunt if you got a brother?"

"Sir Lucas, you're being impertinent."

"Impertinent. That's a great word. I got another, frangible. That means easily broke, like that Venetian lace glass in the cabinet." He pointed to a fragile plate that did indeed look as if it had been made of wispy glass lace, but then he snapped his fingers. "Now I remember. Ross told me your brother is some lord or something."

Prim felt her back stiffen and heard her voice grow cold. "My brother was the heir to the family title."

"And that means he's got a big house and lots of land."

"Sir Lucas, your manners. Such inquiries are not acceptable in Society. Be assured that if my brother could afford it, I would be at home instead of with Lady Freshwell and her son."

"Who's that?"

Sighing, Prim said, "Lord Newton Freshwell."

"Newton, huh?"

"Yes, Newton."

"Sounds a weak-kneed blighter to me. Oh, don't get all stiff and huffy. From what you've told me, you couldn't go to any o' these people without danger to them anyway, and we can't have them here to give you away."

"My reputation has been ruined already. It was destroyed when I didn't meet the servant Lady Freshwell sent for me at the appointed time."

"Don't worry, my ma and pa are here. So everything's all proper, and later when this is all over, we can say you were here all along."

"I doubt such a ruse will suffice."

"Sure it will. I'll get Ross to spread the tale around to his friends, Mrs. Treat-Fotheringay, Lady Mendlehouse, old Cyril Richmond. He'll set you right. But first you got to tell this secret of yours."

Prim glanced around the room. It was one of those imposing chambers decorated in the days of Louis XIV, the Sun King. The white plaster ceiling with its classical motifs, the baroque furniture and the delicate Venetian glass in its various cabinets spoke of Sir Lucas's wealth. She sneaked a look at her host. He was watching her with that quizzical expression that momentarily banished Nightshade's menace. This mercurial ruffian-turned-gentleman had saved her life. She must admit that. Having made the admission, she could not then place his life in danger. Honor forbade it.

He crossed the room, pausing a few feet from her chair and lifting an eyebrow. "Well?"

"I decline to tell you."

"Young blighted Prim, you tell me this instant."

"I shall not place you in danger."

"I've lived in fear o' my life since I was old enough to spit."

"Sir, your language."

"I ain't having no Miss Prim put herself between me and peril. Rot you! First you're afraid of me, and now you're afraid for me, and for no reason."

As he spoke, he approached her and Prim stood, ready to flee. "It's not just you—" She closed her mouth quickly, and her tongue peeked at the corner.

"Oy! What do you mean?" He eyed her closely.

It was then that Nightshade made his appearance. Sir Lucas's gentleness vanished, submerged in the molten fierceness of the black-souled ruffian she'd come to know. Silken tones caused a shiver to run through her.

"Now my precious little imp, tell me, my well-bred lady, my sweet, who else knows your secret."

"I—" Her voice cracked and she had to start again, wishing she didn't sound so fainthearted. "I decline to tell you."

He moved nearer then; she was forced to step back and landed in the chair. Nightshade swiftly bent down and placed his hands on the arms of her chair so that she couldn't escape. He was so close she could feel the heat of his body and catch the spiced-wood scent of him. Prim's mouth felt like an old carpet. She shrank back, all the while trying to meet his dark-eyed, vandal's stare.

"Miss Dane," he whispered. "I've persuaded many to do what I wish. Don't make me have to persuade you."

Shaking inside like a sheet of parchment in a gale, Prim forced herself to hold his gaze. "Sir Lucas," she snapped, "you're going to have to decide whether you're a criminal or a gentleman. You will do me the courtesy of making that decision at once, for I won't be battered by your sudden changes of character any further."

"We'll see whether you will or won't," he murmured.

It was then that a knock on the door made Nightshade whirl around and Sir Lucas seek his place in a chair opposite Prim. He responded to the knock and a parlormaid and footman entered. Relieved, Prim almost smiled at the way the knock elicited in him a sudden attack of civility. It was like watching a dark room burst into illumination from a gaslight.

The footman brought in a heavy silver tray laden with a tea service and china, while the maid followed with a smaller one piled with food. Prim couldn't help watching Sir Lucas's reaction to the intrusion. He beheld the approach of the servants, a general watching the advance of a dangerous and better-armed army. When the footman stopped beside him and looked at him in inquiry, Sir Lucas glared back and said nothing. It was then that Prim realized he had no notion of what was expected, was

embarrassed that he didn't know, and was prepared to
sit glaring at the poor servant to conceal his ignorance.

Prim found that she could not contemplate Sir Lucas's embarrassment with pleasure. "If you will allow
me, Sir Lucas?"

"What? Oh, yes, of course, Miss Prim—Miss
Dane."

Prim gave instructions with the ease and assurance
of a lifetime of being waited on. The trays were placed
on a table situated between a settee and two armchairs.

"Thank you," she said to the footman. "That will
be all."

"Yes, miss."

When the two were gone, she waited for her host
to indicate whether she should serve or not, but
he was occupied with scowling at the door through
which the servants had disappeared.

"Sir Lucas, would you like me to pour?"

"Hmmm?"

"The tea, would you like me to pour?"

"If it will make you happy." He appeared to find
the door of immeasurable interest, for he was still
contemplating it when she tried to hand him his cup.

"Sir Lucas."

"Yes," he said in a distracted tone.

Prim raised her voice and shoved the cup and
saucer at him. "What do you take in your tea?"

"What? Oh, yes, thank you." He took the cup
and began stirring his tea.

"You didn't answer when I asked what you took in
your tea."

Sir Lucas set the cup and saucer down without

drinking and turned a wide-eyed gaze upon her. Prim sipped her own tea laced with milk and sugar while she grew more and more uneasy. He was going to try again to make her reveal what she knew, and she was too weary to endure it.

"You know, Miss Dane, if you told me what it was you saw, or what you know, whoever is after you would have no reason to kill you. The secret would be out, and there would be no profit in killing you."

Prim had already thought of this. "You're wrong. Even if the . . . the secret were known to the world, there would still be the most urgent of reasons for dispatching me." The murderer would have an even more compelling reason to want her dead before she could testify in court.

"Bloody damnation," Sir Lucas said while he gazed at her in wonder. "What could you know that's so perilous?"

"I—"

"Decline to tell you. I know, I know. So what are you going to do, hide for the rest of your life?"

The question caught her unprepared. All at once her exhaustion rushed upon her. With it came feelings of helplessness and isolation. She had been brave for so long, and she was very much afraid that she could be brave no longer. Her eyes stung, and Sir Lucas began to swim before her tear-blurred vision.

"Oy! Don't you be sniffling and blubbering at me."

Her cup and saucer rattling, Prim grabbed her napkin and pressed it to her nose. She was powerless to prevent a great sob from escaping the napkin. The cup clattered perilously on its saucer. Sir Lucas cursed and grabbed both before she dropped them. Prim pressed the napkin to her nose and mouth with one hand and made a fist with the other in an attempt to regain mastery of herself. She lost the battle as the first sob became many. Humiliated, she brought the napkin up to cover her eyes.

Beside her the cushions of the settee dipped. A warm hand took her fist, causing Prim to gasp and peep over the edge of the napkin. Sir Lucas was sitting beside her, making her feel insect-small with his height. He had taken her fist in his hands, and as she watched, he pried open the fingers, clasped her hand in one of his, and covered it with the other. Her entire hand vanished. Prim's tears dried up at the feel of his heated skin on hers. Suddenly the world shrank to those few inches where their hands touched, and Prim felt something inside stir, something that coiled and wound around itself, producing an exciting tension.

"It took you all this mortal time to do what I expected of you the first time we met. Choke me dead but you're powerful brave for a lady spinster."

"B-brave? I'm not brave. I'm frightened." The tears returned.

"Then let me help you," he said.

Another surprise. Nightshade could be gentle. Even his voice could be gentle. Usually it reminded her of a perverse choir—full, harmonious, and singing praises of wickedness. Now she could almost succumb to the images of high battlements and armor and a warrior's skills that it provoked. But what would be the result? Danger for two instead of one; danger for the one who had risked his life to help her.

"I cannot allow you to help."

"You're a wretched blithering fool, Miss Dane."

Prim yanked her hand from his grasp. "Only an infamous creature would so address a lady. But you needn't endure my presence. I shall leave at once."

"You will not."

"Then I'm a prisoner yet."

"Appears so."

Prim stood stiffly.

"Where are you going?"

"I assumed you were going to lock me up again in some barred room, or possibly your dungeon."

"Sit down!" Nightshade bellowed.

Prim started and obeyed in spite of herself. He lowered his chin and looked up at her, his stance recalling dark, mist-filled streets and unseen peril. He was doing it again, trying to intimidate her. Prim squared her shoulders and set her clasped hands in her lap as she returned his stare. They remained in this contest for a few moments before Sir Lucas's smile took possession of Nightshade. She heard him chuckle, and eyed him with suspicion.

"Rot me if we're not at an impasse, Miss Dane."

"I'm pleased that my misfortunes and afflictions provide you with amusement," Prim snapped.

"Now don't get yourself in an infernal stew. I got a proposal."

"Really?"

"Damn I hate the way you get all high-flown and royal and make a bloke feel like a Thames water rat."

"How unfortunate for you."

"See what I mean? But that ain't what I got to say. What I was going to say is that you got to agree you'll have the devil of a time leaving if I set me mind to keeping you here. Right?"

Irritated beyond politeness, Prim merely nodded.

"Right," he said with a grin that made her want to kick him in the knee. "So we're in the same rain barrel we were back in London. Want to give your word you won't run off until we can settle this tangle, or should I pull up the drawbridge and find a nice dungeon for you? I'll put some furniture in it, o' course."

It disgusted her that he could be so logical. A long silence ensued while she did battle with her ire. In the end, Prim realized she had too few alternatives and that leaving Sir Lucas's protection without a plan might cost her her life.

"For the moment," she said coldly, "I shall remain."

"Not just for the moment. You got to promise—"

"Sir Lucas, that is my final offer."

He looked her up and down as if measuring the strength of her resolve. "Very well, Miss Prim."

"Now, if you will excuse me, Sir Lucas." Prim rose from the settee.

"Wait," Sir Lucas said. "You haven't heard everything."

Prim resumed her perch on the settee as far away from him as possible. "Yes?"

"I got something to ask you."

"I won't tell you—"

"Not that." Sir Lucas cleared his throat. "What I was going to say was that since you're here, how about teaching me manners like you got? I'm going to get married, and my fiancée is well-bred, like you. I'm going to need Society manners."

It was the last thing Prim expected to hear. Her mouth fell open; she snapped it shut. He had a fiancée, and she was shocked. No, she was angry. He couldn't be engaged. She did not want him to be engaged. Her thoughts turned into scorpions that battled and stung each other. Damn him. He was engaged, and he wanted her to teach him manners. Teach him manners, manners he intended to use to impress a fiancée!

"What do you say?" he asked.

"Certainly not."

He regarded her silently. Then, without warning, he laughed Nightshade's demon laugh. "Think carefully, Miss Prim. The more manners you teach me, the less you'll see of Nightshade." He leaned close to her, causing Prim to edge away from him as he pursued her to the corner of the settee.

"What do you say, Miss Prim?" he murmured, calling up visions of a pirate captain standing on a deck red with blood. "Who do you want to spend your days with—Sir Lucas, or me?"

Prim thrust at his immovable shoulder and slipped off the settee to land on the floor. Nightshade bent over her, offering his hand. Avoiding his touch, Prim scrambled to her feet and rushed to the door. Turning the knob, she looked back, fearing he'd followed her, but he was standing by the settee smiling at her with all the wickedness of a pagan god.

"We'll begin the lessons at dinner, Sir Lucas."

Nightshade favored her with the kind of grin the devil must wear after condemning a soul, and swept an elaborate bow to her. "I knew you'd see it my way, Miss Dane."

7

Castle Beaufort had once been the home of dukes and princes. Luke bought it from a baron whose family had the distinction of providing mistresses to several Stuart kings, until England had run out of either pretty women or lascivious sovereigns. The castle's massive foundations, its eight-hundred-year history, and the treasures it contained provided Luke with the feeling of permanence he'd longed for all his life.

He could wander across the bailey and survey towers that had withstood the Wars of the Roses and Cromwell. He could admire the suits of shining plate armor in the Old Hall, the renovated residential wings with their Gothic facades and Renaissance, Palladian and Georgian interiors. And each time he did, he could feel his roots delving deeper into the earth.

He would live here, marry, and raise a family here.

Never again would he be the lost, unwanted, and dirty urchin who had to steal in order to eat. Owners of castles never wanted for food or for respectability. Luke remembered how Mr. Tuggle, a greasy and rotund grocer in Pitch Lane, would snarl at him in distaste, as if he were horse dung brought in on a customer's boot. Sure he'd filched an apple once, but that was after his mother died and he'd spent two days on the streets starving. He'd asked for any spare fruit or vegetables first, but the fat old bugger had kicked and spat at him. No one would ever make him feel that way again.

The memory of Mr. Tuggle receded, and Luke glanced down at the letter he was composing. He was in his office, next to the library on the ground floor of the palace. His door was open and he looked down the corridor at a succession of rooms, their doors open to admit air and candlelight.

Beyond his office lay the Mural Room. Its ceiling was painted to simulate a dome that was open to the sky in the center. Ornate frescoes adorned the walls, and the Mural Room was considered a masterpiece of Renaissance art. But to Luke all the busy classical figures, the emperors, senators, ladies, gods, and goddesses, made the room feel crowded.

His study was much simpler. It had a carved frieze consisting of shells supported by palm fronds. Carved overdoors held portraits of unknown castle occupants from the late seventeenth century. These worthies now looked down upon Luke as he wrote.

His pen scratched instructions to his representative

in London—the man who served as intermediary between him and the world he'd escaped. Either Prim had run afoul of someone as dangerous as Inigo Ware, or she'd come upon knowledge that threatened someone powerful. This last was what Luke feared. His agents would have to be careful not to arouse suspicion while making their inquiries, and he was writing to emphasize the need for caution.

Signing the letter, Luke slipped it into an envelope and sighed. He was worried about Miss Dane. He'd seen the look of desperation and resolution in her eyes. She was going to apply herself to thinking of a way out of her dilemma, a way in which she could protect herself and him, *him*.

As if he needed the protection of a wisp of a girl with gray-green eyes. That was one of her most aggravating qualities. Miss Primrose Dane thought she had to protect everybody, thought she knew best for everybody. And what had it got her; it had almost got her killed. Sometimes she was so exasperating he wanted to throw her in the moat. He wouldn't do it, of course, in spite of the temptation. Although why he restrained himself on her account mystified him.

Perhaps her good qualities had impressed him. She cared about children such as he'd once been, cared enough to try to teach them to better themselves. As well, Miss Dane had more courage than a whole company of Her Majesty's grenadiers. Yes, Miss Primrose Dane was an admirable young woman. Odd that she wasn't married. Come to think of it, her whole situation seemed odd. She was cast among relations who obviously cared little for her, while her brother lived well at Oxford and failed to provide a place for her in the home he'd inherited.

Luke took up his pen again, this time to write to Ross Scarlett. He needed to find out more about Miss Dane. If he did, he might find a way to keep her at Beaufort, and a key to her dangerous situation as well. In any case, he needed her with him long enough to teach him propriety, etiquette, all the things he still had to learn if he was going to marry.

His engagement had been almost as easy as the purchase of Castle Beaufort. Years ago when he'd first acquired his wealth, Luke had learned that it bought respectability. Many families of ancient lineage were willing to overlook his humble origins, as long as he was rich now. Luke would never forget his amazement at discovering how titles seemed to drain all the sense from a family. People whose ancestors had been clever bullies in the age of knights and sieges had descendants who couldn't keep a shilling in their pocket if it was glued there.

The Randolphs, the family in possession of the earldom of Benfield, were such descendants. In danger of losing the family seat to debt, the earl had gladly consented to a marriage between Luke and his daughter, Lady Cecilia. However, the earl insisted that Lady Cecilia approve. Luke had already made inquiries about the lady before offering marriage. All that remained was for her to assure herself that she desired the connection. In a few weeks she was coming for a visit, suitably escorted by an aged lady relative.

Luke had promised the earl he would make himself agreeable to Lady Cecilia and accept her decision. He knew many ways to make himself agreeable to a woman. He could use none of them on Lady Cecilia.

This was another reason Luke needed Miss Dane. She was a true aristocrat. Without thinking, she knew how to command servants, how to wear luxurious clothing as though it was ordinary, how to behave among the toffs. She had a fine spirit and delicate sensibility that he'd come to admire. He respected her all the more for her ability to set aside her lady's decorum when she was required to survive in the stews of London.

"Choke me dead," Luke murmured to himself. "I'll never forget how she downed old Jowett with a brick."

He was addressing the letter to Ross Scarlett when Mrs. Snow appeared in the open doorway. Luke swore under his breath, for he'd been thinking so hard he hadn't heard her heels tapping on the polished floorboards. The housekeeper loomed before him, a black, disapproving raven.

"I beg your pardon, Sir Lucas, but Miss Dane does not answer when the maid knocks at her door, and dinner is ready."

He remembered Miss Dane's tone and manner and tried to adopt them. "I will attend to it, Mrs. Snow." He cracked a cheeky grin, forfeiting his lordly demeanor. "Cheer up, old soul. Featherstone will be back tomorrow, and then we won't have to deal with each other direct."

All he got was a stiff nod. Swiveling as if on rollers, Mrs. Snow retreated. He could hear her keys jingling on the chain she wore at her waist as she marched through the Mural Room and disappeared. Leaving his letters to be collected for the post, Luke set off for Miss Dane's room. Mrs. Snow had put her in the wing opposite the one containing his own suite. He was certain that was the thing to do, since proper ladies and gentlemen seemed to fear being left alone together in close proximity.

Luke made his way across the palace, through the Old Hall and into the western wing. There he came to the central bastion of a hollowed half-tower into which had been set a gracefully turned staircase with a delicate banister and rails in black and gold. The landing and hall began the rooms designed in the style of Robert Adam, with ceilings and plasterwork of white picked out in gold.

When he'd first acquired Beaufort, such grand surroundings had intimidated him. Then he learned what he should have guessed all along. A man could accustom himself to anything, even grandeur. Now there were times when he hardly noticed the marble pilasters, the paintings by van Eyck, Reynolds, and Holbein, the Mortlake tapestries, or the pier glass mirrors.

Once upstairs Luke proceeded to the rooms known as Princess Caroline's Suite. He didn't know why they were named after a princess. Almost every room in the castle had a name, and there were about two hundred rooms in use. He was still discovering others that hadn't even been drawn into the plans he'd received when he bought the place. His estate manager said no one knew exactly how many rooms there were.

At Miss Dane's door, he knocked softly, then louder when he received no answer. He waited a minute, then opened the door quickly when it occurred to him that Miss Dane might have scarpered. Rushing across the Princess's Sitting Room, Luke charged into the bedroom, but his steps slowed as he neared the Hepplewhite four-poster bed. Upon it lay Miss Dane, her hair loose and tumbling over her shoulders, her small stocking-clad feet peeping from beneath the skirt of her heavy traveling dress. In one hand she still held the comb she'd been using, but she was in a deep sleep.

Luke noted the blue tinge to her eyelids, the slight pallor of her cheeks. Her lashes were dark gold, as were her eyebrows. Her hair color reminded him of the gold embossing on a rapier in the Old Hall. She sighed, drawing his attention to her face and the deep rose color of her lips. Then she whimpered in her sleep, as if pursued by monsters. She stirred and began to breathe rapidly.

Reaching out, Luke put his hand over hers and squeezed, thinking to give reassurance and restore her to peace. At first she appeared not to notice his touch, but then her hand moved, taking his with it. She tucked them both under her chin against her neck and cheek, forcing Luke to climb onto the bed. He sat there feeling the baby-bird softness of her flesh.

"This wasn't well thought out," he whispered to himself.

His arm was lying between her breasts. In such a position Nightshade would have done more than sit there like a flustered cleric. Luke sat on the bed and wavered between barbarity and civilization, between Nightshade and Sir Lucas. Clamping his teeth together, he forced Nightshade back into the shadows of his soul. With his free hand he extracted the comb from her grasp and slipped it into his coat pocket. Then he eased his hand from hers and slowly removed himself and his desires from the bed.

He took a moment to straighten his clothing, not daring to look at her. His glance fell on a boulle *bureau mazarin* which served as a dressing table. On it lay Miss Dane's drawstring bag, the one that matched her traveling dress. It had an odd shape for a bag. It had a corner. Luke went to the dressing table, picked it up, and withdrew what he first thought was a gold box. Turning to catch the light from a lamp, Luke realized that it wasn't a box but a book with a gilded cover.

The front was decorated with an embossed border studded with emeralds, rubies, pearls, and amethysts. In the center was a figure of Christ set in an oval formed by more stones. Luke opened the two jeweled clasps that held the book closed and found thick ivory pages laden with a neat, handwritten script and illustrated in brilliant colors.

The initial letters of the first word on each page had been elaborately decorated. Although the book was in Latin, Luke recognized the letter O, which had been outlined in thick gold bands enclosing blue roundels. Within the O sat two regal figures, a man and a woman, who wore long robes and crowns.

Shutting the book, Luke looked from it to Miss Dane. All the while that she'd been in hiding, she'd had this book with her. If she'd sold it, she could have escaped and lived anywhere she wished. The thing must be dear to her. It was obvious she wouldn't go anywhere without it. Luke smiled.

"Sorry, Miss Prim, but this is for your benefit," he whispered.

He waited a moment to assure himself that Miss Dane was still sleeping, then left on tiptoe. Hurrying back across the Old Hall, Luke stopped beside a suit of jousting armor and drummed his fingers on the book. Miss Dane would suspect him of taking it. She would demand that he return it, and when he refused, she would search for it herself. He needed a good hiding place. There should be plenty in a castle this large, but Miss Dane was right clever. He must then be even more clever at choosing its place of concealment.

Pacing back and forth over the red-and-white floor of Venetian marble, Luke surveyed the castle in his mind. He couldn't put the book in his rooms or his office. Not the library. She would look there on the principle that he might hide it among the thousands of volumes already there. Knowing Miss Dane, she would search every room in the residential quarters.

What about the towers? He could find a place in the Water Gate Tower, the Clock Tower, or the Armory, where the Treasury was located. There were the dungeons of the Prison Tower or the Plantagenet Tower. No, he had already mentioned dungeons to her. She would remember. What about the Garden Tower? No, too pleasant a place to explore. What he needed was an unpleasant but simple place to hide the book.

"I know!"

Luke shut his mouth and glanced around to see if anyone had heard. He was still alone. It was getting late. Meager light from two lamps caused the suits of armor to cast grotesque shadows. Taking one of the lamps with him, Luke hurried out of the Old Hall and down the steps to the inner bailey. Crossing the lawn at an angle, he reached the Plantagenet Tower and entered through an arched door.

He ascended the dark spiral stair and didn't stop until he'd reached the third floor of the great drum tower. There he found a small landing leading to a single narrow door. Shoving it open, Luke entered a room in a smaller tower that protruded from the Plantagenet. This was the latrine tower. A shaft extended from the top of the Plantagenet Tower down to the moat.

No longer in use, the shaft had been filled in with rubble. The small closet in which he stood contained a bench set over the shaft and fitted with a wooden seat. Lifting the seat, Luke wrapped the book in his silk handkerchief and set it on top of the rubble. He would return with a suitable container for the book later.

Luke stepped out of the latrine, shut the door, and held the lamp high as he descended the spiral stairs again. Soon he was seated at the table in the small dining room eating fresh roast beef while Mrs. Snow lurked in the background. She alternated between scolding the footman who served him and curling her lip in disapproval of Luke's manners. Luke vowed to himself that he'd begin lessons in etiquette as soon as Miss Dane woke tomorrow. Meanwhile he dismissed

Mrs. Snow. After dinner he would go to Vyne Cottage and visit Ma and Pa.

Luke smiled at the thought of his parents. Much older than his real parents, at least that was what Luke guessed, they'd taken him in when he was barely four. He didn't remember his real mother well, and his real father not at all. What he did remember was a dark, frigid room with a bed and a dresser with a broken leg. The only other clear memories he had were of men knocking at the door, his mother answering, and then setting him outside the door to shiver on the dark landing while she entertained.

Glancing down at a forkful of roast beef, Luke put it in his mouth and concentrated on chewing. He seldom thought of his real mother. Thinking of the Hawthornes, Tusser and Louisa, was far more pleasant. They'd been poor, like everyone he knew, but that hadn't stopped them from taking him in after his mother had died leaving him to fend for himself on the streets. They couldn't do much more than write their names; they had no fine manners or knowledge of the world outside London, but they had saved his life and brought love into it. He'd brought them with him when he left the stews, and later to Castle Beaufort. But neither Tusser nor Louisa felt comfortable in such imposing surroundings. Both hated Mrs. Snow, which Luke felt was a testament to their natural good taste.

"She looks like she thinks I'm going to snaffle the silver plate," Tusser complained.

Louisa just gave the stained glass in the Gothic

chapel a dismayed look and said, "Oh, Luke, bless your bright eyes, we don't belong here."

He wanted them to be happy, so he refurbished a country manor house on the Beaufort lands for them. Persuading them to tolerate a maid-of-all-work had been the most he could do in providing servants. He was worried about them, however. They were getting on in years and really needed assistance. His latest scheme to get his parents to accept servants was to convince Louisa to take in a young woman from St. Giles who needed employment. If his mother believed she was giving refuge to another stray who needed her, she might let the girl stay.

Luke finished his dinner and prepared to ride to Vyne Cottage. He thought Miss Dane would sleep through the night and possibly the next morning, which suited him. He wanted her in good health so she could teach him manners and that air of unconscious authority that so intimidated Mrs. Snow. Perhaps by the time his agents in London discovered her secret, he would be as mannered and elegant as the finest nobleman at court.

"Curses on your head and black death on your heart, Mrs. Snow."

❧

Much later that same night Mortimer Fleet skulked down a quiet street near Park Lane in London and crept down the steps to the kitchen entrance of a town house. The first time he'd come, he'd tried the front door and been ranted at by a footman. Now he

knocked softly at the back entry and was admitted by
a disapproving butler, who led him through the rear
of the house, up several flights of servants' stairs, and
finally into a room guarded by carved doors.

His employer—The Gentleman, as Mortimer called
him—had been most particular that he not appear
before this hour, when even the most elegant of balls
would be over and his fine friends asleep. Mortimer
had been in this room several times since The Gentleman had hired him to do for Pauline Cross. Funny
that she'd been the one to introduce them several
years ago.

Mortimer smirked at the thought. The butler shut
the doors in a snit, and Fleet sauntered into the room.
It was of massive proportions compared to the
cramped spaces he was used to in the East End. And it
was painted all over. The Gentlemen had referred to
the painter as if Mortimer should have recognized the
name, but he'd forgotten it. Too amazed at the subject
of the painting.

"Rape of the Sabrines," his employer had called it.
Fleet had lived among the lowest all his life, but he'd
never imagined that fine gentlemen lived in the midst
of paintings of naked women being carried off to
their doom. For a while he indulged himself by ogling
the breasts of one distraught female. Then he wandered over to finger a carved box that held cigars.

The finger was clean, but the nail was crooked. His
skin was cracked and dry from exposure to the ele-
ments. His neck and face were laced with fine
crevices caused by the lack of oils in his skin.

But Fleet had groomed himself in preparation for

this meeting with his distinguished employer. He'd combed his light brown hair, making sure to conceal the balding spot on the crown of his head. He wore his flash outfit with the checkered trousers and orange waistcoat. His coat had been tailored, a major expense. But Fleet had wanted it padded to make up for his hollow collarbones and the fact that his shoulders were nearly the same width as his waist.

Some blokes were stupid enough to mistake his build and his lack of height for weakness, and Mortimer was always happy to prove them wrong by ambushing them on a dark street and beating them near to death. It helped a fellow's reputation to do that once in a while.

The doors opened, and The Gentleman came in. Fleet shoved his bowler hat to the back of his head and said, "Evening, governor."

"Have you found her?"

"Not yet."

"Bloody hell, man!"

"Now don't get h-upset, governor." He was careful to put in his H's when he was with The Gentleman.

"I told you to find her. Do I have to tell you what will happen if she reveals what she saw?"

Fleet let The Gentleman go over this well-trodden ground. His employer was one for repeating himself, as if Fleet weren't bright enough to realize what would happen to him if they were convicted of murder. Fleet's thoughts wandered and he noticed with envy The Gentleman's impeccable dress. He had a polished manner and elegant appearance that nevertheless failed to be effeminate. His hair was brushed straight back from his head to reveal a high forehead that promised more intelligence than perhaps its owner possessed. Thin nostrils quivered when he was disgusted or agitated. And The Gentleman was agitated at the moment.

"Find her, damn you!"

"Look," Fleet snarled. "Me and my men have been combing the stews for days and days. Caught sight of her a few times, but she h-escaped. I told you not to worry. She's hiding somewhere where she can't tell nobody nothing. She ain't going to the traps and peach on us; she ain't going h-anywhere. While my men is looking for her, I been going around the gin shops making h-inquiries. After I leave here, I'm going to the Black Fleece. Been too busy to get to it until tonight."

"See here, Fleet. If you don't get results soon, I'll hire someone else."

Fleet's eyes narrowed and he rubbed the rough, dry skin of his jaw. "Wouldn't do that, governor. Seeing as how it's you and me wot's in this thing together. Wouldn't be a healthy idea to bring in h-another bloke."

"Are you threatening me, you common little weasel?"

"Take it as you like, governor. Just don't be bringing anyone else into this. It would be bad for both of us."

Fleet left the way he'd come and made his way by omnibus cab to the Black Fleece. He hadn't told The Gentleman the whole truth about the reason he was going to this tavern. Although he would sound out the customers there regarding Miss Primrose Dane, he was really going to this particular tavern because he'd heard that Nightshade was back. If he could kill Nightshade while he was looking for the lady, so much the better.

Nightshade had always stuck in his throat, even when they'd been apprentices to Inigo Ware. Nightshade had what Fleet secretly envied—height, a beauty that made women do silly things to get his attention, and clever wits.

He'd always wondered why—things being as they were—Inigo had chosen him as his man instead of Nightshade. Fleet had been the butt of Nightshade's nasty humor; Fleet had come away from every comparison between the two looking inferior. In the end, perhaps Nightshade's very superiority had frightened Inigo Ware.

Fleet knew the streets; he knew crime and how to survive among cutthroats. But Nightshade had a creative intelligence that Fleet knew he could never match. He'd been much less of a threat to Inigo. He'd been so proud to be Ware's ally. So it made Fleet choke to think that Nightshade had become a far more successful thief. Years of watching his rival's brilliance while he struggled just to be adequate had curdled Fleet's small, mean soul.

Even taking Nightshade's woman from him hadn't brought relief from the galling envy. In the end, she'd tried to go back to his enemy. He'd stopped her, but what good was killing her when he knew he'd lost? As long as Nightshade lived, Fleet could never establish himself in his rightful place as king of the stews of

London. Too many still looked up to the bastard no matter how long his absences. Only when his rival was dead could Fleet take the crown and put it on his own head.

Mortimer shoved open the door to the Black Fleece. He wanted to grind the heel of his boot into Nightshade's pretty face. Some day he would celebrate the bastard's demise here, in his rival's favorite haunt. Fleet paused inside the door to take stock of the place. It was crowded as usual, and when he came in there was a slight pause while every thief, prostitute, and cardsharp eyed him. He was recognized, and the buzz of conversation resumed, if a bit warily. Fleet knew most would watch him secretly, but he didn't care. No one knew his business and few would be foolish enough to inquire of it.

When his eyes adjusted to the dim lamp glow permeated by smoke and gin fumes, Fleet searched the clumps of drinkers, finding little of interest. Then he saw what he'd been looking for. Badger and Cyril Prigg were huddled at the end of the bar talking to Big Maudie. He started toward them, but the two lads scarpered at his first step. Reaching Maudie, he watched them scuttle into the kitchen and heard the door to the alley slam behind them.

Maudie regarded him without expression. He had developed a taste for big, strong women, and Big Maudie topped him by nearly a foot. Her bosom was substantial and projected nearly at his eye level. She had curly brown hair that refused confinement of any kind, and Fleet liked the way she fingered the cudgel at her belt. But Maudie had never liked him.

"Evening, Maudie." He doffed his hat, just in case she'd mellowed.

"Humphf."

"Heard Nightshade was back."

"He's gone again," she snapped.

Fleet ordered gin and leaned on the bar. "You wouldn't know where he's gone, I suppose."

"He don't confide in me." Maudie began to stroke her cudgel.

Wiping dust from the rim of his glass, Fleet watched Maudie's busy fingers. "I could pay well to know where he's gone."

"Then you'll be paying for lies, 'cause he don't tell nobody where he goes."

"But if you heard—"

Big Maudie shoved away from the bar and turned her back to him. "I got things to do."

No use taking offense at Maudie's rudeness. She behaved the same way to everyone, even Nightshade. Fleet gulped down his gin and called for another. While he waited, he glanced around the room, noting the absence of women. Some would be upstairs, many more would still be out finding business. Just as he was about to join a group of card players in hopes of eliciting information, the door opened again, this time to admit Larder Lily.

Fleet drew up his hollow shoulders inside his padded coat and sauntered over to her. "Evening, Lily."

"Hallo, Fleet. What brings you here on this prime filching night?"

"Things is precious dull, my girl, and I thought I'd find some entertainment."

Lily sidled up to him, no doubt scenting money, and Fleet wrapped an arm around her plump, inviting shoulders. "I always like a man with money in his pocket to pitch and toss with," she said. "I'm hungry, though."

"Join me. I was just going to have a bit of supper."

They were soon perched side by side at a secluded corner table with Maudie's popular steak-and-kidney pie and ale to wash it down. Fleet waited until Lily's pink mouth wasn't constantly full before resuming conversation.

"Heard Nightshade was back, Lily."

"Aye, he was, but he's gone again."

"Too bad," Fleet said. "Him and me got unfinished concerns between us."

Lily had finished her steak-and-kidney and was digging into apple pie. "I know what you got between you."

"It ain't like that no more," Fleet said in his best aggrieved manner. "I'm a successful man of h-affairs now, Lily. I got legitimate concerns having to do with business in the City."

"You got business with banks and such, do you?" Lily asked in an insultingly skeptical tone.

"H-indeed I do, my girl. Why, h-only this evening I was in Park Lane."

"No!" Lily paused in the midst of raising a forkful of pie to her mouth. "Have you brung me a present?"

"You was the first lady I thought of when I saw all them fine shops in the Strand."

Lily dropped her fork in her pie plate and leaned across the table to him. "Show us the present, Mortimer, dear."

"Not until the proper moment, Lily." Fleet patted his coat pocket, indicating the place where the present was stored.

Straightening, Lily eyed him and crossed her arms over her ample chest. "And when is this proper moment going to come?"

"After I've finished the business I come here for." He paused to increase her curiosity. When she was leaning toward him again, he went on. "I am making h-inquiries as to the whereabouts of a young woman. She's gone missing from her family, what wants her back. She's got thick, gleaming hair with lots of shades of gold, and she looks all refined and proper. Got gray-green eyes."

Lily shrugged and stabbed at a piece of pie with a disgruntled air. "What you want *her* for."

"You seen her!" Fleet hadn't expected Lily to recognize the description. He had been leading up to asking her about Nightshade. Startled, he had raised his voice and called attention to himself. He glared around at the people staring at him to warn them to mind their own business. Then he moved his chair next to Lily's. "Where is she?"

"How should I know?"

Fleet's dry fingers curled and made fists. He could get Lily alone and beat the answer out of her, but that would take time he didn't want to waste. Reaching into his pocket, he pulled out a parcel tied with twine. He opened it to reveal a cameo locket on a gold chain. It had come from his latest graveyard haul. Fleet held it up so that the locket dangled in front of Lily's eyes.

"Tell me where she is, and look what I got for you."

Lily stared at the locket with hungry eyes. "She was here, but he took her away."

"Who! Who took her away?"

Lily reached for the locket, but Fleet yanked it out of her reach, gathered it into his fist, and held the fist out to Lily with a silent, inquiring look. Lily wet her lips, then began pushing the crumbs on the table around with her forefinger. When she didn't say anything, he opened his hand palm up.

"Them's real diamond chips all around the locket."

Lily devoured the locket with her gaze while gulping down ale. "Real diamond chips." She gave him a suspicious look. "You sure you give up your grudge against Nightshade?"

"What's that got to do—bleeding damn—you mean Nightshade has the lady?"

Lily clamped her lips shut over a slice of apple and chewed in silence. Fleet withdrew another parcel from his coat and displayed it next to the locket on the table.

"It's got a matching ring, Lily. Now I promise upon my word that I ain't interested in Nightshade. I'm only concerned with the lady." He shoved the two toward Lily. "When I find the lady and return her to her family, I'll earn enough blunt to keep my little business snug for life. And I'll be in debt forever to whoever helps me to it."

Lily shoved her pie plate aside and propped her elbows on the table as she studied Fleet. Fleet looked back at her with an open, unconcerned gaze. A plump hand reached for the locket.

When Fleet didn't stop her, Lily clutched it to her breast and whispered, "I seen Nightshade bring the lady here, but they left. I don't know where they went."

Fleet unwrapped the cameo ring and held it up to the glow of a lamp, moving it so that the gems sparkled. "Now, Lily, my girl. Let's have a long, long chat about Nightshade and his lady companion."

8

Prim was finishing her late breakfast at a table facing the windows in her sitting room and worrying about the Kettles. What would happen to them? Had anyone discovered their connection to her? Her greatest fear was that one of Fleet's men would recognize little Alice as the child witness to the murder. How she wished she could take the whole family out of that unwholesome apartment and put them somewhere safe.

She had awakened to find that she'd slept through the night and into the next afternoon. She'd been able to sleep so long only because of her exhaustion. Her one comfort was that she'd at last found a resolution to her dilemma—America. She would sail to the former colonies and start a new life there. It would take courage, but it couldn't be any more frightening than being hunted by killers.

There was little to keep her in England. Her brother was her only real family, and after he left university, he would settle in the family home. Everyone expected that she would serve as his hostess and housekeeper until he found a suitable wife. Once he'd done that, she would be superfluous. Without a husband of her own, she would be dependent upon the charity of her brother or Aunt Freshwell. She had never liked being dependent, but had accepted her fate as inevitable because she lacked a fortune. But after learning to survive in the rookeries of London, Prim had discovered that she could take care of herself. Without Aunt Freshwell or her brother.

Her life wouldn't be lived in Society, true. Yet it could be interesting and even amusing. In America her little fortune would afford her more luxuries. She might be able to afford a home and a maid. Who knew what other opportunities that young country might offer? It was a fearful prospect, though, and Prim had to be firm with herself. She would not succumb to dread.

Sipping her second cup of tea, Prim gazed out the windows at the inner bailey, now an expanse of green lawn dotted with trees in sun-burnished autumn shades of red, yellow, and gold. It was a much more calming vision than the one she had of the future. At one time, the bailey would have been crowded with people carrying on business at a blacksmith's forge, a dovecote, an herb garden, an alchemist's shop. There would have been children playing with tops and wooden swords, dogs being readied for a boar hunt, falconers attending to the mews, knights at sword practice, all raising a din. Now there was a lawn and trees with leaves like jewels.

Perhaps it was in just such a place that her book of hours had been kept. Prim took another sip of tea, but the hand holding the cup paused on the way to the saucer. The book! Hastily she set the cup down and went to the bedroom. It had been tidied and the bed made. She searched under the covers, between the mattresses, under the bed. No book. Hadn't she been looking at it when she fell asleep? Or had she left it somewhere?

Prim rubbed her forehead with the tips of her fingers. It could be that she only *thought* she'd been looking at the book. Whirling around, she rushed to the bureau and grabbed her drawstring bag. It was empty.

Prim's hands were suddenly cold and damp. She began to pace. Had a servant stolen the book while she slept? Prim's steps slowed, then halted. Wait. Wait. Could she imagine Mrs. Snow employing anyone inclined to steal? Who in the castle stole things?

"Nightshade!"

Prim hurried to the bell pull and yanked on it. Then she raced to the wardrobe where the maids had stored the garments her host-captor had provided. A quick search revealed a black riding habit and boots. Prim began undressing and was pulling on the habit when the maid assigned to her entered.

"Yes, miss? Oh, let me help, miss." The girl pulled the skirt down and fastened it.

"Thank you, Rose."

A military-style jacket followed along with a riding hat in the male style.

"Rose, you did say Sir Lucas wasn't in the castle?"

"Yes, Miss. He left after breakfast to visit Mr. and Mrs. Hawthorne at Vyne Cottage."

"Direct me to the stables, Rose. I'm going to pay Sir Lucas a visit."

It wasn't long before Prim was riding a fast little roan mare behind a groom she had asked to guide her to Vyne Cottage. The journey took her through Beaufort park lands and into a dense wood. She followed the groom along a winding, sun-dappled path that eventually meandered down to the stream. There she glimpsed the ruins of a great abbey, its hollow shell soaring above the trees. They walked the horses across a shallow place in the stream, climbed the bank and entered the wood again.

Suddenly the trees thinned, and through them she saw a stone cottage of three stories, its walls draped with thick curtains of ivy. The house appeared to have sprouted in the midst of ancient oak trees. Their limbs sheltered the place, and they only gave way at the front, where a sunny garden had been planted with so many varieties of flowers that there seemed little room for people.

A plump woman with dark gray hair in a knot on the top of her head was sweeping the brick walk that wound through the garden. Her clothes were covered with a fine coat of dust, and she attacked the bricks with her broom as though they'd committed some terrible offense. The exertion had reddened her face to the cherry color of her skirts. Freckles dotted her nose and cheeks, giving her a cheerful yet practical air.

As Prim dismounted and handed her reins to the

groom, the woman looked up and smiled. Her front teeth protruded a bit, and her grin gave her an extra chin. She came to the gate in the white fence that surrounded the house and opened it.

"You must be Miss Dane. Welcome, dearie. Our Luke has been telling us all about you."

Before she could respond, Prim was swept along the brick path, around a bank of enormous pink flowers, and into the shade of an oak where white wicker chairs and lounges had been grouped.

"Sit, dearie, sit and let's get acquainted."

"Mrs. Hawthorne?"

The lady put her hand against her damp cheek. "Where are my manners? Yes, dearie, that's me. Louisa Hawthorne. Pleased, I'm sure."

When Prim removed her riding glove, her hand was taken and given a good shake. The broom waved at a chair, and Prim had to sit in it quickly in order to avoid the burst of sweeping that followed. Mrs. Hawthorne brushed a pile of fallen leaves off the path before sinking into the chair beside Prim and letting the broom fall to the ground beside her.

"Whew! A rare warm day, this is. I'll send for Elsie to bring us some lemonade in a moment." Mrs. Hawthorne blew a wisp of hair off her forehead and paused to catch her breath.

"Mrs. Hawthorne, I have some business with your son."

"Oh, he's around, dearie. We'll find him, never fear. Our Luke has been telling us what a terrible time you've been having."

"He has?"

Mrs. Hawthorne leaned closer, and Prim found herself gazing into brown eyes that beamed contagious sprightliness. It was all Prim could do not to return Mrs. Hawthorne's smile.

"Don't you worry. Our Luke will keep you safe until your little problem can be got rid of."

Prim twisted her gloves and looked away from Mrs. Hawthorne's cheerful honesty. "I'm afraid there is no remedy for my situation, Mrs. Hawthorne. At least, not here. And through no doing of my own, I find myself in circumstances of deep disgrace."

"What are those, Miss Dane?"

Unaccustomed to being asked such direct and intimate questions, Prim pursed her lips and glanced out at a bed of late-blooming crimson roses.

"Oh, you mean being in the stews without an escort all that time, and being alone with our Luke."

Prim started when a plump finger touched the sleeve of her habit.

"Fie! Our Luke will arrange everything. You'll go home with your character unbesmirched, safe as houses, don't you know."

What could she say to this woman? Mrs. Hawthorne appeared to think her son a cross between a magician and King Arthur.

With a shake of her head Prim said, "I doubt if that is possible, Mrs. Hawthorne, but I thank you for your good wishes."

"Good wishes, says she." Mrs. Hawthorne gave a bird's-chirp laugh. "Bless your bright eyes, Miss Dane. Our Luke is the prime thief in London. Was, that is. He can do anything."

The woman spoke of thievery as if it were just another occupation, but Mrs. Hawthorne was quick to perceive Prim's disapproval. She contemplated the younger woman for a few moments in silence. Then she began to chatter again, and Prim found it hard to take advantage of the infrequent pauses in her speech to again request the presence of the lady's son.

"Ah, what fine weather. Not like what we have in London most days, is it? Lord bless me, but I remember the foul weather the night I found our Luke. He was just a little bit of a thing, not more than four. His mother had died of the cholera in the night. The poor thing thought she was asleep. He tried to wake her and couldn't, so he ran away."

Mrs. Hawthorne lowered her voice and cupped her hand around her mouth. "A fallen woman, don't you know. Anyway, I found the little thing asleep in my doorway. He'd been wandering the streets with the urchins, filching food, running from the shopkeepers and police. Mr. Hawthorne said we should take him to an orphanage or a workhouse, but I couldn't."

Tears glistened in Mrs. Hawthorne's eyes. "Lost three of my own babes, don't you know. He looked at me with those great big eyes with them long lashes, pleading like. You should have seen him. I gave him milk and porridge, and he took his bowl and cup and went to a dark corner and ate it so fast he nearly made himself sick. The poor little thing thought I might take it back, don't you know."

"How terrible." Prim felt a pain begin in her heart, one she'd felt for the Kettle children and their like.

"You know what was more terrible? When he

heard Mr. Hawthorne talk about the workhouse and all, he didn't cry or nothing. He just put his bowl and cup on the table and started to walk out of my kitchen. I couldn't believe it. He pushed the door open with both his little hands and stepped outside. He just stood there, looking out at the dirty street. Then he hung his head, and I heard this tiny sigh.

"But after that, he straightened his thin little shoulders and started to march away. That was when I told Mr. Hawthorne if that boy went, he might as well go too. But you know what? Mr. Hawthorne had already made up his mind, and he fetched Luke back at once."

"I'm so glad."

"My only regret is that we were too poor to give Luke a proper upbringing. Then he wouldn't have had to do thieving to provide for the family. But Mr. Hawthorne got injured at the docks, and my cleaning money never brought in enough to make up." Mrs. Hawthorne's whimsical smile reappeared. "But I always talked to the Lord about it. Kept him informed about our Luke, so there would be no misunderstandings in heaven, don't you know."

"I see," Prim said faintly, wondering at this novel approach to Christian morals.

"So, Mr. Hawthorne took to rag-and-bone work, but times was hard. Still, I don't think Luke would have took to a bad life it he hadn't found out what his mother was. Some foul young idiot told him. Fleet was his name. And after that, I think Luke felt thieving was all he deserved. It's a good thing he was so expert at it, don't you know."

"Then it is a curious thing that he left his chosen—er—profession and became a gentleman."

Prim had made this remark to provoke Mrs. Hawthorne into revealing more about Sir Lucas's past, but before the lady could reply, an elderly man came out of the house and limped toward them using an ebony cane with a gold top. The elegance of the cane contrasted with his worn suit and soft, crushed hat. A fine gold watch chain made the age of the suit even more obvious. His jaw had the mushy appearance of those unsupported by teeth, and his hands were stiff and gnarled from years of hard labor.

Upon reaching them, he doffed his cap to reveal a dome of bare scalp. "Mother, I see we have a caller."

"Yes, Hawthorne. This is Miss Dane, that our Luke told us about."

"And I suppose you've been telling her all about him, which you shouldn't."

"Why not? He's respectable now."

"And don't you apologize for him, neither. He was the finest thief in London, and he only took from those that deserved to lose." Tusser Hawthorne sat down beside his wife and beamed with pride. "Our Luke has a proper talent for stealing the finest—silver, jewels, paintings. Paintings bring a high price from the right purchaser, he says. What I don't understand is why he stole all them books. To read, of all things."

"Hawthorne, you're nattering."

"Speaking of books," Prim said.

She got no further, for a screech shattered the balmy quiet of the garden. Then a young maid came skittering around the corner of the house. Right behind her clattered an angry goat, yammering and shaking its head. Luke Hawthorne followed, calling to the maid and laughing at the same time.

Mrs. Hawthorne sprang from her chair, grabbed her broom, and charged across the garden to meet them. She bashed the goat in the head with the bristles of the broom, then shooed the creature around to the back of the house. The maid had already raced inside and slammed the door. Still chuckling, Luke joined his father and Prim.

"Good afternoon, Miss Dane."

Prim gave him a startled nod and looked past him to see if any more mad goats threatened.

"Never fear," Luke said. "The rest of the animals are still in the pens. Rose has never gotten the right of milking, and the goat knows it."

"Mr. Night—Sir Lucas, I think you know why I've come here."

"Must be a treat to get out in the good country air," Luke said as he braced himself on the back of his father's chair. "You being in London for so long."

Prim frowned at her host, but Tusser Hawthorne forestalled her reply.

"Don't see how she can enjoy herself up at that mountain of stone you live in. Near drove me mad having to live inside that great warren." Tusser leaned toward Prim on his cane and winked at her. "Got lost so many times I kept a ball o' string in me pocket and let it out if I was going someplace I hadn't been before."

Luke groaned and said, "Pa, Miss Dane don't want to hear all that."

"And you should have seen Mrs. Hawthorne. The place gave her the vapors, and she never had them in her life." Tusser leaned back, took a deep breath and let it out as he surveyed the garden, the secluded house and the wood beyond. "No, this place suits us much better. Mother was right. That castle was too grand for the likes of us."

Prim watched Tusser pat Luke's hand, then said, "I should think no accommodation too grand for persons of the character of Mr. and Mrs. Hawthorne, but certainly a castle can occasion great difficulty for domestic comfort."

Tusser gave her a puzzled look and glanced up at his son. Luke grinned.

"She thinks you and Ma are right fine folk, and she agrees that the castle is too big."

Whistling and shaking his head, Tusser thanked Prim. "You'll have to excuse me, Miss Dane. Mother and me, that sort o' conversation ain't in our way."

"Don't worry, Pa. She doesn't talk like that all the time."

"She's a right proper lady, is Miss Dane."

Wishing to prevent the two men from discussing her any further, Prim rose suddenly. "Sir Lucas, I would have a private word."

She got no further, for Mrs. Hawthorne appeared at the front door and called them inside. With Tusser preceding them, Sir Lucas offered his arm. Prim stepped aside—ostensibly to allow room for Tusser's cane on the path—and moved into a pool of sunlight. Sir Lucas gazed at her with a strange expression on his face, as if he was seeing something he hadn't expected. Prim frowned at him again, and he abruptly bent down and whispered to her.

"Afraid to touch me, after all this time."

"You are absurd, Sir Lucas."

Prim felt her cheeks grow hot as she placed her hand on his arm. How had he known? She'd suddenly remembered how his arms felt and had been reluctant to provoke the unsettled feelings that had sometimes beset her when they were locked together in their various struggles. She wouldn't allow him to embarrass her. They strolled toward the house in silence. As they mounted the front stair, Sir Lucas glanced down at her.

"Sunlight suits you, Miss Dane."

The unexpected compliment flustered her, and all she could do was murmur a faint thank-you. They went to a front parlor fitted with sturdy furniture that was comfortable and had no pretensions to antiquity or elegance. Prim was conducted to an overstuffed chair. As she sat down Mrs. Hawthorne appeared, to ask Tusser's assistance in the kitchen, a request that obviously surprised Mr. Hawthorne. However, he made no objection and followed his wife out of the room.

Sir Lucas strolled down the wall of high windows that looked out on the front garden, then turned to her. "Ma left us alone on purpose. She knows you're angry and is giving me a chance to palliate you."

"To what?" asked Prim, distracted by the word.

Luke clasped his hands behind his back. "Palliate. That means to reduce the violence or intensity of something. Got it from my dictionary book this morning."

"I see." Prim also saw that Sir Lucas was in a playful mood, and he had a most smug look. Swallowing her irritation, Prim continued. "Sir Lucas, I am worried about the family that took me in, the Kettles. What if one of those—those criminals discovers they've helped me?"

"Did anyone see you in their place?"

"I don't think so, but . . ."

"I can't help if you won't be plain with me."

Prim toyed with her gloves. "Alice, the oldest girl, was with me."

There was a long silence during which she paid minute attention to the grain in the leather of her gloves.

"Tell me where they live," Luke said quietly. "They got to be moved, and quick."

She looked up then to find hard black eyes drilling into her.

"There is a drunken father."

He shrugged. "Drunk or not, he'll be given a choice."

"What kind of choice?"

"Do what I say standing up, or laying down."

"Laying down," she repeated in mystification. Then she gasped. "You're going to—"

"Look, Miss Prim. There ain't no use dealing with some blokes like they're members of the flash set."

Prim reflected upon Mr. Kettle's grasping selfishness, nodded, and gave Luke the address. He gave her a quizzical look as if surprised that she had stayed in so desolate an area. She watched him rub his chin and noticed the way his hair kept falling over his forehead.

He brushed it back as he scowled at the garden out-side, evidently contemplating some nefarious plan to rescue the Kettles. Prim set her gloves on the chair arm and stood.

"Where is my book, Sir Lucas?"

"What book?"

"My book of hours—oh, no. I shan't play games with you."

He turned then, his hair swinging forward to screen his face. "No games. What a pity."

"What have you done with it?" Prim grew irri-tated again at the return of his smug expression and mocking tone. "It's quite valuable, but I suppose you know that." A sudden suspicion came to her and she narrowed her eyes. "You can't sell it. It would be recognized."

Luke's smug look vanished. "Watch your tongue, Miss Primrose blighted Dane. I didn't snaffle your book to sell it. I don't need to do that no more."

"From what your parents said, I was certain you stole from the rich to give to the poor," Prim snapped.

It was Luke's turn to flush. "Never you mind what I done in the past."

"You stole from the rich and gave to yourself." Prim glanced around the room. "I can see that for myself. But I have no intention of becoming one of your victims."

All at once he was before her, looming and glower-ing like some wrath-possessed demon. "You're already a victim, and with that razor tongue of yours, I'm not surprised."

"I, sir, am known for my pleasant temperament and accommodating manners."

Luke threw his head back and laughed. "By who?"

"Whom."

"What?"

"One says 'by whom,' not 'by who,' " Prim said through clenched teeth.

"There. That's what I need. We can begin my lessons today."

The man was infuriating. "Not until you return my book!"

"No book until you've given me my lessons."

Prim set her riding crop down, folded her arms and glared at Sir Lucas. "Now you listen to me. Only the most cold and sordid person steals from a guest under his roof."

"As you like, Miss Prim. No lessons, no book."

Uttering a sound of frustration, Prim whirled, turning her back to her tormentor. Gradually her irritation gave way to reason. If she was going to America, she couldn't take the book. It wasn't really hers, and she would have to return it to her brother so that it could be stored at the estate. All at once, she felt Sir Lucas behind her. She couldn't see him with her back turned, but for some strange reason, she was able to feel him. Her body tingled as he came nearer and leaned over her shoulder.

"Give up?" he asked with a smirk.

Prim cried out and skittered away from him.

"No!" Her voice broke, and Prim paused to clear her throat. "No. I have reconsidered. You may keep the book. I'm certain you'll care for it well, and you may return it to my brother soon."

Luke began walking toward her, his gaze fixed on her face. "Why? I know that clever look. What foolery are you up to now?"

Prim backed away, then walked quickly around a chair to place it between them. Luke stopped.

"I will always be in danger here. And there is a stain upon my name in England. Therefore I have decided to go to America and begin a new life."

"Bloody hell."

"Your language, sir."

"My blood—blast my language. You ain't going anywhere."

"I shall."

"You can't!"

"Why not?"

He stared at her, a small muscle in his jaw twitching. Prim had never seen Nightshade at a loss, but he seemed confused—even desperate. Why? Could it be that he didn't want her to leave for some other reason? Prim's mouth formed a small O as she contemplated the idea that Luke Hawthorne might desire her presence for its own sake.

"Why shouldn't I go?" she asked.

He was still glaring at her, speechless. Then he brightened.

"You can't go until you teach me etiquette and manners. You promised."

"Any gentlewoman can teach you."

"Not anyone," he replied with certainty. "You

saying that any lady could put the fear of God in Mrs. Snow like you did?"

"Of course. Well, perhaps not."

Luke stuck his hands in his pockets and sauntered around the chaipr. "Tell you what, Miss Dane. Let's make a bargain. You teach me manners, and if your situation is no better by the time my fiancée's visit is over, I'll send you to America myself."

So, that was the cause of his alarm. Prim berated herself for suspecting that he'd conceived an attachment for her. What conceit. She—who seldom gained anyone's notice at home, the object of Mr. Acheson's charity—would hardly catch the eye of so handsome a charmer as Sir Lucas Hawthorne. What a foolish fancy. No, better to direct her thoughts to practicalities. She needed Sir Lucas's help in getting to America.

"Very well. I shall help you until your fiancée's visit is over. No longer. Then you will help me leave for America at once."

"Agreed. And we'll begin after Ma feeds us." He cocked his head to the side and gave her a most insolent inspection from head to foot. "Can't wait to see what you got to teach me, Miss Prim."

Fleet hunkered down under an awning across the street from a respectable lodging house on the out-skirts of Woolwich. Neither Jowett nor Stark had been able to discern the connection between the old lady who owned the place and the infamous Night-shade. Lodgers came and went. Tradesmen called at the service entrance around the side of the three-story brick building. It had a wrought-iron fence and gate, but the iron was rusting.

"Shabby genteel," Fleet muttered.

Countless hours of sneaking about and spying had revealed the wash day, the manner of disposing of rubbish, the type of young men the maids walked out with, and the zealousness with which the cook shopped for her provisions each day. The cook emerged from the service door now giving instructions to her assistant as she pulled her mantle about her and settled a basket on her arm. A small boy trotted after her, evidently assigned to carry packages.

Fleet turned to stare into a shop window, and watched her reflection appear when she mounted the stairs that led up to the street. As the cook opened the gate and let herself out, the lady owner herself appeared with a stack of letters in hand. Giving them to the cook, she exchanged words with her, whispered words pronounced while each shot furtive looks around the area. The cook shoved the letters in her basket, called to the boy who had been hanging on the wrought-iron fence, and set off for the local market street.

Fleet watched the woman go and rubbed his stubbly chin. It appeared Cook had been sent off to dispatch the mail. Fleet had a cousin in service at the home of a prosperous tradesman, and from what he'd observed, cooks were jealous of their rights and keen to demand respect for their position. Cooks, even those employed in lodging houses, would take offense at being employed on such a paltry errand. What was in those letters?

Pulling his collar up around his ears and stuffing his hands in his pockets, Fleet set off after the cook and her assistant. He caught up with them on a busy street that suited his purpose. It was the work of a few moments to draw up behind her, then jostle the woman and stick his foot out so that she tripped. Cook gave a loud squawk and hurtled to the pavement, causing several pedestrians to stumble and fall as well. The basket flew off her arm. While a crowd gathered—

some to watch and some to help—Fleet searched among the scattered contents of the basket. He filched the packet of letters, rose and walked off at an unhurried pace.

Finding a refuge in a dry goods store, he riffled through the stack of letters. Five were by the lady of the house to people he'd never heard of. Two were by the servants, and one was by some lady named Mistress Eve Shadow. There was something queer about that one, for it seemed to be a letter and envelope placed within another envelope.

"Eve Shadow?" Fleet muttered as he tossed the remaining letters behind a stack of fabric. "Eve Shadow. Strange name, that." He stood beside the bolts of material tapping the letter against the tips of his fingers.

His lips curled. Fleet tore open the letter. "And I used to think you was clever, my lad."

He removed a sealed letter from the envelope. This one was in the same handwriting, with no return address. Its recipient was a solicitor's chambers with a respectable but not exclusive West End address. Fleet opened the letter and found Miss Primrose Dane's name right off.

The smile that spread over his lips would have been at home on a gargoyle. Giving the letter a cursory perusal, he stuffed both it and the envelope in his pocket, glanced out at the street to make sure the cook was gone, and set off for home. He began to whistle. He'd need Stark, who was a passable forger, and he'd need Jowett's help in breaking into the solicitor's. Progress at last.

❧❧❧

Luke sat at a round mahogany table with clawlike legs in the Duke's Drawing Room. It was one of those cavernous chambers more suited for functions of state than taking one's ease. Its ceiling was twenty feet above his head, decorated with a floral rosette in white and gold from which hung a crystal chandelier. Luke eyed it distrustfully.

The thing was heavy with thousands of crystals and situated directly over the table. If it dropped . . . Luke rose, snatched up the sheets of paper he'd been reading, and strode over to the fireplace. Throwing the papers on a red damask couch, he seated himself, stretched his legs toward the fire, and crossed them at the ankles. He rested his head on the cradle of his arms and leaned back to stare at the ceiling again.

"A duke," he said aloud, "is addressed as 'Your Grace.' A duchess, 'Your Grace.' A marquess is 'My Lord.' He's the Marquess of Such-and-Such. His wife is 'My Lady,' as are the wives of earls, viscounts, and barons. A baron is called Lord Such-and-Such, not Baron Such-and-Such, which is foreign. A count is a foreign title. A baron's wife is addressed as Lady Such-and-Such, not by the family name, but daughters of dukes, marquesses, and earls are Lady Ann, Lady Mary, and so on."

Luke frowned and glanced aside at his notes. "Somewhere is ladies with men's names. I know it. Where was that?" He shuffled through the notes to no avail. "God rot them all. Bloody honorables and viscounts and knights and dukes. And why in hell do some ladies get called Lady Henry or Lady James instead of Lady Mary? Where is that paper?"

His head spun. The Duke of Newcastle whose real name wasn't Newcastle, Lady Edbury, Lord Robert Paget, whose name was indeed Paget, the Earl of Donoughmore, Cecil Waring, third baron Revingstoke. The list was endless, and he was supposed to know it. Luke groaned and slumped down on the couch.

Learning the ways of Society was much harder than learning to be a thief. Right now he'd rather be breaking into a town house in Portman Square than waiting for yet another lesson in manners and etiquette from Miss Dane. She had turned out to be an exacting instructress who actually expected him to memorize what she told him each day and repeat it back the next.

Luke sat up quickly when he heard the door open and the rapid tap of dainty boots on the polished wood floor. He watched Miss Dane come toward him and wondered why he hadn't noticed how she came into a room before. He couldn't quite describe it, but she moved so smoothly. The tapping ceased as Miss Dane gained the carpet. Luke hurried around the couch to make his bow.

"Good morning, Miss Dane."

"Good morning, Sir Lucas."

"I hope you had a pleasant evening."

"I did indeed, Sir Lucas."

"May I escort you to a chair?"

"Thank you."

Offering his arm, Luke settled Miss Dane in a chair beside the couch. Three days ago, when their lessons began, he'd sat beside her on the couch and earned a snippy rebuke.

Today, Miss Dane didn't begin at once. He remained on his feet and asked if there was something wrong.

"Yes, Sir Lucas. Tell me, is there word about the Kettles?"

"Yes, they're a pack of little monsters."

"They're not monsters. They do what they can, considering what their father is. It's my fault that Alice is in danger—"

"Don't fret about them, I've seen to it."

"You have?"

"Sent round to see how they did. They were all there, including your little Alice." He gave her a sideways glace. "Sent them out of the city to a friend. He'll give them a place to stay and see to it that the family is taken care of proper."

"Thank you, Sir Lucas."

He could see the tension ebb from her face and was rewarded with a smile that, without warning, strummed a tight little tune inside him. Heartily desiring to ignore such inconvenient feelings, Luke sat down again in the midst of his notes and sighed when Miss Dane called for his recitation.

He launched into the morass of terms of address and did well until his thoughts strayed, and he recalled how Miss Dane had come into the room. She seemed to drift like a sailing ship on calm waters. She was wearing a gown of royal blue with salmon and gold stripes, and flared sleeves that revealed undersleeves of darker blue. He'd been right to ask her to instruct him. In appearance, demeanor, and character she was the ideal lady. Miss Dane could enter a room in her bell-like skirts and create the impression of a soft western breeze gently stirring a garden. She didn't wiggle her hips and make her hoops swing like the women he was used to.

Also, her grammar was perfect; at least he thought it was, and her voice modulated like one of those piano pieces by that fellow Chopin. Miss Dane knew when to wear a bonnet rather than a cap. She knew which parasol was appropriate for morning use, which handkerchief suited a day gown, which of the countless spoons in his silver service should be used for serving as opposed to eating soup. Miss Dane seemed to know everything.

"No, Sir Lucas. One does not address a knight as Lord Such-and-Such. You are a knight. Your title isn't hereditary. You are called Sir Lucas, not Lord Hawthorne."

"Rot the titles and the peerage. They don't make no sense."

"They make no sense."

"See. You agree with me."

Miss Dane pursed her lips and sighed. "No. I was correcting your grammar. It's 'They make no sense,' not 'They don't make no sense'."

"Either way, I'm sick of titles."

"I thought you might be, so I made some notes on decorum and manners."

"Like at table?"

"No, Sir Lucas. Your table etiquette is not as bad as you seem to think. No, I'm speaking of a gentleman's behavior, especially in regard to ladies."

"I don't sit them in me lap, if that's what you mean."

He couldn't help reminding her of their more intimate dealings. He liked to see her blush. It made a wondrous sight, all that creamy skin turning pink and contrasting with the amber, gold, and wheat of her hair. He wished she wouldn't gather it up in that knot at the nape of her neck. What was she saying?

"It is as well to be plain about these standards of conduct, I think, for it may be that what I think is understood may not be by you."

"Right."

Miss Dane read from a sheet of paper filled with her writing. "Never do the following: Go on a journey, dine, go to a play, go to a concert or other function alone with a lady who is not a near relative."

"What, never?"

Miss Dane nodded.

"You sure?"

"Certainly."

"What about a picnic?"

"Especially not a picnic, which may be considered a journey as well as a function."

Just then a diffuse ray of sunlight shot through the window glass and turned her hair to fire, and he stopped listening again. It was a funny trick of the imagination that happened to him. A tantalizing feeling came on him—of being whisked into a dream world where the air was silver mist and sound had a chimelike quality. This was a world he'd created for himself when he was young and lost and nowhere was safe.

He remembered sleeping in doorways, if you could call it sleep. His body lay prone, but his mind wouldn't rest. So many things to fear, but most of all, he was afraid of the older boys who lurked in darkness ready to amuse themselves by beating him. When the hunger and fear came, and he couldn't sleep, he would retreat to his silver mist world and listen to the magical sounds in it—bells, fairy chimes, a stream rushing over stones, a breeze fluttering leaves. In that world he'd been safe. And now this young lady seemed to take him there just by sitting in a sunbeam.

"Sir Lucas, you're inattentive again. Which is rude."

"Sorry," he said faintly, dragging his attention back to the real world. "No going places together without a chaperone."

"Correct."

"No being alone with a lady at all."

She nodded.

His gaze drifted over her sunlit hair, and he couldn't prevent himself from saying softly, "We're alone, Miss Dane. And sunlight becomes you."

"Sir Lucas," came the sharp retort. "Please refrain from familiarity." At his lifted eyebrow, her shoulders slumped and she looked away. "My case is different. Because of my situation, I am lost to good society forever. Ordinarily, I would never visit you alone, or engage to instruct you in anything. However . . ."

"However?"

Miss Dane's tongue peeked out. Luke smiled and shifted his position so that he was nearer to her chair.

"However, I am in your debt, and soon to be in greater debt. I can think of no way to repay you at the moment. Besides, you drove a most unfair bargain, sir."

"So there are times when I can be alone with a lady."

She scowled at him. "Yes. When she's ruined."

"Don't snarl at me, Miss Primrose blighted Dane. I didn't ruin you. I'm only trying to help."

"You can help by sending me to America at once, before he finds me!"

"Who finds you?"

She almost said it without thinking. He could see her lips form the words, but then she caught herself. She realized her near mistake and jumped to her feet. As she rose, the papers in her lap toppled to the floor.

"Oh, you are an infamous creature to bait me so!"

Manners in mind, Luke got up when Miss Dane did, and stooped when she did—and hit her head with his. A spike of pain sent him bouncing back to land on his heels, swearing. He heard Miss Dane cry out. Still swearing, Luke grabbed her as she lost her balance. She fell into his arms and curled into a ball. Luke shut his eyes. Little gasps came drifting up to him, and as his own pain became an ache, he looked down to find Miss Dane clutching her head.

"Let me see." He turned her in his lap and pried her hands from her head.

"I—I shall be fine."

Luke ignored her, touched her chin with his fin-

gers, and tilted her head. He touched her hair at the
spot she'd been protecting, and Miss Dane cried out.

"Quit your blithering and let me look at your
head."

"I'm quite well, sir. Please allow me to rise."

Luke dropped his arms and let her slip to the
floor. Giving him a scowl for such indecorous treat-
ment, Miss Dane battled with her skirts, then tried to
stand. Luke was ready when she wavered and caught
her before she fell again.

"Daft little blighter." He gathered her in his arms
and lifted her to the couch. "You got a right good size
knot on your head. Loosen your hair."

"I shan't do that," Miss Dane replied as she lay back
on the couch. "It's improper."

Luke knew better than to argue with Miss Dane
about propriety. He knelt beside her and began
pulling pins from her hair.

"What are you doing?"

"Relieving the pressure on your poor head, daft
creature."

She grabbed his wrists and glared at him. "Stop!"

They had touched each other before, but Luke
couldn't remember Miss Dane ever voluntarily placing her bare flesh against his. Now her fingers pressed
against his wrists and the cuffs of his shirt. Her skin
warmed his. He could feel his pulse throbbing against
the pressure of her hands. And the sunlight turned her
cascading hair to divine fire.

"Divine fire," he whispered to himself.

"What?" she asked, meeting his gaze with confusion.

He was distracted by hues of bottle green, teal, and

gray, and without thinking, drew closer to her. It seemed the most natural action, kissing her. And it was like drinking enchantment. His body warmed as though the fire of her hair wrapped itself around him.

Even as he tasted her, learned her mouth, and taught her how to learn his, he was astonished. Luke had kissed countless women, and he had, without thinking about it, expected Miss Dane to be like the rest. What foolery. She had never been like the rest. When he kissed her, he felt the effect of an entire bottle of cognac.

He could feel her heart against his chest. No, that thumping wasn't her heart. Luke surfaced from his private world of the flesh to find Miss Dane's small fist pounding at him. He pulled back from her, but she kept hitting him. He captured her hands.

"Stop it," he snapped.

She went still and gaped at him, her eyes wide and her hair in a tangle around her face. Kneeling before her with his eyes closed, Luke came back to himself slowly. He controlled his breathing and willed his body into a more respectable state. And when he opened his eyes this time, he looked at Primrose Dane with transformed vision. How had she remained a spinster, a girl who could kiss like that? Of course, quite likely no one had ever bothered to kiss her before.

"God rot my soul," he said in a wondering manner.

Miss Dane was still looking at him in startled confusion. Luke glanced down to find his hands still on her, slowly released his grip, and stood. He walked away and stared at a rococo marquetry chest. Concentrating on the spiraling curves and sinuous lines of its decoration, he lectured himself. He'd done many awful things in his life, but he was a gentleman now. He couldn't take advantage of an innocent and unprotected young woman in his care. Nightshade stirred inside him, laughed, and asked why not.

"Black death and curses, I don't need this battle upon everything else."

"Sir Lucas, I demand that you stop mumbling and explain your horrid conduct."

He whirled around and stared at Miss Dane.

"Horrid?"

"Most unacceptable," she said.

Miss Dane had managed to pin up her hair again, but in a looser fashion to ease her head. She was standing rigidly, like a starched collar, with her delicious mouth all pinched and her cheeks crimson.

"I must have your word that you will refrain from such actions in the future, Sir Lucas."

"You must, must you?"

"You are mocking me, sir."

Nightshade was laughing inside him, prodding him, daring him to promise. Luke stuffed his fists in his pockets, lowered his chin, and raised his eyes to the woman in front of him. His voice came out in a harsh whisper.

"No, Miss Prim. I'm not mocking you."

"Then I demand an accounting for your conduct, Sir Lucas."

"Don't ask me."

"I beg your pardon?"

He began to walk toward her, slowly, while he

tried to banish the roiling urges Nightshade fostered. "You don't want an accounting, Miss Prim."

"Stay where you are!"

He paused at the tone of panic in her voice, then threw himself in a nearby chair and sprawled there, glaring at the chandelier.

"Do I have your word?"

"What? My word about what?"

"Your word that there will be no repetition of such disgusting behavior."

"Disgusting is it?" How dare she pretend to be unmoved while he was suffering like this? "Don't curl your lip at me like you smell something from a ditch, Miss Prim. I did the teaching just now, but you did a powerful lot o' quick learning."

He was rewarded with a shocked gasp and a flood of color to her cheeks. His grin faded when she marched past him on her way out of the drawing room.

"Not another lesson in etiquette, Sir Lucas, until I have your word."

10

She was dreaming of a ball. Acheson had rescued her from the shame of standing alone and unpartnered. They sailed around the hot ballroom, turning, turning, turning. Couples circled around them, the skirts of the women swishing on the polished floor. The heat and the flickering light from the chandeliers made her dizzy.

Suddenly Acheson was gone, and Montrose was dancing with her. Prim tried to see where Acheson had gone, but she couldn't. Montrose spun her around the room while talking about books. His voice droned on, making her ill. She wanted to stop dancing, but Montrose turned into Harcourt, who whisked her around with renewed energy. They began to spin wildly, careless of the other dancers until they bumped

into a couple. The woman turned, revealing a blood-
ied gown and a knife in her chest. She gave Prim an
unblinking stare.

Prim screamed; her partner grasped her arm. It was
him, the murderer! The dead woman's partner began
to laugh as Prim backed away from the killer and his
victim. The laughter grew loud and mean. Suddenly
it was Luke Hawthorne, laughing so loud she had to
cover her ears. Prim woke wondering if she had really
screamed or if the sound she'd heard coming from her
mouth had only been in her dream.

❧

Prim glanced through the open door of the drawing
room to make sure no one was passing. Then she
scurried across the Aubusson carpet, climbed onto the
window seat, and peered at Luke Hawthorne across
the expanse of green lawn. He paused on his way to
the shell keep to speak with the head gardener. As he
did each day after they finished their lessons in manners and etiquette, he was attending to his business affairs. Prim was going to follow him.

Three days ago, after suffering from bad dreams and
indecision, she'd decided not to keep her agreement
with Sir Lucas. She'd been at the castle only a little
over a week, but the kiss had forced the decision. No
one had ever kissed her like that. He'd done it so
slowly, and with his entire mouth, his entire body, and
she had felt something quite amazing and entirely
wicked. That was when she knew it was Nightshade
kissing her.

With all her other troubles, she couldn't remain in the same house with a Nightshade who had kissed her, even if that house was a labyrinth of a castle. After that kiss, she could feel his presence even if he was in the barbican and she was almost a quarter of a mile away in the most distant tower. No, that wasn't honest. Since the kiss, she had *wanted* to feel his presence, no matter where he was.

That was why she had to follow him and discover the hiding place of the book of hours. Prim couldn't bear leaving the precious little volume behind. She had to get it, break her word, and leave for America at once. Before leaving she would return the book to her brother. Then she would somehow get hold of and sell her modest jewelry to obtain the money for passage. It would mean arriving with less to begin her new life, but she had to escape. For she was very much afraid she was in love with Luke Hawthorne. No, she was afraid she was in love with Nightshade.

Prim ducked aside as Luke and the gardener turned to gaze in her direction. When the two separated, she watched her host continue on his way to the shell keep. She had been following him each day after the lessons. Their meetings had become stiff and guarded, but how else was she to maintain a proper distance between them? He certainly hadn't wanted to. Indeed, he'd been horribly rude when she insisted he promise to use proper decorum—until she had reminded him of his fiancée.

After that, he had behaved. A few minutes ago their lessons had been interrupted by an unexpected visitor. Sir Lucas had received his guest in the room next to the Duke's Drawing Room, pulling the door shut between the two chambers. Prim didn't hesitate to rush to the door as soon as he had disappeared.

Quietly opening it a crack, she spied the visitor. A constable! Sir Lucas was handing him a parcel wrapped in brown paper and tied with twine. He ushered the policeman outside, and Prim was sitting in her customary chair by the fireplace, fuming, when he returned to the drawing room.

"Sorry for the delay, Miss Dane," he said in that artificial, formal manner he had taken to employing since she'd insisted upon the new regime of propriety. "Do forgive me."

"I shan't," she snapped. "You're a vile wretch without principles."

Now he drew himself up in what was becoming his most irritating habit—imitating her proper manner of speech. "I beg your pardon?"

"You've spoken to the authorities about my situation," she said. "Don't bother to deny it. I saw the constable."

Sir Lucas looked down his nose at her. "Have you been spying on me, Miss Dane? How common."

"Don't berate me when you've already broken your word, sir."

Shoulders square, nose tipped in the air, he looked down at her with an excellent copy of her own sneer. "I haven't broken my word. The constable was here on a matter unrelated to you, difficult as that may be for you to imagine."

His decorum and steady, unflustered manner began to make her feel unsure. Prim rose and faced him.

"What possible reason could you have to speak to a constable?"

"I decline to tell you," he said with a mocking smile.

Prim colored and retorted, "Then you confirm my suspicions, and I consider our arrangement null. I shall leave as soon as possible."

"Oy! Now you see here, Miss Primrose blighted Dane. You take yourself off, and you won't live a week."

"Then tell me what you said to the constable."

"You're a precious sly and deceitful creature."

"Tell me."

"Oh, all right, damn you. It was about Feather-stone."

Prim could only stare at him.

Sir Lucas looked away from her, and to her consternation, she could see a flush rising in his cheeks. What could embarrass a man as hardened and dangerous as he? When he mumbled something, she shook her head.

"What did you say?"

He scowled at her. "I said Featherstones have served at Castle Beaufort near as long as it's been here."

"I fail to see—"

"I'm trying to tell you, damn it." He cleared his throat. "When I bought the castle, most of the servants was like Mrs. Snow, but Featherstone, he told them off. And he helped me, you know, understand the way of things. Still does. When I go to dinners and such, he tells me all about the people I'm going to meet. When I visit, he comes with me as my valet. Helps me dress right and such."

"What does this have to do with the constable?"

"Well, Featherstone is a right proper butler and valet. Even you said so." He hesitated, as if uncertain of her response.

"Yes."

"Yes, well, he's an amazing bloke, is Featherstone, but he's got one tiny little fault. He takes things."

"Do you mean he's a thief?" she asked in disbelief.

"Not a thief, really. If he was a thief, he'd be a terrible bad one. Featherstone takes things, but not for blunt. He just takes them."

"I don't understand."

"He can't keep from it. It's like those that can't stop drinking. Featherstone can't stop taking trinkets. Last month I went on a visit, and when we came home, he'd filched a silver cow creamer. He didn't want to sell it for a profit. He didn't want the thing at all, really. He just had to take it."

"Dear God," Prim said. "Was that what you gave to the constable?"

Luke fell to studying the red damask wallpaper. "He'll see to it that it's returned with my apologies. I got an arrangement with the county folk. Most of them are right understanding, probably because of my being the new owner of the castle."

"Am I to understand, Sir Lucas, that you go about the countryside returning articles your servant has purloined and apologizing for him?"

"Featherstone's a fine bloke," came the response. "What do you want me to do, turn him over to the traps? He's always sorry, and he tries not to do it. It's a terrible burden to him, this thieving."

By this time Prim was smiling at him. "And I would be willing to guess that you'd hate it if Mr. Badger or that Maudie woman heard of your kindness."

"Huh."

"Your manner is furtive, Sir Lucas."

He left off staring at the wallpaper, tugged on the cuffs of his frock coat sleeves, and glared at her. "You're a vexation, did you know that, Miss Dane? And now, I decline to discuss this subject further."

Still kneeling in the window seat, Prim found that she was smiling at his embarrassment about being exposed in an act of kindness. Then she stopped smiling. What was she doing crouching here, lapsing into bemused thoughts of a man with the heart of a devil and the ruthlessness of a—a brigand?

She had to keep her mind on her goal—finding the book of hours. Where had Luke gone? She gazed outside again just in time to see him speaking with a workman atop a hay wagon. Luke stepped away, and the workman continued on his way to the stables. Prim waited until Luke went into the shell keep. Hurrying out of the drawing room, she retrieved the mantle she'd placed in a cupboard near the great hall and went after her host.

This was the difficult part, following him without seeming to. She strolled slowly along the gravel drive, passing grooms, footmen, and maids on their various errands. A man was hauling a rake across the gravel to create a more even surface. She paused to admire a spray of roses in a bed beneath the window she'd been using. Eventually her indirect route took her near the keep. She mounted the stairs and ducked inside when she thought no one was looking.

The shell keep was a Norman tower with walls over eight feet thick surrounding a central courtyard. On a high mound, it dominated the castle with its soaring height and sheer stone walls. Prim hugged the wall and descended the stairs that led to the courtyard. Sunlight beamed through at the end of the staircase, and she was careful not to expose herself as she reached the opening. All she saw, however, was another green carpet of grass upon which had been placed a new fountain. Water splashed from an urn held by a woman in a Grecian robe. Around the fountain lay newly dug beds of soil, evidently waiting for spring planting.

Luke was nowhere to be seen, but as she studied the sheer wall faces that looked down on the courtyard, she heard the sound of a boot on stone. Prim ducked back up the stairs and turned a corner. The keep's walls were designed as two circles, one within the other, and the space between formed rooms.

Prim hurried past what had once been the kitchen and mounted stairs that would take her to the top of the keep. She found the going hard, for the stairs hadn't been meant for a lady in a crinoline and corset. She had to pick up her skirts and press them to make them smaller while trying to keep up with the footfalls that told her where Luke was. He stopped only once, and Prim fell back against the wall, her chest heaving against the confines of the bindings that kept her from taking deep breaths. She was almost at the top.

What was that sound? He was coming back down already! Prim shoved away from the wall. Her crinoline flew up past her head, and she had to battle it down and scramble into an alcove on the landing below. She barely made it before Luke walked past her without stopping. Craning her neck, she saw that he had nothing in his hands.

As soon as he was gone, Prim ran awkwardly upstairs to find an open door at the top landing. She ducked inside, but all that greeted her was a bare room fitted with an arrow slit. She looked outside and saw Luke descend the exterior stairs and head to a door in the wall between the Plantagenet and the Lion Tower.

Still breathless, Prim ran downstairs, and had to stop a moment before she could leave the shell keep with proper decorum. Once inside the defensive wall, she saw a swaying glow in the distance that meant someone was carrying a lantern. She followed it through what had once been soldiers' quarters to a winding stair inside the Lion Tower. There she heard footsteps again. Reluctantly, she mastered her skirts again and trudged up the narrow, worn stone steps.

This time she passed a series of chambers that had managed to survive intact. Each was dimly lit by narrow slits and windows hardly more expansive. The lowest held remnants of stones once used for a trebuchet siege engine. The next contained rotting wood timbers, the remains of the trebuchet. By now Prim was perspiring, and gulped in air as if she were suffocating. On the next floor she found a room empty except for a few ancient crossbows hanging from pegs in the walls.

As she breathed hard and stared at the crossbows, a whistle sailed down from the uppermost room. She heard a creak, then a clatter. Her mouth dry, her lungs aching, Prim trudged upstairs once more. There she found another room bare but for wooden racks that had once contained bows, and pegs from which had hung bowstrings. The whistling was coming from the roof. No! It was descending toward her. Luke was coming back.

Prim looked around the tower chamber frantically and spied a shadowed recess that led to a narrow, barred window. Crushing her skirts against her body, she climbed into the recess and pressed as far back into the shadows as she could. As she maneuvered, her foot slipped on a pebble, and her boot scraped against stone. Prim froze. The whistling had stopped.

Footsteps signaled Luke's approach. She heard the steady, easy rhythm of his walk. It grated on her nerves and made her picture the way his legs separated as he walked, how he seemed more animal than man when he moved toward her. Prim put her fingers over her lips to still her harsh breathing when Luke appeared in the doorway with his lantern. She stopped breathing.

Luke came inside, moving with that provocative gait that caused fiery tendrils of excitement to arc through her body. Prim clenched her teeth and wondered if he walked like that deliberately. As she watched, he raised his lantern and examined the pegs on the walls. Suddenly he turned and stared at the recess. Her heart almost stopped at the way he lowered his chin and directed a stare of devouring intensity in her direction.

Certain that he had seen her, Prim was about to crawl out of her hiding place with as much dignity as she could summon when Luke turned with facile grace and left the chamber to its dim solitude. Her relief nearly caused her to sigh aloud. Prim clamped her mouth shut and clambered out of the recess. Her hair caught on the stone above her head, pulling free of the pins that held it knotted at the nape of her neck. There was no time to fix it. She scurried up to the roof where Luke had spent so long, but found no trace of her book.

She descended the Lion Tower in time to see Luke disappear up the stairs of the Plantagenet. She trudged after him, but her efforts were fruitless. He ascended to the top of the tower, spent a few minutes surveying the countryside from the turret, then came down again. Prim was beginning to think him mad.

Previous pursuit had informed her that Luke spent time consulting with his estate manager, conferring with Featherstone, and visiting his parents. Yesterday he had introduced a new servant to the Hawthornes, a girl he'd taken in after finding her begging in St. Giles. Prim had even followed him to the suite of rooms he was having prepared for his fiancée, where he consulted with London merchants about antique furniture and French wallpaper. But today he seemed determined to visit every remote tower and precarious turret in the castle.

Prim was almost grateful when Luke's wanderings took him past the old great hall and down to the ancient kitchen. Little used now, it would be the perfect place to hide her book. Prim rushed down a curving flight of stairs, for Luke had suddenly increased his speed. She ended up in a large, vaulted chamber with wall-sized fireplaces.

Aged roasting spits sat empty, and Prim stood still, gazing at them and trying to hear Luke's footsteps. He could have taken any of five archways. In the half-light she could discern the outline of a grape press, and across the room lay a well that had once been the castle's main source of water. Prim hastily searched the fireplaces, the press, glanced down the well. No book. She looked inside vast cooking pots and empty barrels to no avail. Then she went to each archway and listened. At the third, she heard Luke's whistle. It was beginning to annoy her most sincerely, for it meant she would have to climb yet another staircase.

Lifting her skirts, she had time only to bless her luck that these stairs were wide enough for her crinoline before rushing after her elusive host. She followed the whistle up to the high vault that contained a cistern used to hold rainwater. Then she tracked it out onto the wall walk, through a turret and down into the Plantagenet Tower. It was here that she lost her way. Somehow she ended up turned around, her sense of direction gone.

She was no longer in the Plantagenet. She remembered a long trek through the structures attached to the defensive walls. Perhaps she'd followed that wretched whistle as far as the barbican and the drawbridge. Sighing, Prim chose a direction and marched downward, ever downward. It got dark, then lighter, until she stepped through an archway—into the kitchen, again.

"Wretched castle," she muttered. Then she cried out as a shadow moved.

"Miss Dane?"

It was one of the footmen. Prim let out her breath and shook her head.

"Dinesdale, I didn't see you."

Dinesdale was another of Luke's protégés. He had a habit of recruiting unfortunates from the rookeries and bringing them to Beaufort. Dinesdale had arrived yesterday. He was lance tall and thickly muscled from loading freight for railroads, so he made a gigantic and threatening shadow. He didn't reply to her remark, which made Prim uneasy.

"What are you doing down here?" she asked.

"Got lost, miss."

"Oh."

He said nothing else, and Prim grew more uneasy. He was staring at her as though she were a haunch of meat.

Pointing to the arch nearest the grape press, she said, "That's the way out."

She moved toward the archway, and Dinesdale moved with her. But he moved so that he blocked her path. Prim stopped.

"What are you—"

Luke's voice made her jump.

"Miss Dane?"

Luke came down the stairs near the grape press and

stood in the archway. "What's going on? Dinesdale, what are you doing down here?"

"Got lost, governor."

Prim walked around the footman's bulk hastily and joined Luke. "I'm afraid we both got lost, Sir Lucas. It's lucky you found us."

"Right," Luke said with an assessing look at Dinesdale. "We can get out this way."

Offering his arm to Prim, he conducted her up and into the great hall. Dinesdale followed and was ordered to find Featherstone in the butler's pantry. As Prim watched him go, she realized why she had been so uneasy. For some reason the footman reminded her of that miserable creature Jowett who had hunted her.

"Got your breath again?"

"Hmm?" She was still thinking of Jowett. "Oh, yes, I am recovered, but I'm thirsty after all that climb—" Prim stopped and stared at Luke. "What did you say?"

He gave her a dark-eyed smile.

"Thought I was going to have to come back and carry you a few times. Especially after that last trip up the Plantagenet."

Breasts heaving, face burning, Prim pointed a finger at Luke Hawthorne. "Vile, abominable, wretched, cursed, despicable—you, you led me all over this miserable castle!"

Luke threw back his head and laughed. It echoed off the walls and the distant ceiling. Her legs and chest aching, her mouth parched, her skin clammy from perspiration, Primrose Victoria Dane succumbed to rage for only the second time in her life.

"By God!" she roared.

This made Luke laugh harder. "I didn't ask you to follow me, Miss Prim. Tell me, what is the etiquette for spying?"

"Etiquette?" she cried. "I'll show you etiquette!"

Whirling around, she rushed to a table next to a suit of jousting armor. On the table lay various pieces of a more ornate set. She picked up an elbow cap and hurled it at Luke. He ducked, still laughing, and it hit the floor with a loud clatter. Prim grabbed a vambrace and threw it, forcing him to dive out of the way. He wasn't laughing quite so hard now. She sent a cuisse sailing at him, followed by both greaves.

"Here! You stop that, Miss Prim." Luke dived behind a medieval wedding chest as she heaved a breastplate at him.

"Foul, beastly ruffian," she shouted.

Turning back to the table, she found that she'd run out of armor. Her eye fell on the swords mounted on the wall behind it. There was quite a selection. There was a lovely hand-and-a-half sword, but it was far too heavy. She quickly surveyed a falchion, a two-edged sword with a triangular pommel, and a one-handed sword with a disk pommel. That was the one.

Prim reached up and pulled the weapon off the wall. It was in good shape. No rust. Hefting it in her right hand, she turned to face Luke just as he stood up behind the wedding chest.

She pointed the sword at his chest. "It's time for another etiquette lesson."

11

The Gentleman stood looking out a window that dripped with rain. In the street below a gas lamp flickered, a yellow beacon in the windswept darkness.

I'm not having this. All I've worked for, threatened by a dead whore and a spinster of no consequence. My position and my work are too important. And I'm sick of worrying about it. High time it all ended. High time.

He turned and glanced at his guest, one he ordinarily wouldn't allow in the kitchen yard, much less his study. "Hawthorne, is it? Damnation and hell. Hawthorne isn't a man to cross."

"Who woulda thought?" Fleet mused softly. "Nightshade a gentleman. A bloody miracle, that's what it is. You heard of him, have you, governor?"

"In my line, one gets to know these things. But

that's hardly relevant, Fleet. We have to get her away from him."

There was a short pause. Then Fleet grunted.

"Maybe not, governor." Fleet sat down in one of The Gentleman's leather wingback chairs, purloined one of his host's expensive cigars, and lit it. "Maybe not. If we can get into his place, or if we can use somebody already there." He puffed hard on the cigar.

"What are you saying?" The Gentleman gripped the edge of the windowsill to keep himself from snatching the cigar.

"I'm saying you can bribe a whole castle full o' servants with enough blunt." Fleet turned his cigar so that he could examine the burning tip.

The Gentleman sneered. "More witnesses, you fool."

"Nah. You leave it to me, governor. I'll get someone in there to take care of her. Mark my words, we'll be rid of her in less than a fortnight."

Snake quick, The Gentleman pounced on Fleet, gripped his collar, and dragged him out of the chair.

Shoving his face close to Fleet's, he said, "A week. You have a week. After that, I'll do the job myself if I have to."

The Gentleman released Fleet as suddenly as he'd grabbed him. Fleet dropped into the chair, but before he could say anything, his cigar was snatched from him.

"Get out."

Fleet stood and made a show of straightening his collar and coat. "You should watch yerself, governor. That temper is what got you in this mess in the first place."

A harsh laugh made The Gentleman turn red. "I need no advice from a man with the refinement of a sewer rat." He turned back to the window, placing a hand on the cold pane. "Get out, Fleet, before I decide you're as much trouble as my dead mistress."

The Gentleman heard the door shut behind his guest. It was time to take more direct control. If Fleet failed, he would end up floating facedown in the Thames. As for Miss Dane . . . Servants weren't the only ones who had the run of Castle Beaufort.

❧

Luke beheld a wondrous sight—Miss Primrose Dane coming after him with a sword. He tried not to smile again, for she was already furious with him, but he failed. The sword wavered as she uttered a small roar of combined outrage and wrath. Then she rushed at him with the sword pointed at his chest.

If it hadn't been for the windows, he might have tried to get away, but she came at him through shafts of white light, her hair catching fire in sunbeams. He forgot to move as he watched. Prim almost reached the wedding chest, but as he stood there gawking at her in the rays of the sun, she suddenly halted. The sword froze at his chest level; it dropped to point at the floor. They stood in the aged hall, their breath sounding loud in the vastness of the place, and stared at each other.

He was awakened from his foolish stupor when her little face seemed to crumple and tears appeared at the corners of her eyes. "What's wrong now?"

The only answer he got was a long, strangled cry. Prim dropped the sword as if it burned her, and it clanged on the marble tile. Turning her back, she lowered her head. He could see her pound her fist against her leg repeatedly, but he couldn't hear what she was saying. He left the shelter of the wedding chest and approached her with caution.

Edging around her, he could see that her tears were still falling, slowly, and that she appeared to be in some grave discussion with herself. As a precaution, he nudged the sword out of her reach with the toe of his boot. Then he eased closer. She seemed to have forgotten him in her agitation.

"He's turned you into a barbarian," she muttered. "Soon you'll be stealing jewels and paintings from the finest houses and taking drink with those—those creatures at the Black Fleece. Abominable! Look what you've become, crawling across the rooftops of London, consorting with fishmongers and ruffians. To actually attack him with a weapon. It's not to be believed. Lost to all propriety and decency. Stripped of decorum. Mad. Utterly mad."

He remained silent while she scolded herself. Ever since he'd kissed her, he'd had trouble with Miss Primrose Victoria Dane. After that, she'd gone all proper on him, like some clergyman's wife. Now he realized he'd underestimated the burden she'd been under for so long. Separated from everything she'd known, everyone she was used to, no wonder she had lost her temper. *I suppose now is not the time to tell her how much I liked it.* No, that might give her a brain fever. At least he could stop her from berating herself.

"Now, Primmy, there's no call to go thrashing yourself."

She jumped and whirled to confront him. Her hair swirled in from of her face, and she appeared to notice it for the first time. She began frantically gathering it at the back of her head again.

"Indeed there is every reason to thrash myself, as you put it, Sir Lucas. Although your behavior was reproachable, I should not have descended to such an ill-conditioned response."

He watched her struggle with her hair, then stooped and gathered a few pins. "Here, let me help."

"I beg your pardon?"

"No need to apologize."

"I wasn't. I was trying to let you know how improper it would be—sir!"

He scooped great lengths of soft hair in both hands as he stood behind her. She tried to pull away and cried out when he didn't let go.

"Daft creature, hold still."

"Sir Lucas, you mustn't touch my hair."

"Quit yer wiggling."

When he didn't let go, she had no choice but to turn from him and allow him to smooth her hair away from her face. While she kept up a stream of protests, he caught silken tangles and unsnarled them. Each time his fingers brushed her shoulder, her cheek, her neck, she jumped. The first time she started, he was jolted by his awareness of her. Her taut wariness only provoked a wild urge to capture her. He could smell the scent she used in her bath—honeysuckle.

His fingers worked through the softness of her hair, making trails through its thickness. It took all his resolve not to sink into a haze of downy texture, sunlight, and honeysuckle. From his position behind her, he could see the curve of her cheek, the blush of her porcelain skin. It was like the breast of a little robin. The thought diverted his attention to the way her breasts rose and fell. Touching her this way was like the first time he'd heard a symphony by Mozart—exhilaration almost unbearable. And he didn't want it to end. He twisted a length of hair around the knot he'd placed at the nape of her neck. The gauzy tendrils there distracted him.

He wasn't sure how long he would have remained with his hands on her neck if he hadn't noticed that they were trembling. What was he doing? Any moment she would fly into a rage at his ruining her propriety again. He made himself step back and lift his hands. She remained where she was for long moments, testing his control, so he said something in a voice made rough from craving.

"Done."

"What?"

He cleared his throat and tried again. "I've finished, Miss Dane."

She turned, but he looked away from her because she was still standing in the white light of the windows and looked like she belonged in one of the stained-glass windows in the castle chapel. And because she seemed as dazed as he was. She recovered first.

"Please accept my regrets for my conduct, Sir Lucas."

"Now, don't go all proper and etiquettey on me."

Her shoulders drooped and she sighed. "I have been too long separated from the necessities of genteel life, thrust among people it is necessary to detest. Oh, not you, Sir Lucas."

"Right."

"I seem to have lost the principles expressive of good breeding, my refinement of mind." She threw up her hands and gave him a lost look. "All I ever wanted was a home of my own and the opportunity to study."

"Study? What, book study?"

"That's why I was carrying the book of hours, you see. I am greatly interested in old books, manuscripts, history. Our library at home was quite good. The family had many old documents and books from Elizabethan and earlier times."

She threw up her hands. "But, of course, I don't really belong at home. The lot of a daughter, you see. Daughters must go away." Her gaze suddenly darted to the tips of her boots. "And if they don't, they are an inconvenience and a burden."

"Whoever told you that, Miss Prim?" he asked gently.

Tossing her head, Prim smiled and didn't answer his question at all. "Do you know how rare my book of hours is? The quality of the illuminations, especially of the calendar, is almost unequaled."

She was grieving inside. Why hadn't he noticed

before? Too busy thinking of himself. This valiant little Miss Prim, she wanted to belong somewhere. Rot
her blighted family. Brother too selfish to give up a
few pleasures at university to afford her a home. Aunt
too illiberal to provide her with the means to attract
marriage offers, but only too willing to use her as an
unpaid companion.

"Curses on their heads and black death on their
hearts."

"Sir Lucas?"

"Oy! I got an idea."

"Please, Sir Lucas. I have spoken to you about your
expressions."

"Oh, I say," he said in a nasal whine. "I've got a
most convivial idea, Miss Dane. Would you like to see
the library?"

"If you will refrain from speaking in that odious
manner, but I've already seen it."

"You mean the one downstairs. That's the New Library. I mean the one upstairs, the Old Library."

"There are two?"

"As far as I know. Could be more I haven't found
yet. Come along, Miss Prim."

He offered his arm in the most gentlemanly manner he could summon. Prim gave him an agitated
look but took his arm and walked with him to the
rooms above the great hall. After taking time to light a
lamp, they came to a door larger than most, its oak
panels shining with age and bound in iron. Luke took
a key from his pocket and opened the portal. It swung
back to reveal what he always thought of as a cavern
lined with shelves.

"Featherstone says this was once the lord's chambers." Luke followed a silent Prim into the Old Library.

"Heavens," she said faintly.

Luke stood beside her and surveyed the shelves of books that reached to the ceiling. A balcony had been added to give easier access to the topmost racks, and it extended around the perimeter of the library. Long tables bore document boxes, caskets, reading stands, and glass display cases. He set down the lamp and opened several shuttered windows. Then he went to a pedestal bookstand and opened a thick volume bound in stained leather that had been chained there.

"Have no notion what this thing is."

Prim joined him and turned several pages. She stopped and closed the book to examine its binding.

"Dear heaven," she breathed.

"What?"

"My, my."

"What? Is it bad?"

She opened the book again and pointed to a yellowed page. "You see that this book is written by hand, not printed."

"Yes."

"On parchment with these faint guidelines. There are eight leaves to each gathering or signature—a gathering of pages. The signatures are laid on top of each other and bound."

"But there aren't any pictures like in your book," Luke said. "Can't be as valuable."

She turned to stare at him with wide, sparkling eyes.

"Oh, I think it is probably as valuable or perhaps more valuable, Sir Lucas." She pointed to the writing, which was still clear despite its age. "This is a later script. Later than the seventh-century insular majuscule or Caroline minuscule. It is, perhaps an eleventh-century clerical style, and it's in Latin of course."

"Of course."

Luke stuck his hands behind his back and watched her pore over the book. He loved the way she seemed to brighten just from looking at the old thing. When she glanced up at him, he assumed an expression of polite interest so that she didn't become offended at the way he was staring.

She turned her head to the side and gave him an amused look. "You still don't understand, Sir Lucas."

"Yes, I do. It's an old book."

"Eleventh century."

"A very old book."

"Sir Lucas, this book most likely dates from the years shortly after 1085."

"Right."

"The reign of William the Conqueror."

"Good man, William."

Prim shook her head and pointed at the lines of Latin. "Sir Lucas, I think this is a copy of a portion of the *Domesday Book*."

"Sounds dreary."

"The *Domesday Book*, Sir Lucas, is the only record of its kind in the world, a complete survey of the lands and resources of England commissioned by William the Conqueror, and it's almost eight hundred years old."

Luke narrowed his eyes and repeated, "Eight hundred." He looked at the book, at the script written with a quill on animal hide, and the antiquity of the record before him finally came home. "Did you say eight? Eight hundred years old?"

Prim nodded. "It's only a portion of the whole. The entire survey comprises many books. We must be certain to close the windows when we leave. The light isn't good for old documents."

Luke was still staring at the *Domesday Book,* but Prim was moving among the tables and shelves. Her cries of delight attracted his attention, and he found her leafing through a book with illuminations similar to her own.

"Look," she said. "A book of carols." She picked up another volume. "This is a psalter, and here is an herbal. See the drawings of plants and herbs? It's written in Secretary script, which has spiky letters. Did you know—" She stopped and bit her lip.

"Know what?"

"I shouldn't babble on so."

"You're not babbling. I'm interested. Go on."

It was too late. She was conscious of herself, blushing and uncertain. He had to distract her.

"You know, Miss Dane, I know almost nothing about you except what little Ross Scarlett told me."

"You know my father was a baronet, Lord William Harold Dane. My mother was Frances Cornwallis."

"That's not what I mean. What was it like growing up a lady?"

She smiled and sat down with the herbal in her lap.

"Not nearly so wonderful as you think. When I was born Mother handed me over to a nurse, and later to a governess. My parents might as well have lived on a remote mountain, like the Greek gods. Father had a temper, and everyone crept around the house like ghosts when he was angry. Mother used to signal to us when he was in a temper by tugging on her sleeve three times."

"What a blighter."

"My brother and I had the whole east wing of the house to ourselves when we were growing up." Prim rested her clasped hands on the open herbal in her lap. "We had Nanny Peace, who was more like a mother to us than our real one. She used to feed us porridge and toast for breakfast. She sliced the toast into strips and called them little soldiers. 'Do you want your toast in little soldiers?' she would ask us."

Prim lapsed into silence and lowered her eyes.

"What happened to her?"

"Oh, nothing terrible." Prim pressed her lips together. "We grew too old for a nurse. My parents sent Nanny away, and I never saw her again."

"You mean they sent away the only person you had for a mother?"

She gave him a pained smile. "They didn't mean to be unkind. They didn't think of it that way."

"Right. So then you went to school."

"No, I had a governess. My brother went to Eton and later to university."

"And you studied with the governess."

"I suppose one could call it study. Lessons in

languages, grammar, spelling, geography, music, deportment, dancing."

"More studies than I got," Luke said.

"Hardly any mathematics, no politics, no classics or science, very little literature. My father said that boys should go everywhere and do everything and that girls should go nowhere and know nothing."

Luke gestured toward the *Domesday Book*. "But you know a lot, Miss Prim."

"I used to study on my own. I would stay up at night reading. Until the housekeeper had to account for all the candles I used. Then Father ordered that my candle was to be taken away once I was in bed."

She sighed and ran a finger down the spine of the book. Her shoulders slumped, and Luke swore under his breath. She looked up in surprise.

"Sorry."

"What's wrong, Sir Lucas?"

"I just reasoned it out, Primmy."

"I don't understand."

"I was thinking about your grand house and blue blood and fine breeding, and then I realized what made you so sad."

She looked away, but he went on.

"I was thinking how terrible it would be to grow up in such a fine place and have everyone assume your existence was trifling or inconvenient, like you were a pet goose with a limp, or something."

Lifting her head, she turned glittering eyes on him.

"Sorry, Miss Prim. I've offended etiquette again."

He was startled when she placed her hand on his and whispered, "Do you know what a rare, fine soul you have, Luke?"

"Primmy, no one has ever bothered much about my soul."

12

No man had ever looked at her as Luke was looking at her now. Never had she encountered such gentleness; never had she expected it from Nightshade, whose gaze most often seemed to bore through the back of her head and out the other side. Perhaps the very softness acted upon her as laudanum, teasing qualms until they were fine wisps that floated away in the air, leaving her captivated.

She was still sitting in a hard little chair with the herbal in her lap, but somehow Luke was kneeling beside her. His hands were over hers on the book. They were warm and clean and beautiful, and she had never seen anything so wondrous as those hands—strong, lean, but so careful not to bruise her own. Yet even after gazing upon them, she might have remained composed, if he hadn't spoken in that rough, hoarse voice she seldom heard him use.

"Do you think I have a soul, Primmy?"

He asked, revealing dread, uncertainty, and a hurt longing that sent jabs of compassion through her heart. In spite of the Hawthornes' care, Luke doubted his own humanity. The things he'd been forced to do to survive had left wounds that had never healed.

"Of course you have a soul," she said. "All of us have souls. Some are good, some not very good, some evil."

"Like me."

She shook her head and smiled. "My dear Luke, no man who tries to help as many as you have is truly evil."

"I hope you're right, Primmy. I hope what you say is true after I do this."

"What—"

His mouth stopped the words. She would have protested, but his hands slid up her arms, bringing with their touch the memory of their appearance. Touch and memory provoked a desire to discover what the rest of him felt like. It was a desire she had been experiencing since he'd first kissed her. Once he was doing it again, she lost the battle to resist temptation. With small, tentative movements, her hands slid to his forearms.

When lightning didn't strike her for her licentiousness, she pressed her hands against his arms to feel their hardness. She hadn't realized how the feel of him would feed the sensations he evoked with his mouth. Never had she imagined the way he would respond.

When she tightened her grip, he surged against her as if propelled by a tidal wave. Emboldened, she moved her hands up his arms and flattened them against his chest. At this, Luke began to whisper endearments, placing his lips near her ear while his hands moved over her.

The whispers made her brave. Her fingers found coat lapels and brushed them aside. As his lips trailed kisses down her cheek to her neck, she grew impatient with the waistcoat that formed a barricade against her questing hands. Her fingers worked on buttons and slipped inside the garment, only to meet another frustration, a cursed shirt.

She might have given up if Luke hadn't breathed in her ear. A hot wind soared into her body, setting fire to her most private flesh and to her mind. A fever possessed her and drove her inexperienced hands. They kneaded his flesh through the fine cambric of his shirt, causing Luke to gasp. He pulled at the garment; she heard it tear. Shaking now, her hands slid under the material to press against warm, surging flesh.

The feel of him seemed to stoke the blaze inside her. Luke must have known how she felt, for he responded to her touch by lifting her to him. Prim discovered that her bodice had come loose and was falling away from her shoulders, but before she could worry about it, his lips grazed the flesh that swelled at the top of her corset. Then he pushed her back, dragging her hands from his body. She opened her eyes in confusion to find him looking at her breasts. Again without warning, another garment came undone.

This time it was her corset, and to her amazement, Luke gently cupped her breast and lifted it free of all concealment. Then his lips touched her nipple, and Prim's body jerked. Spikes of sensation stabbed through her, and she cried out.

It was the sound of her own voice that jolted her from the hot whirlwind that engulfed her. Sucking in her breath, she pushed Luke away and clutched her chemise and corset to her breasts. He fell back and gave her a startled look.

"No!"

His chin came down; he raised his eyes and Nightshade was suddenly before her. He uttered one word.

"Yes."

Prim scrambled to her feet and retreated. He followed with much more grace and began walking toward her like a cat stalking some terrified field mouse.

"Come here," he said.

Struggling to fasten her bodice, Prim shook her head and kept walking backward. His lip curled, and he took another step. She did, too, and hit a bookshelf. She wasn't quick enough, and he was on her, pressing his body against hers, blocking her flight with his arms and capturing her mouth with his. Prim tore her lips free, desperate to stop whatever implacable force possessed him—and her. Her heart had betrayed her, and now her body.

"No! You are preparing us for inexpressible misery."

"You don't know what you're talking about, Miss Prim."

His hips worked against hers, but she grabbed a fistful of hair at the back of his head and hissed at him.

"Salacious wretch, stop this at once."

"I mean to have you."

Prim yanked on his hair, causing him to wince and stop moving his hips. "Are you making me an offer, Sir Lucas?"

That made him look at her with sense in his gaze. "What?"

"Are you making me an offer of marriage?"

"Course not."

Until he denied it, she hadn't realized she'd had any hope. Prim fought the tears that threatened to expose her foolishness and snarled at him.

"Then you will condescend to remember my honor, sir."

Breathing hard, he stared at her. She watched him swallow, and was relieved when he stepped back and walked over to a window to gaze out at the bright autumn day. It took her a few moments to right her clothing, and she fumbled with buttons and fabric in misery.

She didn't know how it had happened, but she was so in love with Luke Hawthorne—or was it Nightshade—that she was ready to abandon all principle, all honor, simply in order to touch him. She must have an inherently low nature to succumb to sin like this. Even more terrible, she wanted to touch him though he had no attachment to her and no intention of making her an offer. Her fingers tangled in buttonholes as truth came home to her—Luke did not return her regard. She didn't understand how he could kiss her, touch her, and yet feel nothing but duty toward her, but then, he was a man, and men were contradictory, unfathomable creatures.

I must get away from him. I cannot remain here, seeing him, knowing he has no love for me. Dear heaven, I can't stay and meet his fiancée. That would be the ultimate wretchedness.

Prim lifted trembling hands to shove pins back into her hair and cleared her throat. "Sir Lucas, we had best come to an understanding."

He was still looking out the window. She watched a muscle work along his jaw. The hand lying on the windowsill clenched into a fist.

"You're the one who started—What kind of understanding?"

"I have decided that our arrangement is unacceptable. Indeed, it is the height of impropriety, and I wish to end it. I wish to leave at once and therefore I ask you to return my book of hours."

He turned his head, exposing her to a black-eyed and menacing gaze. "Leave. Why?"

"I told you, Sir Lucas. Our arrangement is unacceptable and improper."

"That's no reason." He cocked his head to the side and inspected her with skepticism. "There's something else."

To avoid his eyes, Prim stooped and picked up the herbal. Under the guise of inspecting it for damage, she kept her gaze away from his while she searched for a suitable excuse.

"After . . ." Her courage failed. She stiffened her

backbone and tried again. "After what has just occurred, I think I am justified in distrusting the frail ruse of your parents' chaperonage." Finally she was able to lift her eyes and face him. "Sir Lucas, you cannot be relied upon to behave toward me with respectability and decency."

Luke shoved himself away from the window. "Me? I can't be relied upon? Who was it that fondled me like I was a Hell Corner harlot?"

Her face aflame, Prim set the herbal on the table. "It is scarcely delicate of you to speak in that manner, sir."

He was before her with the table between them so quickly she nearly gasped aloud. Planting his hands flat on the tabletop, he leaned toward her and scalded her with that Nightshade glare.

"Scarcely delicate, she says. Bloody hell, Miss Primrose blighted Dane, you got a lot to learn. There ain't nothing delicate about sex."

"Your language!"

"Rot my language," he shouted as he banged his fist on the table. "You and your etiquette and your manners be damned. You don't mind me as long as I clean myself up and behave like some trained dog, but you sure as eggs don't want to dirty yourself with my touch."

Luke banged the table again. "No, that ain't right. You want me. I been with too many women not to recognize one who's stirred, like you were. You want me, all right, but you're ashamed of wanting me. So don't you go blathering to me of impropriety and indecency. You're the one who's indecent."

She wanted to cover her ears; she wanted to hide. But most of all she wanted to throw his accusations back at him. He was the one who desired and yet had no good intentions. She wanted to shout at him as he shouted at her, but if she did, she would lose her tenuous hold on her composure. She would go too far and reveal how much she wanted him—and how much she wanted his affection. Such an admission would expose her to a ruthlessness of which Nightshade was the master. He would use her weakness against her. And after he had done with her, what would happen? He would still go to his lady fiancée, and she would be sent off to America—alone.

Taking refuge in her breeding, Prim clasped her hands and forced her voice to remain steady. "I will not be addressed by you, sir, in that manner. It is clear that my remaining under your protection is impossible, and I intend to leave for America at once. Please give me my book so that I can send it to my brother, who is its rightful owner."

"No."

"I thought you might refuse. Very well. I shall leave without it, and you will be forced to return the book yourself. Since you're accustomed to returning things that don't belong to you, it shouldn't be a difficult task."

She cried out when his hand lashed out and gripped her wrist. He pulled her so close she could see the glittering bronze flecks in his eyes.

"You leave," he said softly, "and I'll burn the damned book."

"You will not."

The gaze he directed at her had spent millennia

encased in a glacier. "Miss Dane, I have knifed a trap and dropped a bloke what cheated me off the roof of a storehouse. What makes you think I wouldn't toss that book in a fire?"

"You are hurting me," she said.

He looked down at her wrist as if he'd forgotten he was holding it. He let go. Prim rubbed the reddened skin, and as she did, Luke swore.

"I beg your pardon?"

"Nothing. I said you ain't leaving."

"Do you intend to keep me here forever?"

"Daft creature, I'll keep to our original bargain. If you still want to leave after my fiancée's visit . . ." He straightened and walked to the door.

"It seems I have no choice."

Luke stopped and gave her a cold smile. "No, you don't."

"However, I decline to give you any more lessons."

"We're keeping our original bargain, Miss Dane."

"Hardly, sir, since you've threatened me."

He folded his arms over his chest. "Did you know you're a bloody stubborn little—"

"How many times must I warn you of your language, sir?"

"Thought you wasn't giving any lessons."

"One of us must uphold standards of decency," Prim said stiffly.

"Then I got your word that you'll stay?"

"I do not give my word to dishonest ruffians."

He began to walk toward her. "If you don't promise, I got to think of a way to keep you from doing something foolish."

Prim thrust out her hands to forestall him and he stopped.

"You have my word."

"Sure?"

"Are you questioning my word after you've asked for it, Sir Lucas?"

"Don't set up a hue and cry. I was just asking."

Prim turned her back on him. "I believe our business is finished. Pray excuse me."

"I suppose that's your high-and-mighty way of getting rid of me."

"It is."

"Choke me dead, Miss Dane. And here all this mortal time I thought you liked my company."

Turning swiftly she encountered Nightshade's insolent smile.

"Go away!"

She had to listen to his laughter, fading with his progress toward the great hall. But she could still hear it even when he stopped there, and Prim rushed to the ironbound door and hauled it shut. She want to the farthest corner of the Old Library and sank to the floor. To her dismay, she could hear him whistling as he left the hall and walked along the gravel drive. Prim lowered her head, covered her ears, and hummed to herself to drown out the sound of his voice.

After a while she moved her hands and listened. Silence, thank Providence. She drew her knees to her chest, wrapped her arms around her legs, and succumbed to misery. For the second time in her life she was in love with a man who did not love her. But the devastation of her heart was incomparable.

There had been times in her life when she felt grief. When her parents died, of course. And then there had been another time of misery, when she had left childhood behind and become a young woman. Suddenly everything changed.

Countless restrictions upon her conduct appeared. No longer could she be silly or careless or climb trees or raise her voice or explore the park that surrounded the house. She had to wear her hair up and her skirts long—which made life uncomfortable and cumbersome. She could go nowhere alone, while her brother could roam as he willed. In the space of a birthday, her world shrank and her freedom vanished.

In return, her governess and her mother had promised rewards, marriage and children. At first Prim hadn't been impressed with the magnitude of these rewards, but one day her parents presented her with an arrangement, a betrothal to Lord Percival Percy, the younger son of a duke. Lord Percival was a most eligible young man of rank and fortune. Neither of these qualifications mattered to Prim.

What mattered to her was that Percy brought laughter and carefree grace with him. He took her to operas, gardens, exhibitions, and he took her riding in Hyde Park. She was free again. As free as a young lady could be. Prim fell in love with Percy's charm and effortless refinement, his dashing mustache and blue eyes fringed with golden lashes. She basked in the knowledge that she was important to someone at last, for Percy seemed discontented unless in her company. And he brought her primroses.

Then her father lost his fortune, most of it anyway,

and without leave-taking, hints, or excuses, Percy vanished. Prim remembered waiting for him to call. She would sit in the drawing room and jump each time a servant opened the door, her heart filled with hope. It was all she could do to refrain from rushing to the door. When the visitor was announced and wasn't Percy, her heart sank. Day after day she waited, bewildered and afraid. Finally her father received a letter in which Percy withdrew his offer of marriage. Apoplectic, her father threatened a suit.

His shouting and threats only worsened Prim's anguish. At first she believed Percy the victim of family pressure against an unfortunate match. She blamed herself, knowing that if she had been prettier, more charming, he would not have abandoned her. To this day, a secret mean little voice inside her hissed rebukes at Prim for her lack of beauty, saying that it had cost her Percy's love. As weeks passed, Prim understood that among her kind, marriage was an economic arrangement, a social machine oiled by facile wooing. Percy had been good at oiling. She doubted he would have been good at love.

Her father eventually forgot his ire, and Prim was spared the humiliation of a public airing of her troubles. Her pride and sense would not permit her to contemplate spending her life with a man who didn't want her and who would resent her for forcing him into marriage. Her reduction in fortune made it unlikely that she would attract a suitor of proper rank. She was not allowed to consider one of lower station, except in one instance. After her father's death, Lady

Dorothy and her son Newton thought it most advantageous for her to take a wealthy merchant who was Newton's ally in Parliament. But Prim had had enough of arranged matches.

She busied herself with teaching and doing her duty as Aunt Freshwell's companion. Now she could admit, however, that she had secretly hoped to find someone for whom she could form an attachment. She had engaged in the idle wish that one of her three self-appointed saviors—Acheson, Harcourt, or Montrose—had not been married. Without telling anyone, she searched among the men at operas, balls, dinners, and country house parties, but in Society, falling in love and then marrying was rare. One married for position and fortune. Then, after producing an heir, one was allowed to fall in love—as many times as one cared to—with someone other than one's husband.

All the eligible young men, she soon discovered, were looking for girls with fortunes. The married men cared nothing for fortune. They were looking for a lover and companion among the wives of their peers, but they left unmarried girls alone if they knew what was good for them.

So Prim hadn't married for rank and fortune, and she failed in her quest to marry for love. She retreated to her teaching, her duty, her studies, and she had been content. Until Nightshade.

Why did she have to love him? He was as ruthless as he was beautiful, as likely to mock as to charm. Perhaps he made her feel safe, in spite of her dreams of stifling ballrooms, the woman who danced with a knife in her, and the killer, the familiar, well-bred murderer. Nightshade's very ruthlessness chased away such nightmares.

Prim sighed and got to her feet. Brushing her skirts, she returned to the table where the herbal lay and closed the book. Somehow she had to survive the next weeks without making herself ridiculous. She opened a psalter, but the illuminations on the pages blurred and she wiped her wet cheeks. She hadn't even realized she'd been crying.

She couldn't allow Luke to suspect her true feelings. Luke—Nightshade was ruthless enough to take advantage, amuse himself, and then send her off to America. He had proved that here in the Old Library. No, she had to carry on as she had been. But it would be so much harder now that she'd glimpsed what being with Luke meant. It was like being consumed by starfire.

"Useless to think of it. Don't think of it."

All she had left was her pride and the promise of escape. Escape she could count on, but if she wasn't careful, she would end up humiliated and pitied, too. She had lost enough already without forfeiting the right to hold her head up in the presence of Luke Hawthorne. And she was damned if she was going to be pitied by Nightshade.

13

A week after the scene in the Old Library, Prim escaped the castle by riding to visit Mr. and Mrs. Hawthorne. It was a cold afternoon made heaven-bright by the sun and a nighttime shower. She was grateful for the sun. Too much rain and clouds depressed her spirits. Living with Aunt Freshwell and Newton had made her feel as if she lived in a world of perpetual rain. Being with the Kettles, despite their poverty, and with Luke, had made her aware of the contrast between the households. Aunt was totally absorbed in furthering her son's social position. And as for Newton—Newton's most distinguishing attribute was his utter lack of curiosity about anything unconnected with himself. Prim suspected this lack was due to Newton's not being very intelligent.

How else could one explain the man's ability to sit in a room and do nothing for hours? He even found counting dance steps a challenge. She remembered the time Robert Montrose had tried to show Newton how to waltz. Montrose had called on the family on a rainy afternoon, and Prim's aunt had suggested the attempt. In his perfectly tailored suit, with his exquisite manners, Montrose walked Newton through the steps. For an hour. Newton didn't dip, he stumbled. He didn't turn, he jerked. Prim finally rescued the man before he was tempted to strangle her cousin.

Sighing, Prim patted her mare and reflected on one of the few advantages to being forced to flee England. She wouldn't have to endure Newton Freshwell any more. She was trotting down a path bearing a carpet of yellow and orange leaves. Passing beneath the thick branches of an oak, she heard a thud behind her.

Prim pulled up and turned her mare to see a heavyset man wallowing on his back rather like an overturned crab. It was the footman Dinesdale. She walked her horse back to the man.

"Did you fall, Dinesdale? Are you hurt?"

The footman grunted, sat up, and clutched his head.

"Oh, heavens, you've already got a knot on your forehead," Prim said. "You stay there and I'll fetch help from Vyne Cottage."

"No!"

"Nonsense." Prim turned the mare and kicked her. "Don't try to get up. I'll return in but a few minutes."

She went to the cottage, and to her dismay found

Luke there before her. They returned to the oak tree with a gardener, but Dinesdale had gone.

"I told him not to move," Prim cried. "What if he becomes dizzy and falls?"

Luke surveyed the path and surrounding wood. "He can't have been hurt badly or he wouldn't have been able to leave. Still, I'll search for the poor bloke a bit with the gardener. You go back and assure my mother all is well, or she'll have the whole country-side looking for Dinesdale. He worries her."

Prim rode back to tell Mrs. Hawthorne what had happened. Soon they were seated in the parlor drinking tea.

"It was his pa that did it, don't you know."

"I beg your pardon?" Prim asked.

"Oh, I know Dinesdale is a large boy, but when he was little, his pa would beat him whenever things went wrong. Lucas says he was throttled in the head too many times."

"Then falling on his head couldn't have been good for him."

Louisa shook her head and sipped her tea. "What was he doing in the tree?"

"I don't know. I rode under it, and after I'd passed, he fell out."

Louisa clucked and sighed. "I'm not at all chirpy about this one, Miss Dane. Usually the ones Lucas brings home have a bit of sense. But it can't be got over. He's here, and he's got to be provided with a living."

"Don't concern yourself, Mrs. Hawthorne. There

are many tasks suitable for Dinesdale. He may not be as clever as most, but he certainly can do worthwhile work."

"Oh, I don't quarrel with that, my dear." Mrs. Hawthorne frowned as she stirred her tea. "But what was he doing sitting on a branch over the path?"

"Perhaps climbing trees is one of his pastimes."

"Ah, that must be it, don't you know. What a clever girl you are, Miss Dane."

❧

It was a sunless afternoon, and a bank of nearly black clouds was rolling over the horizon. Luke was in his room dressing with Featherstone's help. The butler's fingers worked expertly on his tie while Luke strained to look past him at the threatening weather.

"Do you think it will snow, Featherstone? Rot this weather. Why did it have to turn ugly on the day Lady Cecilia is to arrive?"

Featherstone grabbed Luke's shoulders and turned him so that he could reach the tie again. "I doubt it will snow, Sir Lucas. Please be still while I finish this tie."

"Remember your promise," Luke said with a scowl. "No filching Lady Cecilia's things, or any of her servants' things."

"I remember, Sir Lucas. You may trust me."

"You said that before we went to that house party at Lord Tringle's."

"I have endeavored to improve since then, Sir Lucas."

"If you haven't, I'll scrag you meself."

"Yes, Sir Lucas."

Luke shoved Featherstone's hands away from his lapels. "Oy! That's enough. You're going to give me a brain fever."

Featherstone retreated, found a clothes brush, and attacked Luke's coat with it. Luke groaned but remained still and endured.

"Mrs. Apple is ready, Sir Lucas."

"Good."

Prim had insisted that appearances be preserved for Lady Cecilia's visit. Thus he'd been forced to produce a suitable chaperone for his unwilling guest. She had carried her point by telling him Lady Cecilia would be scandalized to find her in residence without the company of a mature lady relative.

Luke had asked an old friend to play to role. Mrs. Apple, a woman of Mrs. Hawthorne's age, had been in the music halls and could act. Prim had given her instructions about her role, and now the household was ready for the visit. Ma and Pa had moved to the castle temporarily, and the whole place had been scrubbed. He'd redecorated the rooms assigned to Lady Cecilia. But something was bothering him. He wasn't looking forward to meeting the lady as much as he had been.

It was because of Prim. From the time she'd come after him with that sword, he had been unable to get near her without wanting her. Rot her! She made him furious with her etiquettey ways and stiff manner of speech. She hadn't been near so proper until the day he'd led her on that chase through the castle, and he wished she'd become more like her old self. After all, he knew she wanted him. But after what happened in the Old Library, he recognized that she hated herself for it.

Prim was the first lady he'd ever truly desired. And now he was glad he'd escaped any previous intimate encounters. Miss Divine Fire, Miss Primmy, she wanted him all right, but she knew too much about him. She knew the truth, and it repelled her. She desired Sir Lucas; she detested Nightshade.

Unfortunately, Sir Lucas was a sham, a ramshackle hut in which he concealed Nightshade. Prim saw through the knotholes and cracks. He couldn't hide Nightshade from her. She'd met Nightshade before Sir Lucas, and because of that, their relationship was doomed. He might have her desire, but he would never have her admiration, in spite of her kind words about his soul. And he would have liked to have her admiration.

It would be a fine thing to see those gray-green eyes light up with pride when he came into a room. Right now she hardly looked at him. What was worse, she saw through his most accomplished lies and masquerades.

He had only loved one woman, poor Jenny, and she had worshipped him. Jenny had been common, like him. Prim was a lady, and she had made it clear that she thought him lower than a stoat. Which didn't stop her from wanting him, the little dissimulator.

That was his latest word—dissimulator, which meant liar. Prim was lying to herself.

And torturing him because of it. He could make her respond to him. It would be easy considering how many times he'd done it before. But she would hardly look at him, and she hid behind a barricade of proper speech and stiff, Primmy manners. So he spent his days resisting temptations and his nights pacing his rooms, sleepless and nearly succumbing to the urge to go to her.

Once he'd got as far as her door before he'd been able to master himself. He only did that by remembering how she would hate him afterward for robbing her of her precious honor—which she evidently valued above her affection for him.

Affection. Was that what it was? What did he feel? Hell and damnation. No, he couldn't feel this way. Not when Prim . . . And Lady Cecilia was coming. He wanted Lady Cecilia and all she meant—home, family, a foundation of security and peace. Everything he'd ever wanted, since he could remember.

"I'm not giving that up!"

Featherstone paused in brushing Luke's trousers. "Sir Lucas?"

"What?"

"Give up what, Sir Lucas?"

"Nothing. Damnation, Featherstone, that's enough brushing."

"Sir."

"Do I look right?"

"If I may say so, Sir Lucas, there are few gentlemen

as handsome or so well groomed. The tailor has cut that coat to set off your figure, and—"

"Enough about my figure, Featherstone. Leave my figure in the future. I can do without you talking about my figure."

"Yes, Sir Lucas. Miss Dane said she would await you in the drawing room."

Luke started out of the room.

"Sir Lucas."

"What?"

"Stuffing your hands in your trouser pockets will ruin the line of your suit."

"Choke me dead, Featherstone. I'm never going to learn to be a gentleman."

"If I may be frank, Sir Lucas? Once Lady Cecilia catches sight of you, she will disregard any minor lapses you may commit."

"You're a good bloke, Featherstone."

"Thank you, Sir Lucas."

Luke left his rooms and passed bustling servants on last-minute errands in the residential quarters. Lady Cecilia was due in a few minutes from the train station in town. He opened the drawing-room doors and found Prim standing before one of the tall windows. She was looking outside and hadn't noticed him. Just then a break in the clouds allowed sunlight to flood the room briefly and bathe her in a golden glow. He had lately read the tales of King Arthur and the holy grail, and how the grail appeared in an aura of light. That was how he saw Prim, in an aura of light and magic, a fairy-tale princess in distress.

Only this princess didn't want to be rescued. She was going to rescue herself, and in the process, take herself far away where he would never see her again. Suddenly, Luke realized how miserable the idea made him.

Prim sighed and hung her head. Luke wondered what was bothering her. Not that she didn't have things to worry about, but lately she had grown sad. He longed to make her smile, and she could do with a better appetite, too. But what was he doing standing here in a gloom? There wasn't much time.

"Miss Dane, I'm ready."

She turned and came toward him, and the sun went behind the clouds again, relieving him of his most disturbing distraction. She inspected him, and Luke had to refrain from thrusting his fists in his pockets.

"Excellent, Sir Lucas."

"Glad you're pleased, Miss Prim."

"You mustn't call me that when Lady Cecilia is here."

"Right."

"And remember to introduce me as your cousin who is a guest of your mother." He nodded and she went on. "I have given instructions to your parents and to Mrs. Apple. Mrs. Apple is a most unusual woman."

"Oh?"

"Silver-haired old ladies seldom slide down banisters."

"Got a lot of energy, she does. Always has."

"Indeed. I told her not to slide down the banisters while Lady Cecilia was here."

"Good idea."

Prim eyed him, but he only grinned at her, and she walked to the fireplace where several logs were crackling in the flames. "Shall we review a few important points? Lady Cecilia's title derives from the fact that she is the daughter of an earl. If she marries you, she will still be called Lady Cecilia rather than plain Lady Hawthorne."

"The greater rank," Luke said.

"Correct. Now, remember, one always dresses for dinner, and everyone goes down to dinner in order of precedence. You as host will take down the lady of highest rank, which is Lady Cecilia. You always converse with the lady on your right at dinner. And never talk to or about servants at dinner."

"What if one of them spills custard on me?"

"That is unlikely to happen," Prim said severely. "But if it does, Featherstone will take charge. Now, when you make conversation with ladies, you talk about Society, music, and so on. Do not talk about business or politics."

"Why not? I talk to you about them."

"Sir Lucas, this visit will be much more formal than the occasion of our acquaintance."

"Choke me dead, Primmy. Is this the way it's going to be after I marry Lady Cecilia?"

Prim turned her back to him. "I cannot speculate upon such a private matter, Sir Lucas."

"Has someone starched your tongue, Miss Primrose blighted Dane?"

She whirled around and glared at him. "Such rudeness will certainly count against you in Lady Cecilia's eyes."

"You don't look too chirpy. What's wrong?"

"Ah, here is Mrs. Snow. I asked her to come for your instructions."

He stifled a groan. "Right." Summoning his newly learned manners, he greeted the housekeeper. "Thank you for being so prompt, Mrs. Snow."

Funny how, although she wasn't as tall as he was, Mrs. Snow always managed to look down her beaky nose at him. At one time Luke would have glared at her or avoided her gaze altogether. This time he ignored her funereal demeanor as if her attitude was something he would never even consider.

"Now, Mrs. Snow, shall we go over my instructions?" He didn't wait for her consent. "Fresh flowers three times a day in Lady Cecilia's rooms. Two maids assigned entirely to her. Her favorite foods to be served at each meal according to her requests. A fire always burning in all her rooms. Her things laundered immediately and returned, not put with the household things."

Mrs. Snow's meat-clever jaw dropped. She appeared to wake from a daze. "Yes, Sir Lucas."

"And no running out of stationery in her rooms or allowing fires to die down."

"Yes, Sir Lucas." Now the housekeeper was beginning to look like a horse trying to row a boat.

"I know you'll do an excellent job, as always, Mrs. Snow. Thank you. You may go."

Mrs. Snow stared at him for a moment, then woke

up and dropped a curtsy before wandering out of the room. When he glanced at Prim, she was beaming at him.

"Well done," she said softly.

"Thanks to you, Primmy. The old drab is going to have a fit."

"And?"

"And it is a matter of no consequence to me. A servant does not have tempers and fits."

"Excellent."

He heard the clatter of people hurrying in the hall and the rattling of a carriage outside. "She's here."

"Go on, Sir Lucas. You should be at the carriage."

His parents chose this moment to burst into the drawing room along with Mrs. Apple, who was to be known as Mrs. Rosina Longford, a lady relative of Prim's. Luke quelled Ma and Pa's fevered questions.

"It's all right, Ma. I know what to do. Just leave everything to me, and if you're uncertain, talk to Miss Dane."

He stopped them from hurrying after him so that he didn't look like a mother duck with her brood. Instead, they proceeded in a stately manner out to the drive to greet his fiancée. He could hear someone talking inside the vehicle that waited there. The head footman was opening the carriage door. Luke was in time to offer his hand to the elderly lady who emerged first. Mrs. Portloe was a relative of Lady Cecilia's, whom he'd met on his visits to the earl. Luke saw that Mrs. Portloe was safely out of the carriage and turned back to help Lady Cecilia. It was she who had been talking all this time.

He had heard her described as handsome and had seen her portrait, but artists often flattered their aristocratic subjects. When he grasped her gloved hand, he got his first look at her. In Lady Cecilia's case, the artist had supplied his subject with a bit more flesh that she really had. The young woman who stepped down from the carriage was slim and angular, with prominent jawbones and a lift to her head that reminded him of Mrs. Snow. She had a high forehead distinguished by a widow's peak of jet black hair. Her skin was as white as the glaze of the best Chinese pottery, quite fashionable.

As she left the carriage, Lady Cecilia proceeded with a complicated series of instructions to the footmen and a lady's maid who followed her. The maid held a velvet cushion upon which lay a pug dog so fat Luke would have been surprised if it could walk on its own.

Before speaking to him, Lady Cecilia continued to give orders. "Mind the step, Turnpenny. See that you don't drop Oswald. Lady Portloe, you minded the step? Good. Footman. Footman! My jewel case. Turnpenny, my jewel case. No, no, no. Put the handle of the jewel case over her arm, you stupid man. She can carry it and Oswald."

Luke tried to offer the services of the two maids standing by, but Lady Cecilia was too busy sorting out the disposal of her pet and her jewels for him to be able to speak without interrupting her. In a few minutes her maid, Oswald the pug, and the servants all trooped into the house. At last Lady Cecilia turned her attention to him. Luke met her gaze, and he realized she hadn't been paying attention when she first looked at him, for she blinked several times as if surprised. Then she did what she hadn't since getting out of the carriage—she smiled and extended her hand.

Luke took it and bowed. Mrs. Portloe hovered beside Lady Cecilia and spoke in a whisper.

"My dear, may I present Sir Lucas Hawthorne."

"Sir Lucas." Lady Cecilia's voice only seemed loud, coming as it did hard upon Mrs. Portloe's whisper tones. "I am most pleased."

"And I am honored, Lady Cecilia, to meet a lady about whom I have heard so many charming reports."

"Indeed."

He hesitated. He had expected Lady Cecilia to keep talking as she had since her arrival, but she appeared distracted and was staring at him. To his dismay, he almost blushed, but then he caught a glimpse of Prim, who was standing some distance away at the foot of the steps. She gave him a little smile and glanced in the direction of his parents. His parents! Mrs. Apple—no Mrs. Longford. He was to perform introductions. They would be presented to Lady Cecilia, since she was of higher rank.

To his relief, he made no mistakes, and was soon escorting his guests into the drawing room. Escorting Lady Cecilia was more like being a servant scurrying after a busy monarch. The lady stalked briskly ahead of everyone except Luke, who had to extend his stride to keep up. When he walked with Prim, he always had to shorten his stride in order to stay beside her.

Lady Cecilia swept into the drawing room and headed for the best chair beside the fireplace. It had been intended for her, but Luke had expected to offer it as an attention and a courtesy. The others gathered around the fireplace on a settee and a couch and chairs. Prim stood behind his parents, who sat on the couch opposite Lady Cecilia. He saw her pull on the bell to ring for tea. She caught his eye, and her mouth formed silent words, "How was your journey?"

He walked to the mantel, placing himself between it and Lady Cecilia. "How was your journey, Lady Cecilia?"

"Most tiresome, as rail trips usually are. But I endured. Nobody can say that I complain. I do my best, and everyone knows I'm not one to complain. I do hope my rooms are warm, Sir Lucas. Oswald gets cold easily."

"Your rooms will have fires constantly tended, Lady Cecilia. I can have the servants bring in braziers if Oswald is uncomfortable."

"Excellent." Lady Cecilia glanced around the drawing room. "These old places are always full of poky old furniture, are they not, Sir Lucas?" She didn't wait for him to respond. "Of course if we marry, I shall have to redo this room."

Luke opened his mouth. Then he shut it. He looked at Prim, but she stared back at him, wide-eyed. They had never discussed a polite response to this type of comment. Luke recovered enough to incline his head.

"Oh?" he said.

"You will find that I am known for my taste," Lady

Cecilia said. "I am consulted by all my acquaintance in matters of taste, am I not, Mrs. Portloe?"

Mrs. Portloe's answer was drowned out when Lady Cecilia continued. "I declare I am beset with questions of taste from everyone. The Duchess of Portland wanted my opinion of the tapestries she ordered from Brussels. Lady Carington simply could not make up her mind about patterns for plate, and Mr. Gladstone is still waiting for me to help him fix the design of his new house in London."

The list of appeals to Lady Cecilia's taste continued, and Luke found himself growing bewildered from the unceasing discourse. No one else had been able to make a remark. Then he heard it. A moment of silence. He opened his mouth. Too late!

"Well," Lady Cecilia said. "It's best to place these things in the open at once, Sir Lucas, as we're among family and intimates." Lady Cecilia gave a mannerly nod to Prim and her chaperone. "I am here to make your acquaintance, Sir Lucas, and to see if we'll do together in marriage. I will be frank. Nobody can say that I'm not frank. I will acquaint you with my opinions and my feelings during this visit, and then we will see."

This conversation wasn't at all what Prim had led him to expect. He gave her a desperate glance, but Prim seemed as aghast as he. Again, before he could respond, Lady Cecilia marched ahead.

"As I said, nobody can say I'm not frank. I'm known for my frankness and honest opinions, Sir Lucas. So I might as well tell you that I approve of your appearance."

Lady Cecilia rose, causing everyone else to stand. Her gaze ran over Luke from his boots, up his legs to his chest and finally to his face, where they settled on his eyes only briefly. Luke felt as if she would like to run her hands over his legs like a stable master inspecting a racing horse. He almost expected her to pry open his mouth to look at his teeth.

"Indeed," Lady Cecilia said as she gave him another long inspection. "Your appearance is most satisfactory and almost compensates for your low birth, Sir Lucas. No, there is no need to thank me."

"I wasn't—"

"Oh, I am fatigued. Miss Dane, you may show me to my rooms. Come, Mrs. Portloe. We must see that Oswald is settled. Oh, Mrs. Hawthorne, Oswald requires a special diet. Filet, cooked until barely pink, for his breakfast. He likes a good stew or perhaps some roast for luncheon, and at dinner he insists upon mutton or game. And he does so like his little desserts. I will give you menus and recipes."

Lady Cecilia swept out of the room with Mrs. Portloe and Prim in her wake. Luke could hear her comments to Prim as they left. "You will tell Mrs. Hawthorne about Oswald's chills, won't you, Miss Dane? He likes a carriage ride three times a day, but he must wear his little sweaters and a coat in chilly weather like this."

When they were gone, he sank into the chair Lady Cecilia had just vacated and stared into the fire. His mother was the first to speak.

"Oh, dear, Luke. She is very fine, don't you know."

Tusser grunted. "I suppose she's a proper fine lady,

being the daughter of an earl, Mother. Very grand. With a jewel case and a little dog on a cushion. Never seen a little dog on a cushion before."

Luke didn't respond. He was too busy adjusting his thoughts, for until now, he hadn't realized how much he'd expected Lady Cecilia to be like Miss Primrose Victoria Dane.

14

The day after Lady Cecilia arrived, Prim paced the floorboards of the Old Library, her skirts sweeping up dust as they swayed and brushed the polished wood. Lady Cecilia had been an astonishment. The woman was insufferable! Prim had expected Luke to throw her out of the castle yesterday after she'd complained that the gentle sea-green and white colors of her rooms made her bilious. But no, he'd offered to re-paint. The fool.

It made her ill to watch them together. Lady Cecilia vacillated between treating everyone including her host with grand condescension, and ogling Luke. Meanwhile Luke smiled at her and agreed with every-thing she said as if she were a high priestess or worse, royalty. Disgusting.

Prim stalked by the windows and glanced out to

see Luke and Lady Cecilia parade across the lawn in the direction of the shell keep. "Huh!"

Lady Cecilia had taken a liking to Prim, for no explainable reason, since Prim hadn't said more than ten sentences to her.

"She likes me because I'm quiet. More opportunity for her to pontificate."

Prim's mouth fell open when Luke paused before the shell keep door, bowed over Lady Cecilia's hand and kissed it. "Obsequious wretch. There's no need for such overdone gallantry. Men are such fools. They see a fine figure and pretty face and become witless sycophants."

Spinning away from the sight, Prim bit her lower lip and dashed a tear from her cheek. "Primrose Dane, you will not cry again. He wants a great lady for a wife, not some bookish spinster."

She forced herself to keep her back turned to the window. Taking several determined steps away from it, she was distracted from her misery when the heel of her boot got caught between two floorboards. She pulled free and stepped back to examine the wood.

A small carpet usually covered this area, but it had slipped aside, revealing a misalignment of the boards. Prim bent and pulled the carpet toward the uneven spot, but stopped when she noticed a gap that seemed to form a square in the floor. Shoving the carpet under a nearby table, Prim knelt and pressed her hand on the square section. Nothing happened.

She retrieved a letter opener from one of the tables and slipped it into the gap. The section of boards came up as one piece to reveal a cavity in the floor.

Inside lay a wooden box. She was able to pick it up if she used both hands. Once she had set the box on the floor, she examined it.

The box was of carved mahogany, decorated with swirls, complicated knotwork, and abstract designs that she recognized as the distinctive style of artists in seventh-century Ireland. Prim carefully opened the box to find a book with a deteriorating cover lying inside. She lifted it and placed it beside the box. Using both hands, she opened the book to reveal a page of illumination the likes of which she'd only read about.

It was a carpet page, a page the whole of which had been decorated with illumination. The design, in lemon yellow, red, and deep copper green, was in the same style as the box—chevrons, diamond spirals, swirls, and knotwork all woven intricately with animal and bird motifs. The artistry was so delicate that Prim felt its beauty as a physical reaction. She caught her breath and felt a chill run through her body. She turned page after page written in Irish half-uncials.

This was one of a rare type of early book, the insular manuscripts of which the *Book of Kells* was the finest example, until now. Prim was certain that this manuscript would rival even that famous work. With great care she replaced the book in the box and closed the lid. Her hands trembled as she rose and set the box on a table. Prim was just pulling the carpet over the secret compartment in the floor when the door opened and she heard a most unwelcome voice, like the blare of a hunting horn.

"Are you certain she is in here? What an odd place in which to take one's leisure."

"Drat," Prim muttered.

"Oh, Miss Dane," Lady Cecilia trumpeted as she swept into the library. "Dear Sir Lucas feels it his duty to show me all over the castle, even that tedious library, and here I find you in yet another one. Imagine, two libraries."

Lady Cecilia made a progress around the room, hardly glancing at the books, while Luke followed in her wake. "I told dear Sir Lucas that a complete tour wasn't necessary, especially the library. After all, one book is much like another. Don't you agree, Miss Dane?"

Prim sputtered, unable to form a coherent sentence. She mastered herself as Lady Cecilia completed her progress and came to rest in front of her.

"Are you trying to be amusing," Prim asked quietly, "or are you simply stup—"

"Ha!"

Prim jumped at Luke's interruption.

"You're so perceptive, Miss Dane. It's true that Lady Cecilia has a great gift of amusing conversation."

Luke had settled beside his fiancée. He bowed in tribute to Lady Cecilia and avoided looking at Prim, who was staring at him and tapping her foot. Prim nearly snorted in disgust when Lady Cecilia placed her hand on Luke's arm and smirked at him in response to the compliment. However, she had herself under control by the time Cecilia turned to her.

"Miss Dane, dear Sir Lucas suggested that we apply to you for a list of the places most congenial for me to see. Please join us."

"I can recommend the Tudor Wing," Prim said.

"Unfortunately I have a great deal of work to do and will be unable to join you."

"Oh, fah, Miss Dane. You're such a serious little thing." Lady Cecilia's glance took in the dust on Prim's skirt where she'd knelt on the floor and the wisps escaping from the coil of hair at the nape of her neck. "I insist you come with us, and a guest's wishes are always paramount."

Prim was herded out of the library in spite of her protests, and soon she found herself pacing alongside Lady Cecilia. The woman linked arms with her and began a commentary on all the sights of the castle. Prim began to feel the anxiety Lady Cecilia's perpetual discourse usually provoked. Useless to expect Luke to intervene in the deluge of noise, for he walked ahead, leading the way to the Tudor Wing, which lay between the family quarters and the Plantagenet Tower.

"Of course," Lady Cecilia called in her French horn tones, "if I accept your offer, dear Sir Lucas, we will be spending the Season in London."

Luke's pace slowed and he gave his fiancée a distracted glance. "What, the whole Season?"

Lady Cecilia uttered a trill of laughter.

"Of course the whole Season, so we will have to have a new house there. One worthy of my position in Society."

They had just entered a long gallery paneled in dark wood and filled with heavy Elizabethan furniture. Lady Cecilia surveyed the walls, which were covered with paintings of the families of previous owners. Prim caught sight of a few Holbeins and miniatures by Nicholas Hilliard.

"Oh, dear," Lady Cecilia said. "All these musty paintings will have to go, and this ugly old furniture with them."

Speechless, Prim looked away until she felt a sudden pressure on her arm.

"I know, Miss Dane. I shall turn that Old Library into a billiard room. It will be perfect for gentlemen to smoke and play in after dinner. What do you think?"

Prim pulled her arm free. "I think—"

"Ah!" Lady Cecilia clapped her hands. "And the New Library will make a perfect sitting room for me."

"But the books," Prim began.

"Oh, don't worry about them. They can be sold in lots."

Insults threatened to burst from her lips, but Prim found herself unable to utter them because fury had paralyzed her. She could only stare at the woman in horror. No longer listening to Lady Cecilia's interminable list of requirements for her consent to the marriage, Prim began to consider that there were some people who deserved to be kicked in the . . .

"Lady Cecilia," Luke called from one of the windows opposite the paintings. "Isn't that Oswald I see going out the castle gate?"

"What?" Lady Cecilia rushed over to the window. "I don't see him."

"I'm sure it was Oswald. He was scampering under the portcullis."

"Oh, no." Lady Cecilia hurried out of the gallery.

"Pray excuse me, but walking isn't good for Oswald. He gets breathless." She vanished, but her voice could be heard throughout the Tudor Wing, blaring. "Turnpenny! Turnpenny, come here at once."

Luke walked to the door and closed it. He turned and grinned at Prim.

"You may thank me for preventing you from making a most unseemly remark to Lady Cecilia."

"Me? I'm not the one who is unseemly. That woman is—is—I haven't the words."

"See, I saved you from being unladylike."

Prim's foot was tapping again. She allowed her gaze to settle on Luke's pleased expression. Clasping her hands in front of her, she prayed for patience. She thought of how he had bowed and scraped before that woman. How he'd listened to her offensive suggestions and her ridiculous requirements.

"How could you fawn over that awful woman!"

Luke's grin vanished. "Fawn? Fawn?" He stalked over to her. "You were the one who said for me to be agreeable. You were the one who said never contradict a lady. Did you or did you not tell me not to contradict Lady Cecilia?"

"About inconsequential things," Prim said stiffly. "I didn't mean for you to allow her to trod upon you like a muddy rug."

"Oy! You watch your tongue Miss Primrose blighted Dane. You was the one who kept telling me to be mannerly and do what Lady Cecilia wanted. I been doing my part, and now you give me a thrashing."

Prim was beyond rage at this man who seemed to

have lost his common sense along with his heart in the presence of the undeserving Lady Cecilia. "Having manners doesn't imply becoming an obsequious, groveling simpleton."

"Here, what's this 'obsequious'? I haven't got my dictionary book."

"It means cringingly subservient."

Without warning Luke took a step that put him very close to her. Then he said quietly, "Why, Primmy, you're jealous."

She heard that quiet, menacing note in his voice. Nightshade was back.

"I beg your pardon?" Prim felt herself grow hot, then cold.

Nightshade lowered his chin and lifted his gaze to her burning face. The smoke from hell's fires couldn't have been as black as those eyes. In his expression was written a contract with pagans and demons. Prim found it hard not to back down from that stare. She was saved when he laughed softly and shook his head.

"Oh, it's all right. Choke me dead, but I never thought to see it."

"I am not jealous." Her voice boomed down the long gallery and caused Luke to chuckle again.

"Stop laughing!"

He succeeded in complying, only to break out in a ruffian's grin that made Prim want to slap him. Was he laughing at her for being in love with him? *Propriety, think of propriety.* She composed her features before she spoke.

"You have mistaken my outrage at that woman's

behavior and my concern for your excesses, Sir Lucas."

"What do you mean?"

Forcing indifference into her tone, Prim continued. "I mean that I was merely concerned that you have taken civility too far. I was trying to caution you that in doing so you are endangering that respect and acknowledgment of your own distinction which should be accorded you by everyone, including Lady Cecilia."

Luke didn't answer at once. He clasped his hands behind his back and walked away from her to stand studying a portrait of Mary Tudor.

"You mean you're not jealous."

"My temper was tried by that woman's stupidity, Sir Lucas. That is the whole of it, and I hope I may be pardoned for being unable to support the affectations of a person of so little understanding and sensitivity."

"Oh?" He looked at her with Nightshade's glittering derision. "But you think she suits me all right."

"I decline to tell you."

Nightshade vanished. "Damnation, we're back to that, are we?"

"Sir Lucas, your language."

"And now you're going etiquettey on me again." Luke eased nearer with that unconscious grace that marked all his movements. "Your tongue has gone all starched again, and I've just about had enough of you sitting in judgment on me, Miss Primrose blighted Dane. No matter what I do, it's not good enough. God! You're more than a man should be cursed with, did you know that?"

Her body trembling, near tears, Prim inclined her head and muttered, "Then I shan't trouble you any longer, sir."

"Oy, you come back here, Primrose Victoria Dane!"

Prim stopped and turned slowly. "I beg your pardon?"

"I hate it when you turn your back on me," Luke growled as his color rose. "You ain't going to scarper and leave me standing here shouting at you like a fish merchant on a Friday. I ain't finished talking to you."

"I, however, am finished speaking to you."

Turning on her heel, Prim rushed out of the gallery. Her sight blurred by tears, she bolted for the refuge of the Old Library.

"Rot you, Prim, come back here!"

Her speed increased at the sound of Luke's furious bellow. She raced into the hall and upstairs. Out of breath, she burst into the Old Library, shut the door, and leaned against it. Her chest heaved and her corset pinched her ribs. Pressing a hand to her side, Prim dropped into a chair at the table upon which lay the box holding the insular manuscript.

"I will not give way," she whispered to herself as she panted. "I will not. Oh, dear heaven, he's followed me."

She heard the tap of boots on the stairs and their rapid progress to the Old Library door. The portal burst open and slammed against the wall, revealing Nightshade at his worst. The room seemed to grow dark, as if great thunderclouds formed his escort and sucked the light from every corner. He paused, bracing his arms against the threshold, his legs apart, as though he would launch himself at her like a black griffin.

When his chin lowered and he directed that Nightshade stare at her, Prim's tears dried in her eyes. That stare could intimidate a mad dog. It held jungle heat and arctic chill at the same time. And if the effort took ten years off her life, she wasn't going to allow him to scare her.

"I cannot imagine that you would think I desire your company, Sir Lucas."

There, she'd managed to speak without a quiver in her voice. The room brightened. To make sure she kept her courage, she scooted her chair into a ray of sunlight. When she looked up, Nightshade hadn't moved, but his glare seemed to have lost its wicked fury and become distracted.

He gave his head a little shake and said, "I told you I wasn't finished."

"Indeed," she replied. She removed the book from its container, opened it carefully, and began to try to decipher its script.

It seemed to her that he flew across the room like a raven. Nightshade was at her side before she could object. He slammed his hand over the book.

"Sir Lucas, stop that at once!"

"It's my book. I can burn it if I want."

Half rising from her chair, Prim met his glare and hissed at him. "It's over a thousand years old."

Luke continued to scowl at her, but he lifted his hand with care.

"I got some interesting information about the night you disappeared."

She hadn't expected this. Prim covered her surprise by pulling the book toward her and turning a page.

"Seems the traps have caught the blokes who done all the murders that night. Except one. Somebody did for old Pauline Cross that night. You know Pauline Cross, Miss Primrose blighted Dane?"

"No."

His hand was flattened on the table next to the book, and she tried not to look at it. He leaned closer.

"Pauline Cross was found stabbed and dumped in the Thames. A floater, that's what we call it."

"How terrible," Prim said, not daring to look at him. She turned a page.

"Right. Now our Pauline was a harlot. Not your ordinary tart what walks Hell Corner in cheap silk with a pockmarked face. No, our Pauline was a flash bit o' dirty lace."

"Please, Sir Lucas," she said, squeezing her eyes shut to block her memories of Pauline Cross. "The poor woman was so unfortunate."

"Thought you didn't know her."

Her eyes flew open, but she directed her gaze at the half-uncial script before her. "Any woman who is forced to take up such an occupation is unfortunate."

"Well, something we agree on. But you miss my point. According to my agents, Pauline rented good rooms and made a living off the toffs. She had regulars of good quality what saw her provided for, you see."

Prim turned another page, although she didn't see

what was on it. "Sir Lucas, I have no interest in the particulars of Miss Pauline Cross's business affairs."

"Listen anyway. My agents say Pauline had been bragging lately that she'd found herself a real blue-blooded toff. She boasted that she'd be leaving the trade soon and for good."

"I'm sorry she didn't." He was so close she could feel the heat of his body, and it made her want to scream with frustrated anger and desire.

"Wait," Luke said. "The thing about Pauline is, she wasn't above a bit o' blackmail, was our Pauline."

He paused, but Prim kept her eyes fixed on the Irish half-uncials and refused to speak.

"So, my agents think, and the police think, that Pauline was done for by some toff what she tried to snaffle." His voice lowered and he leaned down. "The way I see it, that night Pauline met her bloke in some alley, and he knifed her. There was blood all over her dress."

The half-uncials curled and writhed and swam. She felt sick and too weak to fight the vision of a woman with her mouth open in an ugly scream. Prim cried out as Luke pounded the table.

"That's it! I knew you saw something. You saw the toff that did for Pauline Cross, and Fleet was there too. Who's the bloke?"

Prim wet her lips. "I decline to tell you."

She gasped as Luke grabbed her arms and dragged her out of the chair. "Whoever he is, he'll hunt you down, even in America."

"He won't know I've gone there."

She winced as he tightened his grip.

"You ain't leaving until you tell me."

"Sir Lucas, you're hurting me."

He released her so quickly she fell into the chair.

Nightshade bent down to capture her gaze with his. "I won't let you go."

Don't let him intimidate you, Primrose Dane.

"Then we're at an impasse for now. However, you will lose eventually."

She didn't understand why his voice went soft. "I never lose, Primmy."

"You will lose this time."

"What makes you think so?"

"Because, Sir Lucas, Lady Cecilia is going to accept your offer of marriage. She intended to from the moment she saw you. And if you think Lady Cecilia Randolph will stand your playing host to me on her wedding night, you are much mistaken."

15

Luke was still furious with Prim on the afternoon succeeding their quarrel. Yet he was forced to behave as if he were free of care when in the company of Lady Cecilia. This proved to be a triumph of will over inclination, for Cecilia had begun to lose her appeal within half a day's acquaintance. He had persevered in his duties as host to the lady despite his growing distaste for her, and what had been his reward?

"Cringingly subservient," he muttered. "Obsequious!"

Luke took a swipe at some reeds that grew on the bank of the stream beside the abbey. Behind him lay the soaring ruins, and beneath them, on the grassy meadow that led to the stream, his guests were engaged in a picnic. The weather had bestowed upon them a false summer day. Upon beholding the clear sky, Lady Cecilia had insisted upon an outing, and had bullied his mother into acceding. Even Prim had been forced to come, although she had vouched many protests of letters to write and studies to complete in the library. All had given way before the locomotive of Lady Cecilia's will.

His fiancée had commandeered the finest of his china, his best tables, chairs, and linens, and arranged a tableau on the grassy slope. She declared the abbey the most picturesque setting. Since everyone knew her taste to be the finest, having been assured of it by the lady herself, her arrangements prevailed.

Luke glanced at the group sitting at the table before a stone wall broken by the remains of arched windows. Lady Cecilia sat in state at the head of the table in the best chair, with velvet cushions. His mother and father flanked her. Both were keeping their gazes fixed on their plates while Mrs. Apple, in her guise as Prim's chaperone, did her best to make conversation with Cecilia. It was an easy task. All she had to do was nod her head every once in a while and let the chatter flow over her in a continuous inundation.

Prim sat next to Mrs. Apple. Luke scowled at her, but her attention was fixed upon Cecilia. As he watched, she stiffened at some remark of that venerable lady's. She bent and retrieved the parasol she had propped against her chair. It was one Luke had seen in London and sent for after they came to Castle Beaufort. After being persuaded to accept the parasol, Prim had vowed to repay him for the trunk of clothing he'd provided. Not that he would ever accept her money.

Prim narrowed her eyes at Lady Cecilia, who was oblivious. Then she snapped open the parasol and hoisted it over her head. It jerked once more and tilted so that it formed a delicate screen between Prim and Lady Cecilia. In spite of himself, Luke grinned. He had never seen a finer sight than Primrose Victoria Dane driven to abandon propriety and insult an acquaintance.

His good humor faded when he remembered how she had reproved him for being a gentleman to Lady Cecilia. After all their lessons, all his practicing, she had censored him. And all because she didn't like the woman. Not because she was jealous.

Luke slashed at the reeds again. He would never be able to forget how he'd felt when she'd burst out with that tirade against Lady Cecilia. It was as if fireworks had burst inside him. If Prim was jealous, then she must care for him. And if she cared for him . . .

Kneeling at the edge of the water, Luke picked up a stone and tossed it into the stream. He liked the way it went *plop* as it entered the water. In the distance he could hear Cecilia's hornlike fanfare interspersed with Mrs. Apple's determined comments. He couldn't decide if Lady Cecilia sounded more like a trumpet or a bugle. Whatever the case, he wasn't going to listen to that raucous concert for the rest of his life.

He'd been wrestling with the problem of how to extricate himself from her. He wasn't certain exactly when he decided Lady Cecilia was unbearable. Perhaps it was when she scurried off to hunt down Oswald and prevent him from taking exercise. Or perhaps it had been the first time he'd intercepted that appraising look of hers. There had been something in Lady Cecilia's hard gaze that reminded him of Larder Lily.

Tossing another stone into the water, Luke murmured to himself. "Oh, admit it. You knew she was a hard piece the moment you saw her. You looked at her and realized you'd been expecting another Prim. Luke Hawthorne, you're an ass." He hurled a stone with such violence that he was sprayed by the water it displaced. "You know what you want, and this time Nightshade can't get it for you."

But he could save himself from Lady Cecilia Randolph. He would suggest a drive before dinner. Cecilia liked to ride in his open landau, bowing and nodding to the villagers and servants like a queen. He would take her for a drive, and when they came back from the village through the park, where there was privacy, he would tell her he was withdrawing his offer. She would be furious, but she'd have to accept his decision. He just hoped she didn't screech at him. He had a feeling Lady Cecilia could screech like a braking train engine.

What an odd thing. He had thought marrying Lady Cecilia would wipe out the memories of his childhood. He had wanted to do away forever with that little boy who had stood at the back door of the baker's shop and begged for scraps. Sometimes he still dreamed of that shop.

In these dreams he was small again, so small he had to reach up to work a pump handle. His feet were dirty inside his cracked leather boots; his whole body was dirty. His coat was too thin to keep out the cold, and he had no cap. But he had to wait in the dark of early morning for the baker to open his shop, and when the man arrived he must make himself presentable, tugging at the bottom of the coat that was too short for him. He had to make a low bow and speak humbly as his fellows had taught him. "If you please, sir. Can you spare any old crusts?"

He woke from these dreams feeling that terrible burning hunger and shivering, not from cold, but from humiliation. Luke looked over his shoulder at Lady Cecilia, who was waving her hand at Featherstone and trumpeting orders. Funny thing about Cecilia. She reminded him of the baker's shop. Constantly. If he married her, he would forever feel like that dirty little boy tugging at his coat, looking up into the hard eyes of the baker and trying so very hard to be humble and polite.

❦

Mortimer Fleet hated the country. It was full of empty space where there should be buildings; there were no gin shops, and there were too many animals. Here he was crouched in a hedgerow at dusk, miserable for lack of drink and swallowing the dust from traffic on the road. Jowett and his men were similarly ensconced. They'd been waiting ever since it had been reported that Nightshade was driving out with his lady.

He'd been doing fine on his own when The Gentleman had called a halt to his activities and substituted a plan of his personal devising. Fleet's attempt to bribe that idiot boy Dinesdale hadn't worked, but he'd been hopeful that a larger bribe to one of the gardener's assistants would work. The Gentleman had refused to wait.

From his own sources Fleet's employer produced intimate knowledge of Castle Beaufort, its inhabitants, and its routine. The Gentleman informed him of the particular friendship between Miss Dane and Nightshade. Fleet could have told him that without investigation. Any woman who spent more than an hour in Nightshade's company could be expected to succumb. It was right disgusting.

So now he was waiting in the hedgerow in the growing chill and lengthening shadows. If Nightshade's carriage didn't come soon, it would be too dark to do the job right. Fleet shoved the shrubbery aside and tried to peer down the road. Farther down a quarrel erupted between Jowett and Reg Trunk.

"Shut up, you sods," Fleet hissed. "I think I hear something."

From a distance came the *clop-clop* of hooves, the jingle of bridles, and the clatter of a carriage. Fleet and his men shrank back into the hedges.

"Remember. Don't bleeding move until I say."

Down the road came an open landau, its black lacquered sides and brass shining even in the fading light. Inside sat a woman of august appearance, and beside her—

"Who woulda thought?" Fleet murmured.

He was distracted by the sight of Nightshade in fine duds, walking stick, and tall hat. "Flash clothes and a fine carriage, the bleeding—" He'd almost allowed the carriage to slip past them. Filling his lungs, Fleet bellowed, "For it, me lads!"

Jowett ran in front of the horses, flapping a length of white cloth. The lead pair reared, causing the carriage to stop suddenly. Two more men rushed to capture the horses' bridles while Fleet and his three assistants scrambled out of the hedges and pointed pistols at the coachman and occupants of the carriage. As soon as they came into sight, the woman began to bleat like a ewe giving birth to twins.

Over the noise, Fleet shouted, "Put up or die!" He winced at the shriek this elicited from the lady.

She threw herself into Nightshade's arms. Fleet ignored her babbling, as did Nightshade. His old enemy hadn't moved since they'd set eyes on each other. Keeping his gaze locked with Nightshade's, Fleet approached the carriage with growing pleasure.

Nightshade's lips curled. "Mortimer Fleet. Whoever gave you a pistol is a fool."

"He don't know I never used one," Fleet said as he smiled and waggled the nose of the gun at his quarry. "But it don't appear to be too hard."

"Still, I should have thought it beyond you."

Fleet's smiled turned sour and he noted with irritation Nightshade's aristocratic speech. "Watch that bitchy tongue of yours, Nightshade, or I'll risk my employer's h-anger and shoot you right here."

The lady raised her head and shrieked, causing the men to cringe.

"Oh, we're to be murdered in the road!"

Nightshade continued as if she weren't there. "You aren't going to kill me, Fleet, or you'd have done it already. What do you want?"

"Miss Dane, o' course."

"You fool. This isn't Miss Dane, and you ought to know I won't take you to her."

"You always thought you was so much cleverer than me," Fleet said. Grinning, he flourished the pistol. "You ain't going to take me to her. All I'm to do is let Miss Dane know I've got you. I got it on good authority that she'll rush right into my hands." He stepped closer to the landau. "Now get out."

A stream of ear-piercing protests interfered. The lady clung to Nightshade like a tick to a dog and squalled when he pried her from him. Finally he succeeded in detaching her and stepped out of the vehicle.

Once face to face with the man whose existence had been a running sore on his soul, Fleet found himself squeezing the trigger of his pistol. Then Nightshade glanced down at Fleet's gun hand and lifted one eyebrow. Not a trace of fear could be discerned in his eyes when he lifted his gaze. Fleet felt again the gut-curdling hatred for this man whose composure and bearing never failed to make him feel as small and distasteful as a beetle in a dung heap.

"No," Fleet said. "It won't be a quick one for you. I want it to be slow, so I can enjoy it."

"That's the Fleet I remember," Nightshade said.

Fleet nodded at Jowett, who had come up behind Nightshade. Jowett raised the butt of his pistol and hit Nightshade at the same time that Fleet punched him in the stomach.

"Glad to oblige," Fleet said as his prisoner dropped to the ground.

❧

Prim had forced herself to dress for dinner, although it would tax her composure and fill her with vexation to be in the company of Luke Hawthorne and Cecilia Randolph. Every time she thought of her conduct of the past few days, she wanted to curl into a ball and roll into a dark corner. How many times had she almost betrayed herself?

She was fortunate to have been able to convince Luke that her outburst in the Tudor Wing had been occasioned by her distaste for Lady Cecilia. Her pride had been saved. Its continuance gave her no comfort, however, for she existed in a haze of pain. Never having won Luke Hawthorne, she had just as surely lost him, and his loss caused tremors of anguish to shoot through the center of her body relentlessly. There were many times when she found it nearly impossible to summon the fortitude to continue with her daily activities. She had little will even to put up her hair decently or eat adequately, so as not to attract attention to her despair.

And this waiting was torture. The family were gathered in the drawing room before dinner, and Luke and his guest hadn't returned. Tusser was dozing by the fire. Mrs. Apple and Louisa were talking quietly while they sipped sherry. Prim walked around the room pretending to admire the paintings on the wall or take an interest in a piece of Chinese porcelain. All the while she expected Luke to enter the room and announce that he and Lady Cecilia had settled matters between them and to name the date of their wedding.

A long time ago she had dreamed little daydreams of such an announcement for herself. In these fantasies she was quite young, certainly not the great age she was now. Her suitor came to her father's house, breathless with fear for his reception. Usually he found her in the conservatory among cascades of tropical flowers, but sometimes she had him searching for her in the park and finding her beneath the branches of an aged oak or beside a cascading waterfall. Always he called out her name in desperate longing; always she turned to him, smiled, and answered by holding out her hand. He rushed to her, then stopped to kiss her hand and stumble over his proposal.

Unworldly, naive, silly. That had been before her fortune vanished in the storm of irresponsibility created by her father. She had no more silly dreams. And now they appeared pale and uninteresting compared to the brilliant reality of the man she always thought of as Nightshade. Her parents would never have approved of him, had they lived. Her brother and Aunt Freshwell would rather see her a permanent spinster than attached to such a man.

Prim picked up a gilded container with a pedestal base that fit neatly into her hand. Intricately engraved and pierced, its lid swung back to reveal an Elizabethan watch shaped like an egg with a crystal top. Her fingers played with the top as she thought about Luke and Lady Cecilia. Even running as far as America wouldn't ease the pain she would feel, knowing that those two were—

"What is that noise?" Mrs. Apple asked.

Looking up from the watch, Prim heard footsteps clatter on the marble floor outside the drawing room. Over this resounded a hysterical bleating that seemed to fill the vastness of the hall. Tusser snorted and woke up. Louisa and Mrs. Apple rose as a group of servants burst into the room. In their midst, supported by them, came Lady Cecilia, alternately shrieking and scolding.

"Oh, my heart, my heart. I shall faint." A sudden bellow belied this claim. "Turnpenny, where is that brandy?"

Prim rushed to Lady Cecilia as the servants lowered her to a couch in front of the fire. "Lady Cecilia, what has happened?"

Tusser waved his cane at the footmen and Featherstone.

"Get away from her. Give her air."

Mrs. Apple took Featherstone aside and began a quiet conversation while Louisa took brandy from Turnpenny and helped Lady Cecilia drink. Cecilia downed the glass in one gulp, a practiced one.

"Oh, dear Lord in heaven. My heart is pounding. I shall faint. More brandy!"

Prim glanced through the open doors. "Where is Sir Lucas, Lady Cecilia?"

"I shall never be the same. I shall die of fright, and be lamented forever."

"Lady Cecilia, where is Sir Lucas?" Prim asked again.

"We were set upon." Cecilia swallowed another entire glass of brandy. "Such palpitations. My heart will burst. I thought I should die. Thank heavens I escaped."

"You were attacked? Robbed?" Prim's anxiety was growing. "Where is Sir Lucas?"

Cecilia turned her face to the fan Turnpenny was waving at her. "It is indeed a wonder that I escaped. Brandy, I need more brandy to calm my heart."

Snatching the glass as Louisa proffered it, Prim pulled it out of reach when Cecilia's hand sought it. She planted herself in front of the woman.

"Cease this blithering at once!" Cecilia's mouth snapped closed, and she goggled at Prim, who fixed her with a killing stare and said carefully, *"Where—is—Luke?"*

Lady Cecilia sputtered, then stopped when she saw Prim's hand curl into a fist. "They took him. I'm sure he's all right. What does it matter, when I have almost been killed from the shock?"

It was vital that Prim control her rage. Tusser and Louisa tried asking the same question with less success. Lady Cecilia ranted of her own narrow escape, her nerves, her heart. Prim was considering slapping Cecilia when Mrs. Apple left Featherstone and took her arm. Drawing her away from the others, she whispered to Prim.

"Featherstone got the story from the coachman. They were attacked by a group of men on the road from the village to the park. From his description, I think it was Mortimer Fleet and his lads."

"Fleet? Oh, dear heaven. Fleet." Prim pressed her hand to her stomach, suddenly ill.

Mrs. Apple grabbed her arm and propelled Prim to a chair. "Get hold of yerself, missy."

Vaguely aware that Mrs. Apple's voice had suddenly taken on the vibrant timbre of a much younger woman, Prim clutched the arms of the chair and took a deep breath.

"That's better," Mrs. Apple said. She handed Prim a sealed envelope. "Fleet handed that to the coachman. Said he was to deliver it only to you."

Her hands shaking, Prim opened the envelope and read.

"If you want to see him alive, come back to London. The Laughing Knacker in Whitechapel. Tell no one or he dies."

The message was printed, as if someone had copied it from an original. The letters blurred as she stared at them. Shaking her head, Prim looked up at Mrs. Apple. The woman was staring at the note and tapping a fingernail against her front teeth. Prim stuffed the note into her sleeve and rose.

Mrs. Apple grabbed her arm. "Where are you going?"

"To London, of course."

"You can't. You'll do no good."

Prim jerked her arm free and faced the woman. "I am going. Please do not waste my time in argument. No power in the world is going to prevent me from getting him back."

Mrs. Apple regarded her for a moment, as if assessing Prim's strength and will. "All right, love. But if you're going, at least let me help you."

It was Prim's turn to survey Mrs. Apple. Quelling

her nearly insane urge to rush off at once without forethought, Prim noted that the old lady seemed to be standing straight instead of bent over with age. Gone was the vague fluttering of hands, the sweet and benign expression.

"You aren't Luke's friend at all," Prim said. "You're one of his band of thieves."

"Me, work for Nightshade? Not bloody likely." When Prim tried to object, Mrs. Apple held up a hand. "No time for introductions now, missy. You want my help or not?"

Prim quelled her outrage and her fear and tried to think like Nightshade. "Luke trusted you, didn't he?"

Mrs. Apple's eyes glinted as she gave a sharp nod.

"Help me save him," Prim said in a choked whisper. "I—I must save him."

16

On a rainy night in Whitechapel a cart drawn by an aged horse clattered slowly down Figgin Street past the Laughing Knacker. The sign over the tavern door was askew, and its paint was peeling to reveal cracked gray wood. Tattered curtains blocked out the light inside the place, but nothing could subdue the noise of a drunken brawl that spilled into the street.

The driver of the cart paid no attention to the fighters or to the women in muddy silk, huddled under a street lamp, who stamped their cold feet on broken pavement. He drove on, nearing Cheesewright's Emporium, an abandoned shop with grimy windows. Its shutters and awnings had been clapped over cheap, crumbling brick.

Opposite the emporium flimsy wooden coffins were stacked in front of an undertaker's, and farther down the road men could be seen trying to unload sacks from a wagon without attracting attention. The cart passed Cheesewright's Emporium, drawing close to the alley between the shop and the next building. The driver glanced down the alley with little curiosity. Cluttered with mounds of old newspapers and broken wooden boxes stacked in a precarious pile, it was dark except for the sliver of light escaping from the side door of the emporium.

The old horse trudged on under the gentle encouragement of the driver, and neither saw the bulky figure standing guard in the alley doorway. His hat dripping from the rain, the sentry blew on his fingers, opened the door a crack, and peeped inside. His survey revealed a windowless corridor into which lamplight from an open door cast a yellow swath. Shadows moved across the light. The watchman closed the door upon seeing the movement, and returned to his uncomfortable vigil.

The room down the dark corridor was littered with vegetable crates, old grain sacks, meat tins, and packing material. Debris had been shoved aside to make room for a cage. The enclosure had a wooden top and bottom and iron bars on the sides, and it had an occupant—Luke Hawthorne.

Although he was lying facedown with his eyes closed, Luke was awake and listening to the two other men in the room. He recognized Fleet's nasal whine, and he had guessed the identity of the other man. It was one Percy Grassdale, who liked to be called Doctor Grassdale, although Percy was really only a chemist, and a corrupt one at that.

"No, no, no," Fleet was saying. "I want him to die slow and hard, real hard. I thought about setting fire to the place, but he might be rescued, and if I hang him, his neck might break right off."

"I don't quarrel with it, sir, but these matters are quite delicate. They depend upon a man's size and constitution and the type of poison and dosage."

"So, what have you got?"

"Mercy me, mercy me. Let me think. There are so many, you see. There are chemicals such as boric acid or camphor. There's quinine and antimony, or mercury, or phosphorus."

"Those sound good."

"But then, you might consider the plant poisons such as hemlock, lily of the valley, yew, or spurge. There is always foxglove, or the poisonous mushrooms such as amanitas, which is known as death's cap."

Luke heard a soft sound; Fleet was rubbing his hands together.

"Of course," Doctor Grassdale said, "there are also the usual poisons. Laudanum and opium, or belladonna, which is from the deadly nightshade plant, and there is ether—"

"Stop! Nightshade?"

Luke risked peering at the two through his lashes. Fleet had drawn closer to the fat little chemist in the yellow checked waistcoat and shabby brown suit and gaiters.

"I like that. Nightshade. What is it like?"

"Mercy, my dear Fleet. Most unpleasant. Delirium, hallucinations, fever, convulsions."

"Lots of pain."

"Indeed, but it may take a while to work."

"And he'd suffer?"

"Yes, but if you're looking for something unpleasant, perhaps you should consider boric acid or death's cap, to produce vomiting and flux. I need some notice, though. So that I have time to prepare the materials. When will you need it?"

"I won't be through with him until a certain package arrives, and that won't be until tomorrow night or the night after."

The two continued their ghoulish conversation. Their voices faded from Luke's notice as his head began to ache worse than before. The last thing he remembered was being hit from behind, then waking in pain only to be hit again and thrown into this cage. Fleet must have beat on him while he was unconscious, for his ribs were bruised, probably cracked. He had a cut on his temple—from the heel of a boot?— and there were several lumps on his head.

Fleet was going to draw Prim to this place by dangling him as bait. Then he was going to kill them both. Luke had known this almost from the beginning. And dear, brave little Primmy would try to rescue him. The thought of her coming within a league of bloody Mortimer Fleet made him want to vomit. He had to get away, but he couldn't work on the problem until he was left alone.

Luke was listening to Grassdale expound on the misery of a death by ingestion of a fungus called ergot when Jowett burst into the room.

"She's here."

Luke stopped breathing.

"Who's here?" Fleet demanded.

"The Dane girl, she's here."

"Bloody hell. Already?" Fleet turned to Grassdale. "Get out. I'll send for you later."

When the chemist was gone, Fleet said, "She's at the Laughing Knacker?"

"Pranced in bold as you please. She's sitting at a table right now."

Fleet called out, "Reg, Fergus!"

Men appeared in the doorway and Fleet handed one a key. "Reg, watch Nightshade, and mind you don't get too close to him. I'll be in the Knacker."

Never had Luke felt so helpless. He watched Fleet and Jowett leave. When he was certain that Fleet was out of hearing, he began to groan.

"Wot's that?" Reg said. He was a big man with a head like a slab of cheese and the intelligence of cheddar.

"It's 'im," Fergus said, jerking his head in Luke's direction. "He's coming awake, then."

Reg lumbered over to the cage and gawked at Luke, who was dragging himself to an upright position. "Coo! So this is Nightshade, is it? Don't scare me none. Just another pretty boy."

"Come away from there," Fergus growled. "Fleet said we wasn't to get near him." He pulled a nearly empty whiskey bottle from his pocket. "You got a dram on you, Reg?"

Reg kicked the cage door. "Coo! Nightshade. Show us your tricks."

Luke had managed to get to his knees. Under the

pretense of dizziness he squinted at the key to his cage in Reg's meaty hand. Reg drifted nearer, and he was about to lunge for the key when his quarry turned away.

"What was that?" Reg pocketed the key.

"What?" Fergus asked as he sucked on the last drops of whiskey from his bottle.

"Stark is at the back door, ain't he?" Reg asked.

"Right."

A sudden crash made both men jump. A rock sailed through the room's only window, spraying glass around the cage. With both men's attention on the cause of the crash, only Luke saw a shadow dart into the room. The shadow raced to Fergus, who was bending to pick up the rock. He and Reg turned as the shadow raised a club.

"Hey!" Luke shouted, making both men turn to look at him.

The club struck with a whack, and Fergus dropped. Reg turned on the shadow. Luke shouted again, but Reg ignored him and lumbered toward the invader. Luke threw himself at the cage door and tried to tear the bars apart. The shadow retreated, passing the only lamp in the room.

"Prim, run!" Luke shouted.

Prim paid him no heed, but continued to retreat slowly, passing over the threshold and into the dark corridor. Reg barreled after her. As he rushed out the door, another club appeared out of the darkness and bashed him on the head. Reg turned and grabbed Badger. Struggling, the two fell back into the room.

Luke shouted at his ally, but Reg slammed the

lighter man to the floor and fastened his hands on Badger's throat. Badger's eyes popped wide open, and Luke tried to topple the cage onto Reg. The effort brought on a wave of vertigo. As he sank to his knees, Luke glimpsed Prim. She rushed at Reg, her club raised over her head. He heard a smacking sound. Gripping the bars of his cage, Luke smiled painfully as Reg fell on top of Badger.

"Primmy," he said as she pulled Reg off Badger. "He has the key."

"I'm coming."

She plucked the key from Reg's pocket and rushed to the cage, while Badger stood guard at the door. Luke blinked at her in disbelief as she stuck the key in the lock and opened the cage door. Prim stuck her head inside and grabbed his arm.

"What are you doing here?" he demanded. "You shouldn't have come."

"Are you all right? Dear heaven, your face is covered with blood."

Luke scrambled out of the cage and stood up, too quickly, for he grew dizzy and had to clutch Prim to steady himself.

"Bloody hell."

"Badger," Prim cried, "Sir—Mr. Nightshade is bleeding!"

"How is it, Nightshade?" Badger called.

"Just a cut in the scalp," Luke said, straightening and taking stock of his condition. "There's a man at the side door."

Prim shook her head. "Not any more. I distracted him, and Badger hit him."

"Choke me dead, Miss Prim. You learned a lot in your adventures with the Kettle family, and I want an account. But we must be leaving these accommodations before my host returns."

He led them out of the room and down the corridor to the side door. Opening it cautiously, he stepped over Stark's prone body and motioned for Prim to follow. It had stopped raining, but only recently, and the world was still dripping, the air thick with moisture. Luke went to the intersection of the alley with Figgin Street and glanced up and down the road. Prim tugged on his coat sleeve and pointed in the opposite direction.

"Prigg has a carriage in Leather Lane."

Luke took her hand and set off down the alley at a trot, the safest pace his condition would allow. Badger went ahead, checking each turn and corner as they went. They crossed a street and walked a few yards before Luke stopped and turned to Prim.

"Oy! If you're here, who is at the Laughing Knacker?"

Prim gazed back at him calmly. "Mrs. Apple."

"Mrs. Apple!"

"You should have told me who she was," Prim snapped. "To dress up in that gray-haired disguise and pretend to be an old lady, what kind of conduct is that? When were you going to tell me she was but a girl?"

Luke set off again, pulling Prim after him. "No time for this now."

"She has a—a gang of ruffians!"

"I know."

"You're intimately acquainted with her."

Luke noticed the accusing note in Prim's voice, but he also heard shouts behind them. Turning, he saw Fleet and Jowett racing toward them.

"Come on," he said to Prim, but she had already pulled her skirt up between her legs and stuffed the hem in her waistband.

Prim scurried around a corner and jumped on top of a barrel. Down the street Badger was galloping ahead. Luke followed Prim up the side of the building to the roof. As he stood up on a gutter, Fleet arrived below.

Luke ran up the roof slope, pulling Prim with him. They skittered down the other side and leaped across to the flat top of the next building. As they raced for the next one, he stopped to pick up a thick piece of wood, and stuck it in his pocket. Prim found half a brick and did the same.

Luke regretted his delay when Jowett appeared, hiking a leg over the side of the wall and landing within a few yards of them. Shoving Prim behind him, Luke faced the man as he drew a knife. He was still holding Prim's hand behind his back when he suddenly felt the half brick thrust into it.

Jowett was coming at them slowly, the knife waving back and forth. Luke waited until he was within a yard. Then he hurled the brick. It hit the man's knife hand and sent the weapon flying over the side of the building.

Jowett cursed and hurtled at him, hitting Luke in the stomach with his shoulder. Luke felt a jolt of pain in his ribs as he fell under the man. Twisting like a salamander from beneath his attacker, he hit him in the jaw. The ruffian staggered backward, righted himself and landed a punch to Luke's stomach. Luke doubled over, more from the renewed injury to his ribs than from the blow. He coughed and managed to dive away from the next blow, but he wasn't fast enough to avoid a kick to his leg. Falling as his leg gave out, he saw his opponent pull another knife. Luke's eyes widened in horror as he glimpsed Prim behind Jowett.

"Prim, no!"

Even as he spoke, Prim raised the half brick she'd retrieved and bashed Jowett on the side of his head. The man cried out and staggered, but he didn't fall. The knife darted at Prim.

Luke bellowed in rage and launched himself at Jowett. He tackled the man, sending them both crashing to the ground. Luke shoved himself up and aimed his fist at Jowett's head, but the man didn't move. Prim was beside him in a moment, tugging on his arm.

He climbed off Jowett and nudged him with his boot. When his attacker didn't move, Luke gave him a harder shove, rolling him on his back. Prim buried her face in his shoulder at the sight of the knife sticking out of Jowett's chest over the heart.

Luke heard running footsteps. He grasped Prim's hand and pulled her after him, running across the roof and leaping to the next one. He stopped briefly when he heard Prim's sob. Touching her wet cheeks, he kissed her forehead.

"No time to weep, Primmy my love. Not now."

"I-I'm n-not weeping."

"No," he said gently as he wiped tears from her chin. "Can you manage that roof, love?" He pointed to the steep slopes of the next building. "It's the last one, and then we'll be at Leather Lane."

Prim sniffed and wiped her eyes with her sleeve. "I can manage it."

"That's my brave little spinster."

"There's no need to call me names, sir."

Luke grinned at the return of Prim's usual lecturing tone and set off for the next roof. In a short time they were climbing down the side of a stable in Leather Lane. He could see Prigg sitting atop a hired carriage in the next block. Luke helped Prim jump down from a windowsill, and hurried her down the sidewalk toward the carriage. They were just about to cross the street when Mortimer Fleet stepped out of a doorway holding a pistol. In the light of a street lamp the metal of the gun gleamed, sweating in the drenched air.

"Never knew you to hide behind women, Nightshade."

"I don't," Luke said as he thrust Prim behind him again.

"Sent that tart to fool me at the Knacker, didn't you?"

"What's wrong, Fleet? Did she do for your men? She must have, or you'd have the lot of them after us."

Fleet turned red. "Never you mind. After I've finished with you, I'll find her and settle the score." He rubbed a purple knot on his forehead.

"But I've had enough of you two, no matter what

The Gentleman says." Fleet raised the pistol and pointed it at Luke's heart. "Too bad I won't get to try one o' them poisons on you, but there's no help for it."

Luke felt Prim stir behind him. He squeezed her hand, then shoved her and whispered, "Run!"

She moved, but not as he had commanded. Before he could stop her, she darted in front of him. Fleet's pistol followed the blur of movement. At the same time, Prigg shouted at the carriage horses and aimed them at the group. Luke sprang at Prim with a roar, sweeping her up in his arms and kicking Fleet's gun hand at the same time. Fleet dropped the pistol and Luke kicked it into the street. Prim struggled in his arms, and Luke set her on her feet.

"You're unhurt?"

She nodded, but he was already running, and Prim plunged after him. Fleet had stopped in the middle of the street and was searching in the darkness for the pistol. As Luke came after him, he spotted the weapon and jumped for it—into the path of the carriage. Luke shouted, but he was too late. Fleet grabbed the gun and tried to spring out of the way, only to fall under the hooves of the frightened horses.

Prim cried out and yanked on Luke's arm. He allowed her to pull him out of the way as the carriage barreled past them. He wrapped his arms around her as Prigg fought the horses and managed to halt them. Over Prim's head, he glanced at Fleet. The condition of his skull was enough to tell him that the man was dead. A door slammed nearby. Luke glanced up and down the deserted street.

"Primmy, we must get out of here before more of Fleet's men show up. Can you walk?"

"Not with you squeezing me so that I can't breathe."

He loosened his hold on her and peered into her pale face. She was trembling, and her eyes were gleaming with tears. Badger came running up to them, out of breath but unhurt.

"I can walk," she said.

Feeling her shake, Luke muttered, "Choke me dead if I'll let you."

He picked her up; she was too light. Hadn't she been eating? Luke held her tight against him and ignored her protests. He set her inside the carriage, climbing in beside her and slamming the door. As the vehicle jostled into motion, he gathered her in his arms and kissed her. She was cold and trembling and tearful, and he had almost lost her. When he released her from the kiss, Prim sniffed and pulled away from him.

"You—you have a most familiar way of expressing gratitude, Sir Lucas."

Luke shook his head. "You think that was gratitude?"

"A most understandable emotion."

Shoving away from her, Luke slouched in the seat and glared at her. "Rot gratitude. And you don't understand nothing, Miss Primrose blighted Dane."

17

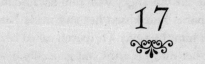

Prim was furious with Luke, a state of some permanence where he was concerned. They had escaped east London, left Badger and Prigg at Big Maudie's, and continued to the deserted town house she now knew had indeed been his. After a night of exhausted sleep in their separate elegant chambers, Luke had been persuaded to seek out a doctor to attend his wounds. Vowing to send a message confirming his safety to Louisa and Tusser, he'd been gone over an hour, and Prim was still angry.

She was angry because she had spent endless hours afraid for his life. Never had she been so terrified, not even when she had seen murder done. If he'd been killed . . .

She was angry because Luke had scolded her for coming to his aid herself. Had she not proved herself as adept as he at sneaking and deceit? But not one word of gratitude had he spoken to her when, by his usual circuitous route, they reached the house. Instead, he scowled at her and nursed some mysterious vexation of his own that he refused to discuss.

And most of all, she was angry with him because in a moment of impulse, he'd kissed her and made her more in love with him than ever. He'd even called her "love" and swept her into his arms and generally behaved like the heroes in her childish dreams. She would never forgive him for that.

Prim paced around and around. She was downstairs in the Italian Room, the chamber in which Luke had placed the treasures he'd acquired in Italy. He had refused to say when or why he'd gone to that country, but he had returned with exquisite mementos of the journey. Prim paused beside a pedestal table upon which had been displayed three bronzes formerly in the collection of the d'Este family. The finest was a dark metal replica of the Apollo Belvedere, the god's arm outstretched, a curved bow in his hand. His hair and scanty robes were gold. Beyond Apollo stood a bust of Bacchus, its patina gleaming in the morning sunlight.

Prim touched the leafy headdress of the god's wife, Ariadne, before her restlessness took her on another circuit of the room. All round her hung paintings by Titian, Uccello, Botticelli, and Raphael. Prim tried sitting down next to a table bearing a red jasper vase with the name Medici carved in it. She studied the lidded vessel, its gilt and enamel mountings, the massive flared base. It was no good. She kept thinking of Mrs. Apple.

The woman had been in disguise the whole time she was at Beaufort. Mrs. Apple was an attractive young woman, not an old lady, and she was everything Prim was not—alluring, confident, an adventuress. Upon learning of Luke's abduction, it had been Mrs. Apple who suggested the plan that ultimately succeeded. Mrs. Apple had braved the Laughing Knacker disguised as Prim. Mrs. Apple had supplied the men willing to take on those waiting to entrap her in the tavern. Prim had done nothing but follow her orders. While she was willing to play any part in rescuing Luke, she wasn't at all happy about how Mrs. Apple referred to Luke in a most familiar and offhand manner. Humiliating as it was, Prim had to admit to herself that she was jealous of yet another woman who seemed to know Luke Hawthorne well.

Ah, well. Mrs. Apple was gone, off on some urgent business of her own. Prim would probably never see her again. Not that she wanted to see her again. Mrs. Apple had turned out to have lovely auburn hair, and green eyes that seemed always to be crinkling at the corners in merriment. She could do without Mrs. Apple.

Prim tapped her fingers on the table next to the red jasper vase and glanced at the delicately carved writing desk in front of the windows. Upon it lay a sheet of writing paper, and upon that, a gilt pen from the inkstand in the shape of a peacock. She had been writing a letter of farewell to Luke. The only way to prevent another threat to him or someone dear to her was to leave at once. Swallowing her resentment of Mrs. Apple, she had borrowed a large sum from the woman. Luke would repay her. Prim could no longer afford to be too proud to take money from him.

Her few possessions, which she had taken with her on the precipitant flight from Beaufort, were packed in a small case waiting for her in the foyer. She had been forced to leave behind her dear little book of hours, but Luke would return it to her brother.

If she could write this letter of explanation, she could leave. Prim rubbed her damp palms against her skirt. She rose and went to the desk where she stood staring at the blank sheet of paper. The Italian Room was on the side of the house and looked out on a lawn with a fountain. Silver sprays of water shot out of it, and sparrows pecked at seeds beneath it. Prim sighed and glanced down at the paper again, then jumped at the sound of a rough voice.

"Curses on your head and black death on your heart, Miss Primrose blighted Dane."

Prim whirled around to find Luke standing not two yards away, her traveling case in his hand. He dropped it, making her jump again.

"You was going to leave, sneak away and go off by yourself."

Prim gripped the edge of her desk, her hands growing cold. The man in front of her was seething with a fury the force of which she had never experienced. It was as lethal as deadly nightshade, and it was in fact Nightshade himself who was stalking toward her. Quelling the impulse to sidle out of his reach, Prim lifted her chin and met his glare. His chin had tilted down. His hair swung forward as he lifted his gaze and directed a look at her that would have made a Borgia retreat. He stopped less than a foot from her.

"Rot you, Prim."

"Your language, Sir Lucas."

"Rot Sir Lucas. You're talking to Nightshade, the ruffian what you promised to stay. You lied to me, Miss Prim."

"I—" Her voice broke under the strain of facing the calm fury of this barbarian. She bit her lip and tried again. "I have to go. I'll always be a danger to you, to anyone near me."

"Not if you'd open your mouth and tell me who did for Pauline Cross. I'll settle him, and it will all be over."

"Over?" Prim's fear vanished and she stuck her face close to his, her voice growing louder with each word. "He almost had you killed." Now she was poking his chest with her finger. "Fleet nearly beat you to death, and you were in a cage. A cage. If we hadn't reached you in time, Fleet would have killed you. I'm not risking that again."

She gasped as Luke roared and grabbed her by her arms.

"Bloody hellfire and damnation, woman!" He was shaking her now. "When are you going to realize I'd rather take a thousand chances with my life than risk never seeing you again?"

The words seemed to hang in the room over their heads. Luke stopped shaking her, and they stared at each other for a long time without speaking. His eyes were still glittering with frustration and anger, but as she watched, something else flickered in them and was gone, mastered by his ruthless will. It was a brief, illusory flicker, a ghost of something, so vague that she might have imagined it. But she hadn't. Prim's eyes stung, and she didn't bother to stop the slow well of tears even as she began to smile.

Luke was still holding her, frozen and rigid. His grip softened and he cursed. "It's the sunlight. I should never have let you stand in the sunlight."

She was still smiling at him while her tears trickled down her face.

He looked away. "Forget what I said. I can see that it don't suit you. Me being what I am."

"Luke Hawthorne, you are a fool."

His head jerked back and he directed a sword-like stare at her. "Well, then, Miss Primrose blighted Dane. I might well be as big a fool as I can."

He pulled her to him, placing his mouth on hers. Prim answered by slipping her arms inside his coat, wrapping them around him, and squeezing. At her response, Luke uttered a wordless cry of disbelief. He turned with her in his arms and sank to the carpet, trying to devour her. Prim felt his body align itself with hers, reveled in its firmness and urgency. His hair fell across her face, a teasing silkiness that echoed the touch of his fingers as they released her from her clothing and traced the outlines of her body.

She searched out his flesh, her hand skimming over the bandages that protected his ribs. Somehow his clothing loosened, and she felt heat and smooth skin. Without warning his mouth searched out her ear, and he began whispering to her—strange foreign words,

Italian, French, she wasn't certain. His breath teased her and sent miniature thunderbolts of desire from her head to her feet. And all the while his hands gently touched her, never too quickly, never so slow that she grew fearful.

With remorseless expertise, he taught her the language of pleasure. Prim began to burn and writhe with impatience, and when he sensed her dilemma, he teased her with private strokes and kissed that sent Prim into a whirlwind of urgency. Still he held back, denying her something she craved but couldn't name.

Only when her nails began to dig into his flesh did he respond. Prim felt him touch her, probe, and slowly slip inside her. There was a brief moment of pain, and then discomfort, and then the slow beat of desire. She felt him move, and answered, pulling him closer and deeper. Her body spun, toplike, and a tiny, sensual spring deep inside her wound and wound and wound—and then broke. Prim cried out, vaguely perceiving Luke's answering cry.

Their mutual violence escalated, then finally subsided. Prim gasped for air as Luke collapsed on her and dug his fingers into her tousled hair. They lay there trying to breathe, each too weak to move. At last Prim found her voice.

"Luke Hawthorne, you are a fool."

She felt him hold his breath.

"To keep this miracle all to yourself," she said.

His head came up, and she beheld an incredulous and scandalized Nightshade.

"Choke me dead."

"That, my dear Luke, is something I've been trying to prevent."

With sudden roughness he scooped her into his arms and began raining kisses on her face and neck. Prim captured his face between her hands and made him look at her. He gave her a mischievous smile that made her think of all the eager women at the Black Fleece tavern and pity them.

"Nightshade, I love you."

"Nightshade," he repeated on a whisper. "Oh, Primmy, my love, I wish you had told me a long time ago."

"You could have declared yourself, too, sir."

Luke touched her nose with his. "We're a couple of right proper fools, you and I."

"I don't care."

Luke's mouth barely touched hers.

"Oh, my divine fire, I'm so glad you don't."

❧

In the kitchen of his town house that evening, Luke was frying bacon and worrying. After spending the day making love to each other, they were ravenous, but only one of them could cook. Prim was upstairs getting dressed.

Self-knowledge was a wondrous thing. It was as if nothing in the world had ever quite fit. Everything had been disjointed, ill-timed. Until he felt her respond to his kisses, until she told him of her love. Then all the great misfitting puzzle of his life righted itself. He was foolish even thinking it, but he felt as if he'd been washed clean and made whole by bathing in her sweetness.

Luke poked strips of bacon with a fork and glared at them. Rot that Primrose Victoria Dane. Why had she kept her affection for him a secret? Of course, he hadn't been honest with her either. But Luke had made a discovery. The knowledge of their love, and the consummation of it, had only magnified his fears for Prim.

He flipped strips of bacon onto a plate and set more to cooking. The fat crackled and spit at him, as if voicing his apprehension. What if she came to regret giving herself to him? In truth, she was too fine for a lowborn wretch like himself. She deserved an honorable man, a true gentleman born to distinction; she didn't deserve Nightshade, even if she had succumbed to his corrupting charm.

"What are you doing to her?" he mumbled. "You're taking advantage of her warm and sensitive heart."

Stabbing at the bacon, Luke contemplated his future. Could he face it without Prim? He imagined the next months, the next years without her, and they stretched before him in endless gray monotony. Then he laughed and shook the pan over the fire. He was a prime fool indeed. Neither of them would have a future if he couldn't get rid of the bloke who did for Pauline Cross.

Luke took a lamp from a cupboard and lit it before sliding the rest of the bacon onto the serving plate. He set the bacon and the lamp on the table in the servants' dining room. Light footsteps announced Prim's arrival. She came down the stairs with her damp hair hanging over her shoulders and sniffed.

"Mmm. I'm so hungry."

She reached for a slice of bacon, but Luke snatched the plate out of her reach.

"No food until we settle something."

"Luke, my stomach is shriveled."

She reached for the plate, but he held it away from her. "Not until you tell me who murdered Pauline Cross."

Prim's mouth snapped shut. She dropped into a chair and folded her arms over her chest.

"Rot you, Primrose Dane. I knew you'd come all over stubborn again if I tried to get you to talk."

"Then why attempt it?"

"And now your tongue is getting starchy again." Luke set the plate down, well out of Prim's reach. He grabbed her chair and twisted it around so that she faced him. "You're still trying to protect me."

"Don't peak to me in that accusing manner, Sir Lucas."

"Sir Lucas?" he repeated with a smile.

Prim sniffed and continued. "If I tell you, your life will be in danger."

"Ha!"

She jumped. "Heavens, don't do that."

"Sorry." He pulled a chair opposite hers, sat, and took her hands in his. "No use protecting me any more, Primmy. You should have realized that once Fleet grabbed me. Whoever your enemy is, he knows I've been protecting you. He'll assume I know everything, and it won't matter what we say or do. He's going to come for us both. So you see, my love, you might as well tell me."

He watched her gray-green eyes widen to the size of overcoat buttons. The kitchen was dark except for the lamp, and the house was empty and silent. Luke lowered his voice and spoke with the soft certainty of a life spent in the cesspools, ditches, and rubbish heaps of the soul.

"I have to end it now, before he kills us both."

"You're too late."

Luke jumped from his chair, yanking Prim to him as he whirled to face a shadow that detached itself from the doorway leading to the kitchen yard.

Prim clutched his arm. "It's him."

The shadow floated toward them into the light, and Luke beheld a man of neat, expensive appearance holding a pistol, the mate of the one Fleet had wielded.

The Gentleman inclined his head. "Miss Dane, this is indeed an unfortunate circumstance. For you, that is."

"Oy! Who are you?"

Prim had wrapped both arms around him, and spoke from the shelter of his body. "That is the Honorable Robert Montrose."

Luke whistled and shook his head.

"Choke me dead. An M.P. No wonder you been hunting poor Primmy like a terrier after a mouse."

"I haven't come here for conversation, Hawthorne." Montrose gestured toward the stairs with the pistol. "To your bedroom, please, Miss Dane."

Luke guided Prim ahead of him. "It won't work, Montrose. Her family will want to know why she was killed."

"And they will have an answer ready to hand."

In Prim's bedroom, Montrose closed the door and ordered them to the bed.

"Now, please undress, both of you."

Standing beside the bed, Luke put his hands on his hips and glared at Montrose. "Not bloody likely."

"I suggest you consider that I could shoot you now and do what I like with Miss Dane."

During the delay, Luke had been assessing Montrose. The bloke might have teeth like piano keys and a mincing kind of voice, but his eyes had the expression of a reptile eating its young. Luke began to unbutton his shirt.

"Luke?" Prim's voice quivered.

"Do what he says, love."

He stood in front of her. He removed his shirt and unfastened his trousers.

"That's enough," Montrose said. "Loosen Miss Dane's corset."

Luke moved behind Prim and began working with the laces. Prim was shivering.

Leaning close, he whispered, "Don't worry, love." Then he raised his voice. "Got the damned laces in a knot. Hold on."

He yanked at the garment and fumbled with the laces. After a moment, Montrose waved the pistol.

"Never mind. As long as it's loose. Come away from her, Hawthorne. To the foot of the bed."

As Luke complied, Montrose moved closer to

Prim. Now Luke was at the foot of the bed while Montrose and Prim were standing beside it.

"Your aunt is quite scandalized by the news that you have run off with Sir Lucas, Miss Dane."

"What?"

"She will be devastated by this tawdry scene. A lovers' quarrel, between the lady and the thief-turned-gentleman. Perhaps you quarreled over that very thing. After all, what lady would want to spend her life with a thief, even one so beautiful as Hawthorne here."

"You bastard," Luke said.

"As I said, I haven't come here for conversation." Montrose raised the pistol.

Luke saw the hammer pull back, and yelled, "Now, Primmy!" Prim snapped a lace in Montrose's face like a delicate whip as Luke hurled the stay he'd pulled from her corset at him. Montrose screamed, dropped the pistol, and put his hands over his eyes. Luke sprang at him, barreling into the man and hurtling them both to the floor. Montrose kicked the pistol across the room as he fell and fastened his hands on Luke's neck. Instead of squeezing, he lifted Luke bodily and sent his head smashing against the floorboards. Stunned, Luke twisted and tried to escape the remorseless grip. Again he felt his head crash against the floor. This time he must have lost consciousness for a moment, for he seemed to wake from blackness and find himself suffocating.

His hands flailed, then grabbed a handful of hair and jerked it. The grip on his neck didn't loosen. Suddenly the weight on top of him doubled, nearly caving in his chest. Luke's eyes flew open to see Prim perched on Montrose's back, clawing at his eyes and tearing at his hair.

Montrose yowled as a tuft of hair came out of his head. He let go of Luke, rose with Prim, and hurled her off his back. She hit a wall and her head smacked against it, stunning her. Luke gave a furious bellow, thrust himself to his feet, and landed a blow to Montrose's chin. Montrose stumbled away, and his foot hit the pistol. He and Luke dove for it at the same time. Montrose grabbed it, and Luke's hands fastened on his.

They rolled over and over, hitting the writing desk near the window. Pens, paper, inkstand, and letter opener were sent flying in different directions. Luke bashed Montrose's gun hand against the leg of the desk, and the pistol flew from his grip. He released Montrose and sat up, aiming his fist at the man. He stopped when the letter opener was pressed against his heart.

Sweating, his head bleeding where hair had been torn from the scalp, Montrose gave his reptilian smile. "I'm going to have her before I kill her, and I want you to know that before you—"

Luke heard a loud crack. Montrose jerked, then turned to stare at Prim, who was holding the pistol in both hands. Luke saw a red hole had appeared in the killer's neck. Rushing to Prim, he took the pistol from her and slipped his arm around her as her knees buckled. Montrose was still staring at them. Luke tossed the pistol aside and turned Prim away from the sight, holding her head against his shoulder.

"It's all right, love."

"Oh, heaven. Oh, heaven."

She sagged against him. Frightened, Luke lifted her, even as Montrose's body hit the floor, and carried her to his own chamber. He laid Prim on his bed, searched in the darkness, and lit a lamp. Taking her hands, he rubbed them while murmuring to her.

"It's all right, love. He's gone. You're safe now."

She shot upright with a gasp. "He was going to kill you!"

"But he's gone now, my love. My brave love."

She clutched his hands and began to repeat over and over, "Oh, oh, oh."

Alarmed, Luke tried more reassurances, but that had no effect. Finally he wrapped his arms around her, tucked her face into his shoulder, and squeezed her hard. Her cheek was thrust against his bare skin. He could feel her shaking through the mattress, but as he rubbed her arms and rocked with her, the trembling subsided.

At last she lifted her tearstained face to his. "I—I killed him. Oh, I feel ill."

"Now you listen to me, Primmy. You had no choice. It was that way from the beginning, the moment you saw him do for Pauline. It was going to be you or him."

"I k-killed him."

Luke shrugged. "You would rather he killed you?"

There was a brief silence.

"No."

"Or me?"

"Of course not."

He kissed her on the nose and wiped her wet cheeks. "There's some things, love, that we ain't never going to understand in this life."

Prim snuggled closer to him and gave a trembling sigh.

"I think I shall be able to bear it, if you will help me."

"That's what I want to do, love. I'll help you, no matter what."

18

Prim stood in front of the full-length mirror in her dressing room at Aunt Freshwell's town house and scowled at the reflection of herself dressed in undergarments and crinoline. How could a few hours make such a difference in her fate? It was really too disorienting to be thrust back into the life she had left so abruptly after the nightmare of Robert Montrose, and it was all Luke's fault.

Last night he had summoned his friend Ross Scarlett. Together they had dealt with Montrose's body and the Metropolitan police, and she had been ordered to submit to the attentions of a kindly doctor and to rest. How could she rest with strange men coming and going in secrecy? She wandered the house until Luke had finally thrust a snifter of brandy in her hands and ordered her to sit in the drawing room where he could keep an eye on her.

From her vantage point she had grown ill watching Montrose's body carried out and taken away in a carriage. She had watched while the house was explored, straightened, and cleaned. More gentlemen arrived, these with an air of calm authority. Luke and his friend closeted themselves in the Italian Room for hours. She finally fell asleep listening to their low grumbling voices.

Not long before daybreak, Luke awakened her looking as severe and menacing as she'd ever seen him. He bundled her into his town coach. On the journey through town Prim tried to get him to tell her what was wrong, but he only replied, "Oy! Give us some peace, woman." The trip ended at Aunt Freshwell's. Luke plucked her from the carriage and deposited her on the doorstep, where the Freshwell butler was already waiting.

He left her with a whispered explanation that was no explanation. "This is for the best, Primmy."

Then he left her.

Prim wiped a tear from her cheek. Luke had abandoned her, and she was afraid it was because he regretted coming so close to making a commitment to her. The horror or Montrose's attack had brought him back to reason and banished all memory of their love. Luke had remembered what he really wanted—a grand lady of rank and distinction. He deserved such a lady, someone who would make him proud and give him children of noble heritage and breeding.

No. No, he didn't. He deserved her. She was the one who had saved his life. Twice!

Turning from her miserable reflection, Prim tried to smile at the maid who came into the room bearing the skirt to the gown she was to wear tonight. Aunt Freshwell had insisted she attend this dinner party. All Prim wanted to do was stay in her room and cry, but her aunt had harped and hectored until Prim gave way.

Another maid followed the first, bearing the bodice that matched the skirt. She helped Prim put it on. Then the two maids positioned the voluminous skirt. It took at least two maids to lift the yards of material over the crinoline and her head. Once the skirt was fastened, Prim felt hemmed in and weighed down by all her garments, even though the bodice was cut off the shoulder and low in the bosom.

With the maids' help she was able to lift the skirt so that she could sit without crushing the pale blue antique moiré. While one girl fastened a spray of tiny white and blue roses in her hair, Prim's spirits plummeted further. She was back home after a mysterious disappearance, and everyone was acting as if she'd never left. Aunt Freshwell and Newton had greeted her at breakfast this morning without mentioning the weeks she'd been absent and possibly dead.

The reason for their behavior, Prim suspected, was the hidden hand of Luke, and that of his influential friend. Both men had been anxious that she not be exposed to public speculation and notoriety. Prim had been skeptical of their ability to control the affair so that no word reached beyond their inner circle. Now, even her hedgehog of an aunt behaved with circumspection. Prim had expected Aunt Freshwell to rain castigation down upon her for risking the family reputation and honor. No such tempest occurred. This miracle caused Prim to realize just how powerful Ross Scarlett was. And she suspected that her views of Luke Hawthorne's influence would also need revising.

Nothing, however, could make up for the fact that she had been abandoned by the man who had transformed her life from one of unremitting sameness to something resembling the flight of a star. He had cast her back among people who spent their lives in pursuit of what Prim thought of as capitals. And this evening's dinner party was a prime case. Aunt Freshwell had recited the guest list to her earlier, and it was full of capitals.

"Oh, Victoria." (Aunt Freshwell preferred Prim's second name, which was the queen's.) "Oh, Victoria, this dinner will be so important for my Newton. He's sure to get an appointment to Her Majesty's household. We're having the Queen's Equerry" (one capital), "and a Cabinet Minister" (another capital). "We snagged a Bishop, and a Personal Friend of His Royal Highness, Prince Albert."

Each capital—whose name was never so important as his or her station and influence—was spoken in a hushed tone and accompanied with a pursing of lips and a look that announced the great rank and consequence of the guest. It seemed that Prim's disappearance hadn't prevented the Freshwells from pursuing their life's ambition. Both the lady and her son lusted after a position at court with all the fervid and grasping selfishness of the wives of an Ottoman sultan. It was to this company that Luke had condemned her without so much as a farewell. She hated him.

With her toilette complete, Prim slouched her way downstairs to the drawing room, miserable and resentful. Several of the guests had already arrived. Aunt Freshwell glared at her tardy arrival, but Prim kept well away from her, joining a couple at the fireplace. The gentleman turned, and Prim came face to face with Ross Scarlett. Her lower jaw came loose as he bowed to her.

"Ah, Miss Dane. So pleased to see that you're well. May I present Françoise Marie de Fontages, Comtesse de Rohan."

Prim curtseyed to the elegant, silver-haired woman. Lifting her gaze, she stared into the twinkling eyes of Mrs. Apple.

"But—"

"The comtesse has only recently arrived from her chateau in Austria."

"But—"

Aunt Freshwell's harpylike voice drowned Prim's protest. "Victoria. Victoria, come here and meet my other guests."

She spent the evening in a daze. Not even Newton's obsequious attentions to the Queen's Equerry and the Personal Friend irritated her. She kept glancing at the "comtesse," who seemed to have changed her hair color, stature, weight, and accent yet again. Luke wouldn't tell her about Mrs. Apple, but Prim was certain she didn't belong at Aunt Freshwell's dinner party, or to the French aristocracy.

After dinner Prim tried to corner the comtesse, but the lady eluded her. Handing a thick envelope to Ross Scarlett, she murmured apologies in an accent so charming that all the men in the room stopped talking. Taking her leave of Aunt Freshwell, she gave Prim a twinkling smile and vanished. Prim slumped down in a chair, preoccupied with this little mystery, until Newton bullied her into participating in the formal leave-taking.

Ross Scarlett was the last to go. Prim found him in the foyer talking to Aunt Freshwell. When she joined them, he nodded to her and smiled.

"Here is Miss Dane. Excellent. Shall we go into the library?"

Offering his arm to her aunt, Mr. Scarlett led the way, leaving Prim and Newton to trail behind. Mystified, Prim took one of the stuffed leather chairs and eyed the guest with trepidation.

"Oh, Mr. Scarlett," her aunt gushed as soon as the door was shut. "I can't tell you what an honor it was to receive your request to be included in our little affair tonight. No! No, don't tell me. I can guess your reason. You have a little communication to make from an exalted personage."

Prim gawked at her aunt. The woman was chirping. There was no other word for it. She peeped like a fuzzy, week-old buzzard chick.

Distaste flickered in Scarlett's eyes and was gone. He shook his head. "You are mistaken, my lady. Such a communication would come from another source."

"Now, Mr. Scarlett, it's well known that Her Maj—"

"I am here on quite a different errand," said Mr. Scarlett with a quelling frown at Lady Freshwell.

Newton piped in. "But what could that be?"

Scarlett produced the thick envelope Mrs. Apple had given him. "I am here to make a proposal on behalf of Sir Lucas Hawthorne."

"A proposal?" Aunt Freshwell said.

Prim's heart did a Spanish dance in her chest, and she thanked Providence that she was sitting down. A proposal. Now she understood. Luke had wanted to preserve her reputation and honor and had gone to great trouble to do it. This was his gift to her and his way of asking for her hand. But he could have told her.

Aunt was staring at her with that startled horse look that exposed the whites of her eyes. Newton merely looked stupid and confused.

"This chap who kept Victoria in hiding wants to marry her?" Newton's brow unfurrowed. "Only decent thing, really."

Lady Freshwell had recovered and was bristling in her usual hedgehog manner. "This—this person of low birth has the temerity to offer for my niece? Unacceptable, sir. Most unacceptable."

"You are mistaken."

Prim's heart, which had just settled down, started banging against her breastbone again, causing a jab of pain.

"Oh?" Aunt Freshwell asked.

"Sir Lucas wishes to settle a sum on Miss Dane so that she becomes independent and may chose her own fate."

Newton brightened. "I say!"

Ignoring Newton and Lady Freshwell, Scarlett went to Prim and placed the envelope in her hands.

"These are the legal papers, the draft for the money and instructions on how to manage it, along with a letter of reference to my own solicitor. He will be honored to help you with your affairs, Miss Dane. This money is yours entirely, with no conditions attached to it."

Prim blinked at him. Scarlett smiled and nodded at her in encouragement. With shaking fingers she opened the envelope and glanced at the figures. Zeros swam before her.

"Heavens," Prim said faintly.

Newton sidled over and looked at the papers. "Good God! Fifty thousand pounds."

Aunt Freshwell gasped and clutched the back of a chair. Newton rushed to her side and fluttered a handkerchief in her face. Scarlett thrust his hands in his pockets and grinned at Prim.

"It's a nice sum, Miss Dane. But you must take care not to become prey to fortune hunters." He paused, but Prim was still staring at the papers.

Turning to Lady Freshwell, Scarlett said, "I must take my leave, Lady Dorothy."

"A moment," Prim said.

Scarlett turned back to her. "Yes, Miss Dane?"

"It seems you and Sir Lucas have my affairs all nicely settled between you."

Frowning, Scarlett said, "It was meant for the best, Miss Dane."

"No doubt," Prim said.

She rose, gripped the papers and the bank draft, and ripped them in half. Aunt Freshwell shrieked.

"I say!" exclaimed Newton.

Prim thrust the torn sheets into Ross Scarlett's hands and addressed him in a trembling voice. "If Luke Hawthorne thinks I'm going to accept this— this charity, he has gone mad indeed."

"Victoria!"

Prim glared at Lady Freshwell. "Be quiet, Aunt." She faced Scarlett. "Tell me, sir. Did he think it necessary to do this in order to get rid of me?"

Scarlett spread his hands and shook his head.

"Or perhaps he simply pitied me."

"Absolutely not."

"Then he's buying my compliance," Prim snapped. "He doesn't wish to marry me himself, but in his gracious goodness, he's willing to purchase a husband for me."

"My dear Miss Dane, this isn't what we intended at all."

Prim was near tears. She had to get out of this room and away from these horrible people.

"Mr. Scarlett, you can tell Sir Lucas Hawthorne to go to hell. I'm done with hypocritical propriety and stifling boredom and tediousness." She marched to the door, then whirled around. "No! Don't tell him anything. I want to do it myself. Where is he?"

Scarlett was grinning again. "An excellent idea, Miss Dane. Luke has gone back to Beaufort."

"Thank you, Mr. Scarlett. I shall take the first train in the morning."

Prim slammed the door on Aunt Freshwell's strident protests.

❧

Late the next afternoon Prim sat in a hired carriage as it rattled under the portcullis at Beaufort. The sky had darkened and charcoal-colored clouds were streaming across the sky toward the castle. Prim hardly noticed the way the wind whipped through the trees and blew petals off late-blooming flowers. Servants scurried past in haste to finish their work outdoors. Gardeners were piling tools in wheelbarrows and the horse pulling a provision merchant's wagon fought his harness and tried to pull away from the man holding him.

As the carriage pulled up to the great hall, Prim was leaning out the window. She saw Louisa Hawthorne flounce out the door and wave at a groom holding the pony and cart she used for her personal transportation. The carriage came to a standstill beside the pony cart, and Louisa rushed around it.

"My dear Miss Dane, what a surprise!"

Distraught, weary from sleeplessness, Prim leaned out of the carriage and tried to be calm. "Forgive my coming unannounced, Mrs. Hawthorne. There is a personal matter of great urgency—"

"I know."

Descending to the ground, Prim swallowed hard and attempted to keep her crinoline from flying up with each gust of wind. "You know?"

Louisa's plump hands were strangling the driving gloves she held.

"Our Luke has been a terrible widgeon, has he not?" She paused to look at Prim's set features, then patted her cheek. "There now, dearie. One thing you'll have to learn about men is that they're proud. The other thing you must learn is how to extract them from the troubles they get themselves into because of their pride."

Clamping her hands on her bucking crinoline, Prim cleared her throat. "I'm sure I don't comprehend your meaning, Mrs. Hawthorne."

"Dearie, I've just spent two hours arguing with my son about his stubborn pride, and I'm in no mood to tolerate a prickly little miss. The two of you must sort things out between you." Louisa shook a finger in Prim's face. "That boy loves you so much he can't say a dozen words without mentioning you, and you're no better off."

Stunned, Prim forgot to hold her crinoline, and it nearly flew over her head. Louisa bashed it down with one hand.

"I can see by that witless look on your face that you've been struck all of a heap. For no reason, too. Do you think our Luke would have done what he's done for anyone? Do you think he'd have employed his influence with Mr. Scarlett for any woman?"

"I had not thought."

"Humph. That's the problem. Neither of you is thinking." Louise grabbed Prim's arm and thrust her toward the hall. "Now you get yourself inside and talk to that boy. He won't listen to me. Thinks he's doing the honorable thing, the gentlemanly thing. And the way I see it, what good is knowing you've done the gentlemanly thing if it makes you both miserable?"

Prim felt Louisa's hand on her back. She was propelled inside. Turning back, she found the doors slammed in her face. She was about to open them when she heard the click of shoes on marble.

Whirling around, she found herself confronting Featherstone. "Oh, good afternoon, Featherstone."

"Good afternoon, miss."

Prim brushed nonexistent dust from her sleeve and said casually, "Is Lady Cecilia still here, Featherstone?"

"No, miss." Featherstone smiled. "She left the morning after Sir Lucas was abducted. Quite precipitately, in fact."

"Oh. Good."

"Yes, miss."

There was an uncomfortable lapse in the conversation. Clearing her throat, Prim ventured another remark. "It's going to rain, Featherstone."

"Yes, miss."

"It will be a great storm, I think."

"Indeed, miss."

Prim intertwined her gloved fingers and rocked back and forth on her heels.

Featherstone gave her a kindly look. "I was just remarking upon that very possibility to Sir Lucas in the Sky Room, miss."

"The Sky Room?"

"Yes, miss, in the residential wing, seven doors down from the room you occupied during your visit." The butler indicated the appropriate direction through the hall. "That way, miss."

"You—you don't want to announce me?"

Featherstone smiled at her. "In this instance, miss, surprise, followed by a certain amount of—shall I say—audacity, is indicated."

Prim glanced down the series of lofty rooms beyond the hall, each as sumptuous and imposing as its predecessor. "Are you sure?"

"Decidedly, miss."

Featherstone bowed and left, but Prim continued to stare at the vista of rooms. Her anger was fading, leaving in its place the wretchedness of self-doubt. What if Louisa and Featherstone were wrong? What if she was right and Luke really did want to rid himself of her? How could she tell? She had never been in this predicament before.

"Better to know than to wonder forever in misery," she muttered.

She had to make herself walk through the rooms and upstairs past an endless line of portraits of dead nobles. She came to her former room and counted doors. One. He couldn't have pretended the love he'd shown her in the town house. Two. He was Nightshade; he could deceive anyone. Three. There was no reason for him to deceive her. Four. What did she know of a man who had been forced to live as he had? Five. He had wanted her love, not just her favors. Six. Then why had he offered her money? Seven. Because even if he loved her, he desired a much better wife.

Prim stopped at the seventh door and touched the handle. Her skin was colder than the metal. Taking in a long breath, she turned the handle and walked into the room before she could think of reasons to be afraid—and stepped into the sky.

The ceiling had been painted in a glorious heaven blue with misty clouds, but the artist had not stopped at the ceiling. The sky continued down the walls of the room, broken only by gilded pillars. The room was empty of furniture, and Luke was standing with his back against a window frame staring at her as if she were one of the castle's many resident ghosts.

"What are you doing here?"

Prim marched up to him, pulled a folded sheaf of papers from her bag, and threw them at him. Torn sheets flew in his face. He batted them away and caught one. He glanced at it, flushed, and gave her one of his Nightshade glares.

"Oy! You got no business tearing up bank drafts, Miss Prim."

Prim's anger flared. He hadn't rushed to her with open arms, ecstatic that she'd come to him.

"So, this revolting idea was yours and not Mr. Scarlett's."

"Ross? Nah, he didn't like it."

"And neither do I, sir. Your conduct in this matter has been woolen-headed, dishonorable, and ungentlemanly."

"Now see here—"

Prim began to remove her gloves and pace at the same time. "To offer money to rid yourself of an inconvenient connection. To do it in so impersonal and public a manner." Her fingers fumbled with the button of a glove. "I'll have nothing to do with your sordid money, sir. You needn't conduct yourself in so desperate a manner. I have no intention of demanding an offer from you."

She gave a sharp tug. The button tore from the glove and sailed across the room to bounce off the wall. Tears stung her eyes as she gazed at the glove in dismay. "Oh, dear." Her voice broke. "My only good pair. I must f-find the button. It is a p-pearl."

She tried to see where the button had landed, but her vision was blurred. Luke hadn't said a word. She turned her back to him and tried to wipe her eyes surreptitiously. Suddenly his hands enveloped hers and dragged them down from her face.

"I wanted to give you an independence, Primmy."

"It is neither honorable nor proper."

"And your coming here alone is? Choke me dead, I'm never going to learn etiquette."

Prim jerked her hands free and nearly shouted at him in her distress. "You're just afraid you'll have to marry me instead of some grand titled lady!"

Reddening, Luke shouted back at her.

"I am not. I was afraid you'd be ashamed to marry me."

"Luke Hawthorne, that is the most insulting, vicious thing you've ever said to me."

"Oh, and I suppose you would marry me?"

"Yes, drat you!"

A startled silence reigned for a moment.

"Then you will?" Luke whispered.

Prim nodded. She started when he gave a whooping yell that echoed around the Sky Room. Grasping her by the waist, he swung her around in a circle. Prim squealed and protested until he finally put her down near the window. The room was growing dark with the approaching storm, but they both ignored it. Prim saw the change come over him, saw the black wickedness flicker in his eyes. Nightshade drew her to him and captured her mouth. Soon she was in a swirling storm of her own.

Lifting his lips, Nightshade said, "You know what I've been. You're certain?"

"There is no greater certainty than mine."

Nightshade touched her lips gently with the tips of his fingers. "Then you must go back to your aunt's."

"No."

"I'll want things done properly, Miss Prim. Think of our future children."

Prim thought, then smiled. "Very well. I'll go if you give me back my book of hours."

"Oh, yes."

"Where is it?"

Luke bent and whispered in her ear.

"The latrine!" Prim gazed up at his smiling face, horrified. "Luke Hawthorne, you take me there at once. The very notion is horrid. The latrine tower."

Taking her hand, Nightshade kissed it and glanced up at her while still bending over it. "I'm at your service, Miss Dane. It's my dearest wish to get you alone in a tower."

About the Author

SUZANNE ROBINSON has a doctoral degree in anthropology with a specialty in ancient Middle Eastern archaeology. She has now turned her attention to the creation of the fascinating fictional characters in her unforgettable historical romances.

Suzanne lives in San Antonio with her husband and her two English springer spaniels. She divides her time between writing historical romance and mystery under her first name, Lynda.

Bestselling Historical Women's Fiction

✖ AMANDA QUICK ✖

____28354-5 SEDUCTION ...$6.50/$8.99 Canada

____28932-2 SCANDAL ....$6.50/$8.99

____28594-7 SURRENDER ....$6.50/$8.99

____29325-7 RENDEZVOUS ....$6.50/$8.99

____29315-X RECKLESS ....$6.50/$8.99

____29316-8 RAVISHED ....$6.50/$8.99

____29317-6 DANGEROUS ....$6.50/$8.99

____56506-0 DECEPTION ....$6.50/$8.99

____56153-7 DESIRE ....$6.50/$8.99

____56940-6 MISTRESS ....$6.50/$8.99

____57159-1 MYSTIQUE ....$6.50/$7.99

____57190-7 MISCHIEF ....$6.50/$8.99

____57407-8 AFFAIR ....$6.99/$8.99

✖ IRIS JOHANSEN ✖

____29871-2 LAST BRIDGE HOME ...$5.50/$7.50

____29604-3 THE GOLDEN
BARBARIAN ....$6.99/$8.99

____29244-7 REAP THE WIND ......$5.99/$7.50

____29032-0 STORM WINDS ....$6.99/$8.99

Ask for these books at your local bookstore or use this page to order.

Please send me the books I have checked above. I am enclosing $____ (add $2.50 to cover postage and handling). Send check or money order, no cash or C.O.D.'s, please.

Name _____

Address _____

City/State/Zip _____

Send order to: Bantam Books, Dept. FN 16, 2451 S. Wolf Rd., Des Plaines, IL 60018
Allow four to six weeks for delivery.
Prices and availability subject to change without notice.   FN 16 2/98